A HOUSE UNSETTLED

TRYNNE DELANEY

annick press

toronto · berkeley

TRYNNE DELANEY is a writer currently based in Tiohtià:ke (Montréal). They were born on the west coast and raised on the east coast in the place colonially known as Canada. Trynne has never seen a ghost, but they've been one.

Cover designed by Zainab's Echo
Interior designed by Kong Njo
Edited by Claire Caldwell and Khary Mathurin
Copy edited by Genevieve Clovis
Proofread by Mercedes Acosta

Front cover image credit: *Vanitas Still Life*, c. 1665/1670 by Jan van Kessel the Elder. Courtesy National Gallery of Art, Washington.
Back cover image credit: *The Silver Tureen*, c. 1728-30 by Jean Siméon Chardin. Courtesy The Metropolitan Museum of Art, New York.

Annick Press Ltd.

We acknowledge the support of the Canada Council for the Arts and the Ontario Arts Council, and the participation of the Government of Canada/la participation du gouvernement du Canada for our publishing activities.

ONTARIO ARTS COUNCIL
CONSEIL DES ARTS DE L'ONTARIO
an Ontario government agency
un organisme du gouvernement de l'Ontario

Library and Archives Canada Cataloguing in Publication

Title: A house unsettled / Trynne Delaney.
Names: Delaney, Trynne, author.
Identifiers: Canadiana (print) 2022017623X | Canadiana (ebook) 20220176256 | ISBN 9781773216959 (hardcover) | | ISBN 9781773216997 (PDF) | ISBN 9781773216973 (HTML)
Classification: LCC PS8607.E48255 H68 2022 | DDC jC813/.6—dc23

Published in the U.S.A. by Annick Press (U.S.) Ltd.
Distributed in Canada by University of Toronto Press.
Distributed in the U.S.A. by Publishers Group West.

Printed in Canada

annickpress.com
trynnedelaney.com
Also available as an e-book.
Please visit annickpress.com/ebooks for more details.

**To everyone who's been a ghost
or known one**

—T.D.

PART ONE

DUST

CHAPTER ONE

*T*raci kills the ignition with a swift hand. Her aging station wagon shudders to a halt and the headlights flick off. It's evening. The old-growth trees that surround Great Aunt Aggie's property make just enough shade to give our surroundings the dark blue illusion of night.

Traci breathes out relief, breaking our silence. "We're home."

Home. I wouldn't have used such a strong word for this place. I understand why we had to move to Great Aunt Aggie's old house, but that doesn't make me any less homesick for the city, its foggy mornings, and our vermin-free house. This place, no matter how many times I visited growing up, remains unfamiliar to me. But Traci needed to come back; she and Aggie were each other's only close living relatives, since she lived with Aggie as a teenager and all Aggie's siblings moved out west before Traci was even born. Traci says their moving away was a betrayal of the highest order for Aggie. When the cousins came out east to visit, she'd tolerate their presence as long as they made no mention of her brothers. We're the only branch of the family left on the east coast. If Traci hadn't stepped up to take care of the house, it would've been demolished. Without Dad around, I had to come with her.

Still, as the sun set over the harbor last night, I thought maybe Traci would decide this was all part of her midlife crisis, same as her losing her job, and that she didn't actually want to move out to the middle of nowhere to an enormous and desperately neglected house where she spent her unhappiest teenage years. Up until last night, I refused to pack in hopes that would convince her to stay in the city. When that didn't work, I got mean. We're both still picking the shards of that argument out of our skin.

Each of us is hanging on to the promise of a fresh start—the only thing we agree on is wanting to get as far out of people's sightlines as possible after what happened to Dad.

As we step out of the car, the house's hulking body blocks out the setting sun, coating us in a damp cool. Traci smiles at me wide. "Isn't it just gorgeous?" she says with a sigh, her eyes glinting against the little remaining light. I squint at Aggie's house and try to imagine what it'll look like when all the repairs and cleaning are done. It's hard. My eyes move over the gaping rottenness of it all, unable to focus on anything specific.

Traci pops the trunk, and we pull our luggage from the car. One thing I share with my mother is a talent for packing lightly. Each of us only brought one suitcase. Jeff will bring the rest of the things in his truck next weekend. He said he couldn't make the three-hour commute with us on a weekday because he needs to be sharp at work if he wants to make CEO when his boss retires. It's fine with me that he couldn't make it. I'm not exactly itching for the three of us to live together—it didn't go so well last time we tried.

"You got everything?" Traci reaches up to pull down the trunk hatch. She hesitates. "You want to bring in your skateboard?"

My board leans against the dented side of the trunk, the scratched purple UFO on the back reminds me of riding through the night back in our old neighborhood with Nia. I checked my phone the whole way here but there were no messages from her to distract me from the distance of the highway between us. She's probably heading to the skate park to practice her rock to fakie with some friends before her flight to Freetown takes off in a few days. Homesickness holds me so tight around the throat I can't breathe for a minute.

"You coming?" Traci is already navigating the path to the house. The structure blurs at the edges, crooked and imprecise. Maybe I'm carsick. "Careful not to get any ticks!"

I shudder at the overgrown grass leading to the door, but grit my teeth and follow. The path often forgets its direction in the alternating weeds and dry patches that eventually take me to the entrance. As much as I try to avoid it, my calves bear the tickling of overgrowth. I ignore the urge to swat away potential bloodsuckers until I'm at the door. I can already feel lumps beginning to swell and simmer beneath my skin.

Traci points to the third step. It's sagging on the left side. "Watch you don't step there. It's rotten." I'm careful to avoid it as I follow her onto the porch.

Even here, in the questionable security of the porch's rotten overhang, the details of the house remain blurred against my memory of it. Me and my cousins played out here in the winter, one Christmas when the adults decided to have a reunion. We raced in circles around the house, climbing the railings of the wraparound veranda. Back then, trips out here were an adventure. We were so close to nature and spent summer weekends swimming in the clear waters of a nearby ravine, jumping onto springy beds of moss . . . that vague memory version of this house is as distant as my cousins, who haven't come to visit in six years.

I wonder what it's like for Traci to be back. Maybe she only sees what it could become when it's restored. I can't tell from her face, which is upturned, searching for the hidden key in the rafters.

"Aha!" she says with glee. She tries to reach for it, but she's too short. "Honey, I need your height."

On tiptoes, I reach up into the cobwebbed rafters. The key is tired brass hardware store stock mangled by years of over-twisting in sticky locks. I'm startled by its warmth in my hand, like someone else was recently holding it. I drop it and it skitters to a stop just before it slips through the wide cracks of the soft porch wood. Holding it gingerly between my fingers, I drop it into Traci's palm.

"Thanks Asha." Traci kisses my cheek. I almost pull away out of habit, but I want to love her just as bad, and my arms find their way around her. She holds on too long. It's as if she's sucking the love out of me. When I was younger, I used to curl up beside her in bed when I had nightmares and melt into the safety of her. Now something about our skin touching is artificial.

Traci unlocks the door and steps inside. The smell of air that's been still too long curls out of the house like smoke. Its undertones are familiar and alive: aging wood, silver polish, yeast, and pine . . . but the result is as strange as looking at someone you knew well in an open casket; all that compressed dust pretending life.

When I glance back at the car, all that falls outside the house's shadow is cut with the lowering sunlight, sharp as shards of glass.

∂∫∂

In the vestibule, Traci swipes her hand over the wall until she finds the switch and dim yellow light flickers into the space.

"Mice probably chewed up all the wiring in here," she mutters as she unties her shoes and leaves them neatly next to an intimidating pile of Aggie's old ones: a rubber boot, a sneaker, a kitten heel she must not have worn since at least the early 2000s, and enormous steel-toed boots that look even older. From my quick glance over the pile, I can't even find matches for all of them. They're just collected there, junk removed of all function. Looking at them makes me intensely lonely.

I hold up one of the steel-toed boots. "These weren't Aggie's, were they?"

"Put those down." When I don't drop the shoe fast enough, Traci pulls it from my hand and throws it back on the pile.

"I could've put it back myself." Traci's wiping her hands off vigorously on her pants. In between wipes, she gives me a warning glance to correct my tone. Maybe she saw something on the boot I couldn't see. "Was there a spider on it or something?"

"You don't know where those shoes have been."

"Looks like they've mostly been sitting in that pile."

"They meant something to Aggie." Traci takes a deep breath, then purses her lips. I get the feeling she could say more about the boots but she doesn't want to get into it right now. Maybe the boots mean something to Traci too.

I kick off my own muddy sneakers and leave them next to hers. She bristles at my carelessness, so I follow her lead and place them neatly on the mat.

"Aunt Aggie liked her shoes. And she never threw any of them out. She was certain there'd be a use for them someday. Typical of anyone who lived through the second world war." Traci picks up one of the kitten heels and blows the dust off, rubs a corner clean with her sleeve. The patent leather takes on a dull shine. "They look like your size, actually. Perfect condition, too. Why don't you try them on?"

I take the shoe like it's a wild snake. Part of me wants to point out the hypocrisy in her offering me one of the shoes right after snatching one from my hand, but I remind myself of the fresh start we both want and can my criticism. Maybe this kitten heel is a peace offering. When I went to prom with Steven Kennedy last spring, I hated every moment I was chained to my shoes, but they were Traci's treat; our first big purchase together after I had to move back in with her when Dad was arrested. She was so excited to share the secrets of femininity I'd been deprived of while living with my father, but wearing them made me feel like a pretender. Was this who I was supposed to be? In all the pictures on Traci's newsfeed, I look so happy.

Traci holds the other shoe out for me. I slip the heels onto my socked feet.

"Walk around in them a bit. You need to do that to make sure they fit right."

"I know." I take a deep breath, paste on a smile for her.

I take a couple awkward steps. Even having walked in heels higher than these at prom, my ankles wobble in their sockets. I pass over the threshold of the vestibule into the dimness of Aunt Aggie's house.

"They look amazing on you! You should keep them. I think she'd want you to have them." I doubt that, but I smile at Traci. Aunt Aggie and I barely interacted over the years. By the end of her life, I don't think she even remembered who I was. She was always kind of scary to me. She had this severe frown line that ran down the center of her forehead and made her look perpetually judgmental. It was years since I'd last seen her, so I don't know what she would have wanted. I didn't even know what she wanted when she was alive.

Positivity, I remind myself. *This move will make everything easier.*

I glance back at the pile of shoes. Was her shoe collection the only company she had in this big house? A crack snags the rough edge of the heel and I trip. The whole heel breaks off. I don't realize I fell until I'm standing back up and watching the can of beans I shoplifted from the Jiffy-Mart roll from my hoodie pocket into a darkened corner.

"Oh honey, are you ok?" Traci squeezes my arm. Her brow is furrowed. If this fall looked bad, she should see the bruises on my legs from last week's skate.

"Only thing I hurt was my pride," I say. The words feel stolen from Dad's mouth. Traci doesn't laugh. It reminds her of him too. Neither of us, me or Dad, could ever stand to be embarrassed. Even the smallest mistakes we brush off or try to cover up. I don't know why we're like this, but I think it's why moving out here feels a little like a relief despite the homesickness. I don't have to face the embarrassment of everyone I know knowing about the charges against Dad. Instead, I swallow it all down.

"Glad you're ok," Traci says finally. "Guess you're not keeping these, hey?" She throws the shoes back on the pile. "Go take your suitcase upstairs." Traci leaves her own suitcase at the bottom of the stairs and flips the light switches for all the rooms all the way down the hall to the kitchen. The whole place is exposed for its dusty, neglected self, when in the dark, it might've pretended grandness for just a few moments longer.

∿

When we used to visit Aggie, I'd sleep in Traci's childhood room. That's where I head automatically. Upstairs, I find myself at the head of a hall on a long threadbare imported carpet. The carpet used to be a rich red, Traci told me, but I've always known it to be a faded pink and gray-beige from the wear and tear of feet. The carpet holds Aunt Aggie's shuffling footsteps. A pattern on the original obscuring it. I try to walk on the places where it looks like she didn't. Something about stepping on her path feels like bad luck or disrespect.

The oak doors to each room are shut, but their crystal doorknobs still glint in the light that rises up the stairwell. Great Aunt Aggie kept all the doors closed except when family would come to stay. Traci says that with the doors closed, Aggie was able to shrink the house in her mind so it didn't feel so lonely. When she was growing up, Traci wasn't allowed in any of the other rooms under any circumstance except holiday visits, not even Aunt Aggie's. She said it was really the only rule in the house. So, of course, she broke it. When Aggie went out to the market on Saturday mornings, Traci looked inside the rooms. She didn't find anything interesting, though. Just a bunch of dust and antique furniture. She supposed, for Aggie, looking into those rooms must have brought up memories. For Traci, the rooms felt empty.

I head toward Traci's childhood bedroom. It's the only room in the house that doesn't look perfectly preserved from the Victorian era. It's another kind of time capsule, though. The walls are pasted with posters of The Cranberries, Prince, Nirvana, and a bunch of local bands long since forgotten. A weird mix of the transition from the '80s to '90s that Traci grew up in. Big hair clips and heavy earrings line the drawers. Hairspray aerosol cans in the closet. When I was younger, I imagined the room smelled a little like Traci's teenage self: all chemical, just like the '80s and '90s before people realized how truly fucked the climate is. Her old books are in there too, mostly ones from school like *The Catcher in the Rye* and *To Kill a Mockingbird*. I can't believe I'm still reading the same bullshit books in class after thirty years.

At least, as I turn the icy doorknob to enter, that's what I expect to see: a time capsule of Traci's youth. Instead, the walls are blank, faded around where the posters used to be. Everything is blank. No combs or big barrettes on the dresser. The mirror reflects the emptiness of the room. The bed's made with fresh white linens. It smells like dryer lint. Clean but dusty. When I pass over the threshold, will I become as colorless and empty as this room? I throw my bag on the bed to wrinkle the sheets a bit and put my jacket on the floor. There. Now, at least it looks like *somebody* lives in this old house. If I'd known the room would be so empty, I'd have brought stuff to decorate. Maybe this is better, though. A blank slate. Just what I wanted, right?

As I leave the room to head back downstairs, I think I see a flash of light on the wall across from the mirror. I swear I could feel some heat off it too. I glance toward the mirror, then out the window that opens onto the woods diagonal to it. I can't see any light from here, not even streetlights. I close the door behind me and walk downstairs to the kitchen.

I find the can of beans in the dusty corner beside the staircase. I cradle them and wipe the cobwebs off the label, then bring the can to Traci in the kitchen. She's staring out the window over the kitchen sink, in a kind of trance. I have to tap her on the shoulder to get her attention.

She's so deep in her head that she jumps at my touch and grabs my wrist hard as she turns to face me. Her eyes hold an old well of fear I haven't seen on her before. When she sees it's me, she laughs. "You startled me! You're a regular Casper. All those old stories must've gotten to me." I don't laugh with her. My heart is racing too, now, but I hold back my fear and shake the can of beans.

"Got this at the Jiffy-Mart." I place it next to the small bag of groceries we brought from home. When Traci sees the can, her eyes well up.

"Oh, Asha. I can't believe you bought these. You remember when we used to eat these together, right?"

I nod. We used to eat beans every Saturday when I was a kid and Dad was out working at the sports center all day. Traci always said it was a treat because they're so sweet they might as well be dessert. Until I pulled the can off the shelf and stowed it away, I'd forgotten about that. Those sweet moments we used to share are buried under all the fights we've had since. Ugly things we've said that sit just behind the corners of our eyes. And even though I didn't buy them and I know I shouldn't be shoplifting, especially after Dad's arrest, it touches me to see my peace offering is understood. Besides, how can it be immoral to take one can of beans from a gas station owned by a company that's destroyed the land of this province again and again until half its people are living in poverty?

Traci wrenches the can open and pours the beans into a small pot. The smell of baked beans and molasses fills my head, clears away the strangeness of being here. Sweet comfort food. Traci hums as she stirs.

"Let's eat." She pours the beans into two cracked cream-colored hexagonal bowls. We sit at the kitchen table in the bad flickering fluorescence. It washes us out, makes us both look sick and gaunt. But for now at least, that's a false image. For now, we're both happy and full and warm. I imagine living here for the next year and it doesn't seem so bad.

Inside me, the beans grumble. Something skitters across the floor, into the shadows.

CHAPTER TWO

*W*hen the scent of coffee finds its way upstairs, I rise from a dead sleep. Voices, low and serious, follow the coffee scent into my room. My hand locates my phone squished between the headboard and the wall, and I check the time. Eight thirty. It's too early. Who's making house calls at this hour? I pull a pillow over my head to try to block the noise out as their somber voices morph into raucous laughter. I thought one of the benefits of leaving the city would be that Traci wouldn't make so much noise in the morning. No more coffee dates, no more running buddies, no more dishes to clean up before people judge us for our mess at seven in the morning. But she's still found a way to interrupt my sleep. I'm a teenager, I'm growing, I need to sleep. Period.

I roll over and bury my face in my pillow, but the pillowcase is dusty as hell. And the pillow itself smells like a wet basement. I try to stifle it but an enormous sneeze bursts through my face and I'm fully awake whether I want to be or not.

It would've been hard to sleep much longer anyway. The morning sun falls through the east-facing window, diffused through the ancient elm growing a few metres away from the house. Something about this house keeps cool, even in summer.

Traci told me it's because people were a lot more thoughtful about how they designed houses in the 1800s, since they didn't have central cooling.

As the sun inches onto my bed, it feels warm, peaceful, so I stretch, throw my legs off the bed and move closer to the wonky panes. Mist rises over the trees, tinted gold against the rapidly bluing sky and thick green of the woods bordering the property. For a minute, everything arranges itself into paradise. Then my eyes wander to the muddy truck parked crookedly behind our station wagon and the elaborate gardens Great Aunt Aggie once so carefully tended, now overgrown with poison ivy. It's strange. All the decay I expected from my first glance at this old place looks more like growth from up here.

I look for the spots I remember having fun in as a kid; there used to be a tire swing hanging from a tall oak that Aggie got some neighbor to put up so me and my cousins wouldn't stay inside denting mahogany and chipping china. Where is that swing now? My eyes comb the blurry edge of the treeline where new growth is emerging: little saplings, wildflowers, weeds . . . nothing to indicate the existence of that big old truck tire hanging from a frayed length of rope.

But then I strain my eyes to gaze farther back, past the saplings to the more developed trees, and I see a pair of legs swinging lazily, without any clear direction, sticking out of the brush. They're so pale, awkwardly crossed, and bruised up so badly, that at first my heart races, thinking I've clocked a dead body. Maybe it's just what I've come to expect of this old house— Aggie's death and the signs of decay tricking me into seeing such morbid traces on the landscape. Or I'm on edge from everything that's happened recently. Just a year ago, I don't think I would've assumed the worst. A year ago, I was a different person.

It's probably some local kid. Traci's always talking about how people let their kids roam free here.

I scan the brush again, and the legs are gone. Maybe whoever was swinging went back into the woods.

It's nice out today. I think I'll try skating to Main Street.

I pull on my ragged jeans, a hoodie, one of Dad's old basketball jerseys, and head downstairs.

In the kitchen, Traci is sitting across the table from a lady who looks like she spends most of her time outdoors. I get the feeling she looks older than her age. Her stiff posture doesn't match her babyface and soft blue eyes. A few streaks of gray salt her auburn hair, pulled tight into a ponytail.

When she sees me, her face opens into a warm grin. "You don't recognize me?"

I didn't expect her to speak to me. I shake my head no. Do I know her?

Traci rolls her eyes as if I should remember this stranger. "Mrs. Levesque-Gerges from next door. You and her daughter, Nicole, used to play together as babies the first few times I brought you and your father to visit Aggie out here. She's been taking care of the house." I find that hard to believe with the amount of dust that's layered up on everything.

"It's a shame you didn't come visit more, Trace." Mrs. Levesque-Gerges reaches out and places a hand over Traci's. It's pointed and overly sympathetic, the kind of gesture I know Traci considers an overreaction. I wonder if Mrs. Levesque-Gerges knows about Dad. Or maybe her sympathy is with Traci's loss of Aggie. Most people consider Traci and Dad's divorce a good call on Traci's part now that Dad's behind bars.

"Well, not until after the divorce. Asha's father didn't like it out here. Maybe you remember, Kel, Asha's great-grandparents were settled out here before they moved to the city."

"How could I forget?" Neither of them moves for a minute. They're frozen in their own thoughts, each waiting for the other to say something. Did something happen with my great-grandparents? Mrs. Levesque-Gerges is the first to break the silence. "It's such a grand old house. Shame Aggie neglected the place. Always made me feel like a princess walking through these halls when we were teenagers."

The grin she shoots my way feels like an overcompensation for the awkward silence. Not wanting to endure another, I follow up: "You were friends?" Mrs. Levesque-Gerges in her John Deere camo fleece across from my mother in her cream Hudson's Bay merino sweater that Jeff bought her. It seems impossible to imagine Traci in this woman's world, let alone as friends.

Mrs. Levesque-Gerges turns to face me, grinning ear to ear. "We weren't just friends. Tied at the hip, we were!" she exclaims. "At least until you got married. But of course, it was silly to stay apart all those years."

"Well, you can't choose your partner's family." Traci's mouth is tight. It gets that way when she's trying to protect other people's comfort at the sake of her own. I wonder what happened between them. I always thought Traci and Dad's family got along.

Traci clears her throat. "Asha, Kelly cleaned my old room out for you."

"Oh, thanks. Do you know what happened to the Prince poster that was in there?" I ask. Mrs. Levesque-Gerges stares at me blankly. I take that to mean it's in the trash. I really wanted that poster, but maybe it's better this way. A true fresh start. Not a trace of Traci's past in the house either. Just us and Aggie's junk.

"Sorry I didn't recognize you, Mrs. Levesque-Gerges. But I'm glad my mum has a friend here." Even if Traci and Mrs. Levesque-Gerges have some beef that's gone unresolved all these years, and I wish I had that poster, I'm being honest: it's good Traci has someone in this town who still knows who she is and cares enough to come by.

Mrs. Levesque-Gerges reaches out a hand and I shake it. Her grip is tight. I remember what my dad told me about how shaking tight signals strength of character and I grip hers equally strongly back. She seems a bit surprised by this and massages her palm as she corrects me: "Call me Kelly. And I think you and my daughter Nicole would still get along." She chuckles and takes a sip of her black coffee. "You used to play so well as babies."

"Oh yeah?" I say. Traci is tapping the side of her mug impatiently. She must want to discuss something specific with Kelly. I hold up my skateboard. "I'm going out."

"Now?" Traci surfaces from her coffee, scandalized that I would leave without breakfast. There's a box of frozen waffles on the counter. She must've gone out to get them before I woke up. It's a nice gesture, but I'd rather duck out until they're finished having whatever strained conversation they were building up to before I interrupted.

"Had a granola bar upstairs. I'll be back in a bit. See you."

As I reach for the kitchen door, Traci says, "Remember how we used to spend so much time on our hair and clothes? See how kids go out now? I'm all for self-expression, God knows . . ." Her comment is not directed at me, but I still turn around. Traci hates when I dress to go skateboarding because she thinks I'm hiding my figure. It takes every ounce of my self-control not to talk back to her in front of Kelly.

"Nobody cares how I dress." I try to tamp my temper down, avoid letting it seep into my tone.

Traci turns back toward Kelly. It's unclear if she heard me. "All the bright colors and the hairspray. And now . . ."

Kelly glances at me then faces Traci, as if I'm not even part of the conversation. "Oh yeah, Nicole is just the same. Don't understand her style one bit. It's all Hassan's dirty old t-shirts and baggy pants."

They both cackle. Traci wipes tears from her eyes. "I do sometimes wish you'd show your body a little more, though, Ash. You're so beautiful."

I try to smile. I don't know how convincing it is. "I just don't think you'd say the same thing if you had a boy, you know?"

Traci lets out a frustrated breath. "You don't need to make me out to be the patriarchy, here, Asha. I just said you were beautiful."

"You're talking about my body, my clothes, as if I'm not even here. Acting like I'm weird for going out in—" I gesture up and down at my outfit. Heat is rising in my chest, threatening to burst out, "—*this*."

"I just want you to look like you have someone to care for you—" Traci is usually so composed in the presence of guests, but maybe something is different with Kelly, who is now fiddling awkwardly with her coffee mug.

"Isn't that classist? What if you couldn't afford nice clothes for me?"

Kelly laughs awkwardly and jumps in to loosen the tension. "Well, your daughter certainly inherited your fire, Traci!"

"The headaches I must have caused Aggie . . . "

It's as if I'm not here again.

"I'm heading out," I say, and bolt before she can protest more. The kitchen door slams behind me. It's not on purpose, it's just heavier than I'm used to. The screen rattles in its frame. I think about looking back, about apologizing, but instead I set out for the road.

♪♪

The long dirt driveway ends with a mucky puddle before the road begins. On the way in, Traci called it a moat. It's not the most welcoming entrance or graceful exit from this grand old house. It also shows how little traffic Great Aunt Aggie got in her last years. The only people coming in and out were probably the Levesque-Gergeses who did their neighborly duty of bringing her groceries and cleaning house when she couldn't do it herself.

The puddle is so wide and deep that as I slosh through it, I soak my shoes, socks, and jeans with thick brown-red water. I can't help but think it's too deep to have appeared naturally. From the stories Traci and her cousins have told, it sounds like something Aggie would have done when she was still able to do hard manual labor. Apparently, she was a notorious misanthrope. That's what Traci said.

I didn't know what "misanthrope" meant until I looked it up: *someone who dislikes other humans and society.* If Aggie did dig this moat, did she do it to keep people out? Or keep herself in? I asked Traci and she told me not to play into the town mythology surrounding Aggie and that the moat is just the gutter stream that floods in the spring and washes the driveway out.

One of my feet sticks in the muck. When I try to dislodge myself, it only sinks in deeper. I pinch my skateboard under my armpit as hard as I can to avoid either losing it to the moat or falling in myself. I tug on my left foot and the right sinks deeper. Shit. I'll never even make it to the road at this rate. I stand still for a second and just breathe. Relinquish all resistance. Other than being stuck in the moat, it's so pleasant out. The mist is burning off, and the sun warms the parts between my braids. There are chickadees in the trees doing their sweet mating calls.

Aunt Aggie taught me what they sound like when they're searching for a partner. That sweet *weee-woooo.* She also showed me how to get them to land in my hands with a few sunflower seeds and a whistle. There weren't many times we connected one-on-one, but that day she made me feel like a fairy-tale princess. Their little mouths so careful in the palm and their claws didn't even dig in. The first time I thought it would hurt. But they're so light and gentle. Their bodies are barely made of anything.

As my body melts into the stillness, I become aware of another sound beneath the slosh of my feet and chickadee calls:

sticks breaking. Something large is farther back behind the trees and moving my way.

Abruptly, I remember a time my cousins told me they saw a coyote around here. I thought they were just saying it to scare me. If that was their intention, it worked. I was scared, even though I wouldn't admit it. The night after they told me, I curled in bed next to Traci and Dad with my eyes wide open to the pitch of the country night. And late, late into the night, when everyone was passed out, I heard it. The snapping of branches and the barking laugh of a coyote beneath our window. Then the laugh became a child's scream.

Everyone in the house woke up. Usually, coyotes or coywolves didn't come that close, Aggie said. Maybe they heard all us kids making a ruckus and thought it had found some kin. That didn't make me feel any better. What if the coyote was disappointed when it saw me? Would it tear me up and devour me? While everybody else got up and turned the lights on, traded stories about how they woke up or what they were dreaming just before, I curled under the covers and pretended to sleep. I pretended to sleep for the rest of the night, even when the excitement wore off and everyone drifted off again, safe in their beds, confident in the security of locked doors. I never told anybody how I couldn't stop shivering, like I'd been the coyote out there in the cold of the night.

Now, the same fear overtakes me. I pull harder at my foot as the rustling comes closer. There's no one out here. I'm stuck and if a coyote didn't like the look of me, it could take me down, easy. I forget that it's not likely for them to be out at this time, not likely for them to approach a human. It's just me and the fear fluttering in my chest. I need to get out of this puddle and skate away as fast as I can to town. And then a bright orange baseball cap emerges between the leaves and I know I've embarrassed myself again.

"Hey!" the person in the cap yells my way. They're short and wearing clumsy work boots and a brown barn jacket that engulfs them so only the ends of their shorts peek out from beneath the hem. "I said hey!" they yell again when I don't answer.

"Hey!" I yell back, trying to sound friendly. I know I can't pretend I don't see or hear them. Who walks through the brush in the morning yelling at strangers? It doesn't really make me feel much safer in my stuckness. Plus, it's embarrassing I'm even in this situation. Maybe I should've just buried myself in blankets and hidden the day away.

They come out into full view, and I can see it's a girl around my age but a head shorter than me. She has tan, freckled skin and long, dark auburn hair. Something around her eyes is familiar. It takes a minute, but I recognize Kelly in her.

I'm not surprised when she yells, "I'm Cole Levesque-Gerges. Your neighbor? You know you could've just taken the easy way . . ." She laughs and points to the makeshift log bridge over the gutter that I hadn't even known to look for. Heat rises to my head, the fear of encountering a wild animal melting to shame at my lack of awareness. "Throw me your board. It'll be easier for you to get unstuck." Cole comes closer to the edge of the moat and I toss her my board. She catches it and I'm finally able to get my feet unstuck and wade out of the moat, panting.

She crosses the rotting log bridge and meets me in the lengthening grass that quickly turns to chunked cement and gravel. I survey the pavement. It's pretty torn up. It'll be a challenge for me to skate at all.

"Yeah," Cole smiles, seeing me survey the road, "Not many skateboarders around these parts. The roads're shit." She says her "r's" hard and rural the way Traci does after she has a couple glasses of wine.

Cole hands my board back to me, and I reach for it with still shaking hands. Her eyes catch on them, but she looks away quickly.

"I'm Asha. I live here now."

"What's it like living in a haunted house?"

I shrug. Her tone is jokey but there's something behind the question that makes me realize just how little I know about the house's history. I don't want to betray my ignorance about the house, so I strike the same joking tone to reply. "Don't know yet. It's only been one night."

She doesn't laugh. Maybe she doesn't know if I'm joking either. There's a moment where we both stare at our feet, not sure what to say. Then she points at my board. "You know any tricks?"

"A few."

"Kickflip?"

I laugh. "Why's that always the one people ask first?"

"Well, can you?"

"Kinda . . . not well." Nia was trying to teach me. Ground tricks freak me out. They take a lot of confidence, and all the momentum must come from you, rather than the sloping terrain of a park. Nia would always make fun of me for being such a chickenshit skater. *May as well be a long boarder.* I can't be chicken now. First impressions . . .

I throw my board down and land on it with that familiar pop of solidity. I skate down the street a bit, then come back and do some ollies over potholes. Cole throws up some *whoops*. I can feel myself warming to her already.

This is what I like best about skateboarding: I can do something so little and feel so proud. Just for a moment. My favorite part of show and tell was always the showing. Why waste time talking about the *whys* and *hows* and *whats* of things when you can just ride and ride until—

"Hey, I think someone's coming!" I turn to see if what Cole says is true so I can get off the road and—

I hit a rock.

I don't remember falling and I don't remember standing back up. My hand's on the back of my head where a lump is already rising. Better it swells out than in. I look around, but Cole's gone. It's just me and an RCMP cruiser barreling toward me, chirping its siren. I scramble off the road, my legs catching gravel sharp as shrapnel as the cruiser kicks up dust. A white man hangs out the window and yells something at me I don't understand as language. I'm still turning my head, looking for Cole, when I realize the cruiser has pulled over and switched on its lights.

Why would this cop car come speeding out of nowhere like that, entitled and reckless? Rage fills me until I can't feel my body's edges. But as the cop swings his legs out of the cruiser and slams the door, I swallow that anger down and let it simmer just above my stomach where it burns like acid reflux. I force a smile onto my face.

Cole appears beside me holding my board, burrs attached to her shirt. My board must've gone in the ditch. She looks me up and down, concern wavering behind her eyes. "You ok?" That concern is misplaced, I think, when the cop is walking toward us, slow and menacing.

"Yeah, just a hard fall." It's a half-truth. What really set me off was the RCMP car. The full truth is that sometimes I crave the crash into the pavement. I should've stayed off the street. "But I'm fine. It was just a shock."

That's what Traci said when Dad called her collect from prison the first time. She cried too. I guess throughout the trial and his sentencing, the reality of the situation hadn't fully kicked in. Even though I know she hasn't loved Dad for a long time, she still cried. Back then, I thought she was being melodramatic. I still haven't cried about it. I thought I was stronger than her for holding back. I try to be stronger than my instincts now, suck all the salt back in. No tears.

The cop shifts from foot to foot. He's bulked up with gear and holds his hand on his hip, just above the holster of his gun. The hair left on his head is beginning to gray from a dirty blond. Even though he can't be much taller than me, he's way more solid, which gives the impression that he could intimidate anyone he wanted to.

I jump when Cole shouts, "Uncle Joe!"

The officer smiles and walks our way. He opens his arms, reaching out the way people do in that moment of surrender when you're not sure if they're going to get shot or make it away safe. Cole falls into his embrace.

"Nicole Mariam, how many times have I told you—stay off the road. It's a blind hill. You and your friend here could've been hit."

Cole pulls away. "I *know*. But I asked Asha to show me a trick."

He squints at me like he's feigning misrecognition. "I don't think we've met? You from around here?" he asks me.

"Asha," I say. "I just moved in." But I bet he says the same to all the other non-white folks in town. *You from around here?* All my history's in this town, I should've said yes.

"Oooooooh—" He draws out his surprise. "You're Traci's daughter?" How did he know that? We just arrived last night. Maybe like Kelly and Cole, we met in some distant past I can't remember. I thought no one in this town would know who I was, that I'd be able to build up an image of myself from scratch. I'm starting to realize how unrealistic that dream was.

"Yeah," I admit.

"She was a fun girl back in the day."

The way he pauses when his lips shape themselves around the word "fun" makes me think he means slutty. Not that that's anything to be ashamed of. Good for Traci. I'm glad she got hers. I don't think this officer is all about sex positivity though. I hold the officer's gaze, hoping he can see past my neutral expression to what I really think of him calling my mother fun. There's an awkward silence between the three of us as I struggle to think of anything else I could possibly tell this balding RCMP officer who almost ran me over, who is related to Cole, who didn't ask us to get on our knees, whose gun is so close to his hands.

Then the silence breaks as he and Cole exchange pleasantries and a brief arm wrestle. I become invisible. She asks him if he's going to come by for dinner. He asks her how the last week of the school year was. Then he gets in his car, salutes us, and drives off.

I don't have the time or guts to talk about how uncomfortable this exchange made me before Cole asks, "Hey, you ever seen baby bunnies?" Her gaze lingers on my hand clenched around my board.

"I should go back home." I don't want to be out here anymore. *Home* stings in my mouth. It's not a lie, but it feels that way. Aggie's big old house is not what I think of as *home*, at least not yet. I miss our warped laminate floors and familiar cracks in the popcorn ceiling, the smooth, easy-to-skate pavement of our cul-de-sac.

Cole sees my hesitancy and grabs my arm, pulling me toward a path off the road. "It's on the way back, come on." And before I know it, I'm following Cole into the woods, my wet shoes squashing out water into the sweet-smelling moss as the new summer canopy shades us, veils us from any onlookers. I remember the bruised legs I saw this morning. Uneasiness crawls like worms in my guts.

Then, I notice Cole's legs, moving through the brush, match those bruised legs exactly. I let go of my breath.

⁂

The moss is moving. It reminds me of the thick skin that sometimes forms on top of a pot of warm milk. The whole thing moves as one, as if bubbles want desperately to escape but can't. It looks alive. And it is.

Cole reaches one hand toward the patch of moss. All our surroundings are dappled; sunlight falls like rain through the thick, humid air right onto the patch of moss Cole overturns with two soft fingers. I lean closer. The hole is well protected, not just by the moss, but prickly raspberry brush and poison ivy that Cole warns me to avoid. At first glance into the hole, I think I see one large rabbit. Then, what I thought was a leg twists and turns, separating into little bunnies. Soon, the little slits of sleepy eyes become visible.

"Come, look," Cole whispers. "There're five of them. I've been coming to check on them every day since I found them."

I let my knees sink into the mulch of the forest floor and put my face closer to the bunnies, closer to Cole too. We're almost touching. I do my best to keep my distance, try not to breathe too loud or heavy. Don't want to disturb the scene with my morning breath. "How'd you find them?"

"By looking." She reveals her buck teeth in a smile. She's soaking up my awe. Gently, she places the moss back on top of the nest and we stand. "I like coming on the trails out here. It's quiet and no one's telling me to clean my room or take out the trash. Plus, I keep the trails fresh. My parents like that."

"Kelly?" Cole looks surprised that I know her mother's name.

"She was at my house for coffee and mentioned I'd get along with her daughter Nicole," I explain. "Assuming that's you?"

"That is me! But don't call me Nicole. I hate it. It's always Cole."

"Cole it is."

We're both silent for a moment. She looks comfortable in it, tilts her head skyward. I dig my hands deeper into my pockets and wriggle my toes in my shoes. I don't know what to say next. It's so weird I would meet someone who seems genuinely cool and nice and who I might want to chill with in the first few hours of my first day here. Minus the RCMP uncle, of course. He can suck it. I don't want to get my hopes up, though. Friendships have never been easy for me. Traci says my expectations are too high. I don't know if that's it exactly. Dad says it's because I don't know who I am yet. That might not be it exactly either. The only person I ever felt I could be truly myself with was Nia, but that's a lot of pressure to put on one friendship, especially when she's flying across the ocean for the summer.

But I don't want to come on too strong with Cole. So instead of asking if she wants to be best friends forever, I just ask: "How come I don't remember you from when we were younger?"

Cole looks down from the place she was observing in the trees. She doesn't quite meet my eyes. "I kind of remember you. Eating popsicles on the stoop or something. But my parents got pretty strict when I was older and I don't think I saw you again."

"Are they still strict?"

"Yeah, but I'm better at lying. And I'm old enough to drive."

We both laugh.

"Your mum seemed pretty desperate for us to be friends."

Cole rolls her eyes. "She thinks I'm lonely. Plus she doesn't like my friends."

"Why?"

"I don't want to get into it." But from the way she waves her hand, almost theatrically, it seems like she might.

"You sure? I'm the perfect person to share gossip with because I don't know who anybody is anyway. Secrets are safe with me."

"I mean . . . it's not really anything, you know? Just petty high school drama and I'm over it. I just want to get the next year over with and get out of here."

I know exactly how that is. That's part of why I'm here. "Is it, like, a boy thing?"

"No? I guess? I don't know."

"So, it is." All the boy-thing stories start like this. I know from listening to all the people in me and Nia's (mostly Nia's since my dad's arrest, if we're being honest) extended friend group talk about their *boy-things* non-stop. I'm always giving advice or zoning out. It's the one subject Nia doesn't really talk to me about, which is fine. I'm not ready to talk about my feelings for anybody and she hasn't ever pushed it. She's a good friend for understanding, but sometimes I wish she could help me understand this part of myself, what I want. *If* I want anyone. I'd have to be able to put how I feel into words first, though.

"I mean, you'll hear it from someone else if you don't hear it from me, so . . ." She takes a deep breath. "It's like . . . I made out with one girl, Maddie Leblanc, at a party and then everyone was saying I made her do it to break up her and Devon because I was jealous."

"Devon?" She's acting like I already know everyone in town. I don't know if it's because we used to play as babies and that's a special bond in her eyes, but I appreciate it. I haven't met many people I feel so immediately comfortable around.

"Devon Paul. We were tight, best friends since primary."

"Not anymore?"

"Nope. Not anymore." Cole takes in a big breath, then lets it all out in a huff. "I'm not saying I didn't break his trust or whatever, but he told her stuff I wanted to keep private between us, like, about my sexuality, and then *she* kissed *me*."

"Oh, shit." I can't believe she's telling me this right off the bat. That's, like, some deeply personal stuff. Not to mention extremely hot gossip for a newbie like me to be privy to. Maybe she's as lonely as me. "I'm sorry."

"It's whatever." She won't look my way. I can tell it's bringing up some emotions for her. "We'll get over it. It's just high school."

"Yeah, I guess it's high school, but it's also a breach of trust on, like, many levels." People just can't help running their mouths. It's better to keep to yourself.

Cole nods. I hitch my skateboard up under my arm. "Dude, look," I say, "that sucks. If you ever want to hang and catch up more on all the stuff that's happened since we were babies, I can give you my number? Or you can call the landline. I think your parents probably have Aggie's old number."

"My phone's in the shop, but I've got the landline. Used to do crank calls to the old, haunted house in middle school."

"You ever get a ghost?"

"A few times, actually, yeah."

I laugh. It hurts, just a little, in my stomach, so I stop. I never thought before about how laughing builds muscle. Mine must be out of shape. I remember Dad told me to keep the ones who make you laugh around. "You want to come to lunch?"

"Thanks, but no thanks. Mum's counting on me to sous-chef from now 'til Sunday dinner. My dad just got back from out west so she's pulling out all the stops." *Sunday dinner* . . . I wonder if their family is traditional Christian. What do her parents think about her queerness? Do they know?

"Ok." Maybe I went too hard, too fast. I have to play it cooler. "You know how I can get home?"

She points to a towering oak that has a lightning split in it. "Just keep walking straight at that oak and then you should be able to see the edge of the roof. From there you should be fine if you just walk in a straight line."

"Thanks."

"Ok, ya city slicker." She chuckles to herself at the phrase. "See you later if you don't get lost and die in the woods."

"Later."

I turn and walk toward the house, the smile on my face as warm as the dappled sun. She turns and walks toward her home. I think of all those baby bunnies so safe in their mossy nest, all curled up tight and close.

I run my hand over the back of my head. The lump's big and tender but the blood has dried. I hope Traci doesn't see me before I clean up and wrap my hair. She'd freak out for sure. I feel some guilt at hiding this morning's adventures from Traci. It's just so she won't worry about me. She already has so much to worry about with the house and moving. Is lying by omission as bad as lying straight out?

Besides, it's hardly the worst information I've kept from her. If she knew what I do about Jeff, maybe everything would crumble and she'd be back on the couch, not eating, not speaking to me. I'd be totally alone.

Cole's directions back home are good. I make it to the oak, and then the edge of the woods, and then I'm back in our yard. I look up at Traci's room. Her shadow moves across the curtains. This house isn't haunted, just depressing and lonely as fuck.

CHAPTER THREE

*I*n town on Saturdays, the market is an event. *Everyone* goes. Traci
drives us to the other side of town, jittery and jerky. I don't know
if it's the third cup of coffee, half-drunk and clenched between her
knees, or nervousness at the prospect of running into everyone
she ever knew in this place, but Traci's talked from the moment
I shuffled downstairs to now. At the (the!) stoplight, Traci cranks
our windows down. She points out town landmarks, Ron's diner,
the fried chicken joint, Riverbank café, a squat brick building
that houses the Bainbridge Library. "It's named after Ellis, Aggie's
late husband," Traci informs me. "There's a whole exhibit there
about how the Bainbridges brought industry to town."

"Sounds like propaganda," I joke. Traci doesn't laugh but
moves on to talking about the clay they imported from Minto to
make the bricks back in the day.

Once we're off Main Street and onto the road that leads to
the market, she switches on the radio to replace my silence with
a conversation partner. I wish I could keep up with her. It's just
so early. I'm still groggy, and watching the mist rise off town is
more appealing than conversation. CBC News streams out into
the open air. It's a segment about how activists are rallying in
favor of healthcare for women, non-binary, and trans people
in the province.

"It's a shame that clinic shut down . . . sometimes I wonder if coming back here was the right decision." Traci shakes her head in shame. "But if no one comes back, how will things improve?" There are a couple more provincial stories, then:

. . . and those affected by the embezzlement of a popular youth sports organization speak out against Raymond Walker, recently found guilty—

Traci swipes at the power button, shutting it off. "I'm sorry." She puts her hand over mine. *Raymond Walker.* Dad. I squeeze Traci's hand back. The light turns green, but she only lets go to shift into gear, then her hand's right back on mine. I don't pull away. In this moment, Traci's hand is the only thing grounding me. Every time I hear his name, an image of Dad's face the last time I saw him pierces me.

"I wish they wouldn't talk about him like that," I mumble. It's painful for Traci too. As much as their romantic relationship has long expired, and as much as me and Traci have our disagreements, my parents were always committed to raising me together. Dad was still a marker of consistency in her life, if only as my father. They had shared custody until Dad was charged last winter. Even with shared custody, these past few years I rarely spent longer than a weekend at Traci's because I couldn't stand to be around Jeff. Most of my life was at Dad's house. Now, he's barely present, and not of his own will. I think Traci doesn't know whether to be angry with him for the situation he's put us all in. I know I'm angry. I just can't decide if it's at my life or the entire world.

"I wish they wouldn't talk about him at all." The words leak through my teeth like a toxic gas that spreads into the car air. If they didn't talk about him at all, maybe things would be completely different. I could forget why I ended up here and make the most of my time with Traci. And if none of it had ever happened at all, I'd still be in the city where the streets are evenly paved and easy to skate over. I'd still have the familiarity of a neighborhood where every neighbor and house was scorched into my brain instead of this overgrown, decaying landscape of Aggie's property without neighbors in sight. A three-hour drive to Nia's. A pre-set amount of time with Dad in the visiting room once he feels like he's ready to see me. What if he never wants to see me? "They don't even know he did it."

"It's what the court decided. We have to accept it as our reality for now." We've talked this through before. My anger is always met with a brick wall of practicality. "I'm sorry, Ash. I thought it would be further away here."

But what if I can't accept his incarceration as my reality? I don't think he did it. I don't want to believe he did. And I hate that he's going down for it whether he did it or not. Why does he have to be locked up? What if people don't look at him the same when he comes out? I know no one looked at me the same once the news hit the mainstream. The lunch table me and Nia used to sit at got a lot sparser. Even Karys and Melanie, who I'd thought were good friends, made themselves scarce. They said it was because they liked going for walks at lunch, but I caught them eating in Miss Moon's room more than once. They didn't even bother to leave campus.

At least people don't know how we're connected to Dad here. The only real clue is my last name, Walker. It's not like Walker's that uncommon a name. If this town wasn't so white, I could blend right in. Hanging with Cole yesterday really made me believe it wouldn't be harder to make friends here than it was back home.

Kids aren't so different here and neither are the police. Cole's connected to them through her uncle. If we do end up hanging out more, I don't know if I want to talk to her about Dad. Kelly probably already told her what happened, but if I don't bring it up, maybe it will seem like something that happened to someone else.

Traci gestures at some distant hills with a waving hand that's supposed to clear the air in the car. "Your Nan grew up somewhere over there." I glance at where she's pointing, then stare back down at my lap. Nan never talks about growing up here except about her horse. It was Dad who told me about his grandfather, who was arrested when my Nan was a kid, for the murder of someone he barely even knew.

Dad used to tell me that story whenever the police came to my school to give a talk. *Don't trust them*, he would say. *They may act nice during those presentations, but not much has changed in seventy years.* He was right about that. Getting locked up for a crime he swears he didn't commit, just like his grandfather. Whether he did it or not, my great grandfather walked with a limp for the rest of his life. The legacy of his pain was visible. What will Dad's legacy be? Even if it's not made visible by the time he gets out of prison, will the scars on our brains be passed down too?

Every time Dad would tell this story he'd finish with, *and that's why you don't call the cops.* I don't know who called the cops on Dad, but if I ever find out, I don't think I could hold myself back from telling them just how much they've taken from me and Nan with him put away. "Put away" like some useless, silly toy. Not even a human. I think of Nan, back in the city. Her father and now her son taken away. And me way far away now . . . I should call her.

I take a deep breath, count two in four out, two in four out, then try to push those thoughts away. I'm here now, with Traci. I have to try to stay positive.

We pull into the "parking lot" of the market, which is a portion of field that's been ground to dirt from all the wheels that drive over it each weekend. The market itself is half open air, under a collection of colorful tents, and half inside a long brick building.

Traci turns to me, grinning. "You smell that?"

I sniff and let a smile creep onto my face. Woodsmoke, bacon, fresh bread, and the earthy scent of fresh produce waft together and push thoughts of Dad and the radio behind. "I'm so hungry."

"Good. Let's get some food."

We wander through the stalls toward the building. The big swinging doors open toward a little breakfast counter where you can order food. You order at one window and pick up at another down the hall. Past that, there's a collection of long tables where you can eat with other members of the community. It's loud in here, full of laughter and people reuniting after a week at work. There's a lineup in front of the window so me and Traci circle back outside and grab a couple of fresh squeezed orange juices then take our places in line. The juice is pulpy. I try to savor it, but it's impossible. I suck it down like it's saving my life, and in five minutes it's gone.

"Nothing's changed." Traci grins. I wonder what it's like to come back to your hometown after a long absence and find it exactly the same. I can't imagine going back to the city and finding everything exactly the same. Gentrification works too fast for preservation. And even if the place is familiar, people change. I wonder if Nia will be the same when I go back. A summer can change you, and she's going to Freetown to visit relatives she's never met in a place where our shared Black Loyalist ancestry and her mother's ancestry are intertwined. That's going to be an amazing experience for their family. Will living here without my best friend change me too?

"What about you?" I ask Traci. Traci, here as she is now, in her pressed adult contemporary fashion, must be different from who she was when she first moved here, after her mum died of cancer. She was younger than me, then. Fifteen.

"Some things have changed about me. But it's funny, maybe you'll notice as you get older, but there's something about going back to certain places you've lived that makes you connect with a history you've almost forgotten."

That's part of why the radio was so jarring. Dad's felt far away, not only physically, but psychically, since we arrived here. I'm thinking about him. It's hard not to when his name's on the radio, but not everything reminds me of him. "I think I get that."

"Like, right now, Asha, I'm remembering how *heavenly* the blueberry pancakes are here. It's not blueberry season, but they freeze up local berries for the year and they're just . . . I can't describe. You have to get them."

So, we both order the blueberry pancakes from the pimply kid at the counter, Traci with a side of bacon, and me with home fries, and take a seat at a table close to a window. The morning light shines through onto us, heating our faces. I realize I haven't seen Traci's face so relaxed in a long while. Maybe this town is bringing her back to youth in more than one way.

I'm halfway through my meal when someone claps a hand on my shoulder. My body jerks away instinctively. I don't know anyone here, so who could be laying a hand on me with such familiarity? When I turn, I see it's Cole's Uncle Joe, in civilian clothes: an army print fleece and beat up chunky sneakers.

"Traci Forrester!" The corners of his mouth stretch too far when he smiles, giving the impression of a hyena on the hunt. The way the word "fun" slithered from his mouth yesterday is the same as the way his hand slithers off my shoulder as it reaches forward to shake Traci's.

A small crease has reappeared between Traci's eyes. "Joe? How've ya been? Can't believe you recognized me. It's been years."

"Good, good. And you're still looking fine. As for work, can't complain. Working odd hours. RCMP, you know."

"This is my daughter, Asha," Traci introduces me with friendly tones, but I can tell something's off when the crease between her eyebrows doesn't fully release. For once, it's got nothing to do with me. She must not like this Joe guy, either. "We just moved back into town."

"Asha didn't tell you? We met yesterday. Thought she'd give my salutations to you. But then, maybe you didn't want to tell your mum you had a run in with the cops, huh?"

Traci's friendly smile drops. "Excuse me?" Now she's looking at me with that same frown again.

"Skateboarding out on the street with my niece, Nicole. Could've flattened her."

Driving like he was, he could've. That's no lie. Traci sighs. "I'm sure she knows not to skate on these roads now. I don't like the danger of skateboarding at the best of times, but Asha's a bit of a risk-taker."

"Like her mother, hey? You'd better stay out of trouble. Your family has a history of causing trouble around here." Joe lets out a belly laugh. But I'm not sure it's a joke from the way his eyes glint. I wait a beat for Traci to contest his claim but she doesn't say anything.

"I'm not planning on causing any trouble." When is this guy going to leave us in peace?

Traci laughs along with him but the way she picks at her food I can tell she isn't interested in this conversation lasting longer than it needs to.

Joe continues, "So how's the move? Need any help unpacking?"

"My husband, Jeff, will be by this weekend with some stuff. We're taking the move slow. Can't say Aggie's house is in the best shape. We don't want to fill it up before we've cleared all the necessary stuff out."

"Well, let me know if there's anything you need. Kelly's told me some of the work that needs to be done, and I have to say, it's a handful. But you two young ladies should be able to do it."

"Nice seeing you, Joe." He gets the signal that it's time for him to leave.

"You too, Trace. And you, Asha." He claps me hard on the shoulder again. "Good to see you back in town with the right sort of folk again, Traci." With that, he wanders off into the crowd.

Right sort of folk. Did he mean what I thought he did? And why didn't Traci say anything about me not being trouble to him? I take a deep breath, let it go. We're here to enjoy our pancakes, not socialize with some off-duty cop. And just because she didn't defend me, doesn't mean she thinks Joe is right.

"Man never knew how to keep in his own business," Traci seethes. "*Right sort of folk.* Like Joe Levesque knows the right sort of folk from the wrong."

I'm surprised to find myself laughing. "He got you heated!"

"He called me trouble! All the trouble when we were younger was started by his hand. Asha, the stories I could tell you about this man . . . I'm glad I left this place when I did. God forbid I ended up with Joe rather than your father or Jeff." But now we're back in this town. And he called me trouble too.

I don't have time to dwell on that before it hits me. "Oh my god . . . were you and Joe a thing?"

"Asha, we need to leave our shame in the past." Traci's entire face goes red. I laugh so hard I almost choke on my pancakes.

After breakfast, we pick up a few groceries from the vendors— some New Brunswick brown bread, jam, cold cuts, and veggies. We place the groceries in the car, then Traci leads me down to the river that runs behind the market.

"I used to come here with my friends every weekend." She points to a little trail that borders the river. We walk until we come to a wooden dock, then we drop our feet into the water. It's cool and refreshing. The day's heating up. Ducks float around and little minnows tickle our feet. I lie back and let out a sigh.

"And you thought this place was going to be hell." Traci tickles my belly. She does that when she's playful, since I was a little kid. It always makes me giggle.

"Fine. It's not that bad. I just didn't want to leave home."

We're joking now, but our fight from the night before we came here is still fresh in my mind. I screamed some unforgivable things at Traci about how she was a failure for losing her job, that I never wanted to be like her, just in a relationship for the money and no real emotional connection. I didn't want to leave home. Our fights sometimes get pretty hairy. I've thrown things and Traci has laid hands on me in the past when we've both lost control. Our chests have burst open with rage, and we've spent days picking up our mess. So it wasn't the first time I'd made her cry, but it was the first time I saw something break in her eyes that I thought might be beyond repair. With our feet in this river, though . . . I'm not certain things between us are beyond repair. In this moment, I know I'm safe. Maybe she'll forgive me. Maybe I can forgive her.

"What was it like moving here when you were younger?"

Waves that roll in from a passing group of kayakers slap lightly against the dock. "Hard. I had a lot of grief after my mum passed away and I acted out."

"By hanging out with Joe?"

"Would you let it go, Asha? Jeez. But yeah, and with Kelly. Me and Kelly got into tons of trouble at school."

"What for?"

"Pranks, mostly. We let some chickens loose in the high school once. That was our masterpiece, I think."

"Can't believe you used to be a rebel."

"Damn right."

"Did something happen between you and Kelly?" She must know she was acting tense when Kelly was over yesterday morning.

Traci swishes her feet back and forth, creating bubbles. Sunlight fractals play on her feet. "Not really. Just, I left and she stayed. I promised her we'd get out of here together, but she never did. She never could—well, maybe in the end she didn't really want to. And when push came to shove, she took care of Aggie for years when I felt I couldn't leave my job. I think she thought I was failing Aggie. It was hard for Kelly to be in that house, but it gave her space when things were hard over at her place with her kids. Kelly's mother and Aggie were close back in the day, you know. Aggie held a lot of knowledge about Kelly's mother but couldn't bear to talk much about her."

"Why not?"

"Aggie was secretive. Took a lot of knowledge to her grave. Not just about Kelly's mother, but everyone in town. She lost a lot of folks over her lifetime. Her husband died, her closest friend went missing . . . she knew more about loss than most. I never felt like she didn't understand what I was going through. And I'm grateful for that. I couldn't bear to live here with her, as an adult, though. Vacations were great. You remember, we used to have a great time. Now that she's gone . . ."

"Now that she's gone, you're back."

"Now I'm back. In my old house without Aggie. But with my girl. I'm happy you're here with me, Asha." We sit in silence, which is not actually silence, with all the activity around us. Voices carry over the water. There's so much peace in the world. With the sun bleeding into me, I feel the peace fully, deeply. Then Traci's phone buzzes. She pulls her feet out of the water and answers, leaves me on the edge of the dock.

When Traci returns, I've pulled my feet out too, let them dry off enough so I can put them back in my socks and shoes without discomfort.

"No—no—you have to talk—she *needs you*."

I know who she's talking to, but when Traci walks back toward me with the phone outstretched, I still ask: "Who is it?"

"Your father."

With determined, even breaths, I hold the receiver to my ear, ready to hear Dad's voice for the first time in weeks. But when I open my mouth to speak, I only hear the tone of a dead line.

"There's no one there." I hand the phone back.

"I'm sure he'll call back when he has a chance." But from the way she says it, I know he won't. We head back to the car. I stuff my hands in my pockets so Traci won't see they're shaking, and swallow the burn in my throat. I try to breathe in and out, counting again, but this time it's harder to make it work. Traci rubs my shoulder and I recoil. From then on, we're silent.

On the way home, Traci calls Jeff and puts him on Bluetooth. They flirt and joke with each other in their stilted, middle-aged way. Traci's looking forward to his arrival next Saturday.

Out of all the shitty, boring men she has dated, Jeff is my least favorite, and she chose to marry him. Jeff works for a company that's in the business of polluting and pillaging. He does their taxes or something. Traci swears it's just his day job and that he's a good guy underneath it all. Maybe to her. He's constantly taking her out for fancy dinners and buying her flowers, corny gestures I never thought she'd fall for before him. That's all nice, I guess, and I can't judge if it makes her happy. But that's the thing: *if*.

Most of the time I'm convinced she's happy, but then I'll notice how she fusses over appearance—*my* appearance, yeah, but also how she appears on social media, what she says about current events, or even feminism. When I was a kid, Traci used to be so outspoken. Now she's all about moderation and not making a scene. I can't help but think it's Jeff's influence. All his talking about "optics" and his dreams of becoming CEO of an energy corporation. It's not only that, though. I've caught him being a hypocrite in more ways than with the environment. I still haven't told Traci about the call I heard him make.

And then, I wonder if this is just me growing up. Maybe this is the way Traci always was and it's not Jeff's fault we grew apart.

Even with my reservations about Jeff, what I know about him that Traci doesn't, I should still try to make this move a fresh start with him too. Whatever I dislike about him, I'm starting to understand Traci's attraction to him a little. Jeff is dependable. He shows up when Traci needs him, answers her calls, lets her talk things out. And he was there to support her through all my fights with Traci, even if his ignorance was the cause of them half the time. He was there for her when Dad was arrested too. And he'll be here with us again soon. This time I'll really try to give him a chance.

I'm tired of fighting.

As we drive, I tune them out and keep a lookout for Nan's old farm on the side of the road. The way Nan talked about it, growing up here sounded difficult, but they always had enough to eat from the land, and working with the horses was fulfilling for her parents and for her.

There's so many trees, so much growth around here. I could get lost. I don't have to think about Dad if I don't want to. So instead, I think about Traci's rebellious past in this town, about the nest of bunnies Cole showed me yesterday, all the treats we're hauling back to the house, really anything but Dad, until Aggie's house looms in our field of view once again. I imagine the modest farmhouse Nan described as her childhood home next to it. Aggie's house would make Nan's old farm look like a garden shed. They only lived a few kilometers apart.

Nan still has a picture of her with her horse, Tamarack, up on the living room wall in her apartment. They're standing together, her hand on the reins that hang from Tamarack's big, speckled head, with her hair sticking out in two braids, her big dimpled smile lighting up the frame. She looks so sweet. How could anybody run that little girl's family out of town?

CHAPTER FOUR

"*A*sha, there's somebody at the door for you!"

Mid-text update to Nia, I drop my phone and race toward the muted evening light of my open window and poke my head out, trying to glimpse who it is before realizing all I can see is the mossy roof of the wraparound porch.

"Asha!" Traci calls again. We've been getting along pretty well this past week. But as I lag in my response, I can hear the testiness in her voice.

"Coming!" I sing toward the stairs, without betraying my annoyance at her impatience.

I throw on a sweater over my torn up old t-shirt and regret my choice for a second, knowing Traci will see this as a way of rebelling against her because of our argument in front of Kelly last weekend, even though it's not; it's just what I feel comfortable in. To Traci, what I feel comfortable in looks like neglect.

I hope it's Cole at the door. Who else would be coming by for me? I haven't met anyone else my age around here yet. My heart races at the thought of hanging out with Cole again. I've been thinking about our walk in the woods for the past few days—not that there's much else to think about around here. I tried to go out and find the rabbit's nest again, but I couldn't. Maybe she can show me how to find my way around in the woods. I ended up getting lost for an hour in there even though the patch of woods is only half a kilometer squared, according to Traci. It felt much larger when I was walking around in circles in there.

"Asha!"

"God! I'm coming!"

I race down the steps, nearly slipping on the freshly mopped hardwood. "Careful!" Traci's eyes bug out. She thinks one day I might break my neck.

"Don't rush me, then," I say. I see her swallow a lump of retaliating words. Instead, the glare she shoots my way burns my cheeks. She turns to Cole, smiling; the perfect hostess. I roll my eyes and guilt floods my gut. She's just trying to make a good first impression. She never used to worry about the house being clean or bother me about how I looked. With Jeff around, she wants me to look as clean and shiny as the floors after they've been swept, vacuumed, *and* mopped.

"Cole, you said you wanted to see Asha?"

Cole looks uncomfortable. Clearly, she's picked up on the tension. I can't imagine what her face would look like if we were really in a fight, not just an argument like Kelly caught when she was over. A real, loud, red-faced, spit-flying fight.

Cole's hands are buried in the pockets of her cut-offs. In contrast to the hunting gear she was wearing the first time we met, she's wearing a hand-cropped button up. From the brown-toned primary color stripes, it looks like it might've been her dad's in the '90s. She has her hair pulled back into a long ponytail. Without the cap, I can see that her eyes are a warm, reddish brown, like a deer's coat.

"Hey . . ." I realize I don't know how to follow up. I'd hoped it would be her at the door, but weren't we supposed to call before running over to each other's houses? I'm surprised at her confidence. As much as I enjoyed seeing the baby rabbits, I'm not sure how I came off when we were together. Her cop uncle showing up really messed with my head. Did she think I was acting weird?

"Hey, I came by to see if you wanted to chill at my place? I'm having some friends over for board games and stuff. Maybe a movie."

"Uhh . . ." I look down at my sweatpants and notice a clump of oatmeal stuck to them from yesterday morning. "Like, now?"

"You can change if you want."

"You'd better, Asha. You can't go out of the house like that," Traci jumps in. She can't resist commenting on how I dress, how I present my body. First with Kelly, now in front of Cole? But because Cole's here, I don't snap at Traci. I can tell from the way she averts her eyes that she feels the same guilt I felt earlier at rolling my eyes at her. For now, we keep the peace, and she fills the awkward silence that follows apologetically:

"But you should go! Thanks for inviting her, Cole. That's sweet of you. I thought Kelly sent you over with a message about some other issue with the house. I forgot that out here people will just drop by to hang out without warning."

Cole laughs. "My mum told me it would be a good reminder of how things work around here. Guess she was right." I can tell Traci is enchanted by her. Or by the fact she's getting me out of the house to socialize with my own teenage kind. "Oh, and she says to watch out for mice, too. She saw a hole when she left last time she came by. I think on the south-east corner? Maybe call her for more specifics . . ." she goes on, but I stop listening and sit down on the stairs, scratch a small patch of rash that's appeared on my wrist.

The longer I watch them, the more I can't help but wonder if Traci wishes she had a daughter like that, who could make small talk and be pretty once in a while. I bet she imagined her daughter would be outgoing, like Cole. Instead, there's me, who doesn't laugh at her jokes, or want to get manicures, and prefers to spend our time together in silence. All me and Traci have in common is a temper and a good sense for packing light. But maybe that's not fair . . .

". . . Asha?" They're both staring at me. I don't know which one of them said my name.

"You can come up to my room, if you want, or wait here. I'll just get changed," I say to Cole.

"You'd better go up with her." Traci beckons Cole in. "She'll take forever to choose an outfit. I don't understand her style, but she certainly takes her time picking her clothes out! I keep telling her, it's not the end of the world if she'd just wear a nice blouse or something other than these baggy shirts she loves—"

"I love Asha's sense of style," Cole interjects, before I can snap at Traci. "Or what I've seen of it so far. It's definitely different from how people around here dress. Not that people are bad dressers. Just different." Her compliment finds warmth in my cheeks.

"Well, it used to be a lot of plaid." Traci watches as Cole undoes her shoes and steps inside onto the threadbare carpet. Cole and I stand awkwardly for a moment, waiting for Traci to leave. She seems to realize her intrusion and says, "I'll go into the kitchen. Just let me know before you leave, ok, Asha?"

"Ok. I will."

❧

"You and my mum seem to get along well." I don't really know what else to say to break the silence. Cole and I barely even know each other, and now I'm trying to make conversation as I pick up dirty laundry off my bedroom floor. I throw some shirts in the old wicker hamper in the far corner of the room. God, it's messy in here. I didn't even realize.

"You jealous?"

"No." I say it too fast. Am I? That would be silly. Jealous of my mum getting along well with a potential friend?

"I'm joking! She seems nice. But I sense some tension."

"No, we're cool." It's clearly a lie.

"Whatever you say. Ooh, I like this shirt." I turn from the hamper to see what she's holding up. It's a simple blue tank top Traci got me on one of Jeff's business trips to the States—Texas or someplace with a lot of oil and a strong sense of American exceptionalism. She chose the shirt because the color "really pops" on me, which means it looks better with brown skin than white. She's not wrong.

"This color reminds me of an artist I did a project on last year." Cole swipes a hand over the smooth fabric. "Apparently, he painted everything this color at one point, or a color close to this, probably because he copyrighted that other color."

"He copyrighted a color?" I laugh. "How is that even possible?"

"No idea. Kind of a dick move if you ask me. But not surprising given the history."

"True." I think she's talking about the history of white patriarchy. It's not a topic I expected her to bring up so readily in this majority white town. We laugh together and I start to relax. I remember Traci mentioning something about Cole's dad being Lebanese, so even though I couldn't tell, she must be mixed too.

Her joke made me feel more comfortable, so I confess, "I never really wear it, that shirt." I just brought it along in case Traci ever asked about it. I keep it in my hamper where I don't have to be reminded of how guilty I feel that she bought me such a nice shirt that I'll probably never wear.

"You don't like it?"

"No, I do." And that's true, I do. Just not on me. I haven't worn it because it makes me feel too tight in my skin. "But for board games? I don't know . . . this doesn't really seem like the right vibe, does it?" I take it from her and hold it up in front of my face.

"What if I told you we weren't going to have a small gathering and play board games?"

"What?"

She has a wicked glint in her eye. "What if it was just a cover and I was actually taking you to a party?"

I'm shocked. "You came over to sneak out to a party with *me*?"

Cole almost looks offended. "What, you think we don't have parties out here like you city kids? We do. They're probably better too."

"What? No!" I don't doubt they're better. The source of my surprise is a lot more shameful. I've never been to a party. Every time someone's offered, I've turned them down. Nia would go every once in a while and complain it wasn't as fun without me. But I couldn't imagine myself having fun at a party. All those people and drinking, drugs, sweatiness, puke, music that's louder than it is good, the same old drama from school hallways . . . none of it really appealed to me. In the city, I was much more interested in spending the evening with a few good friends, drama-free. "I just . . . you did such a good job impressing my mum. Are you sure you want to throw it all away?"

"Your mum will never know. Don't worry. My little sister, Millie, will cover for us."

"Ok . . . yeah. Sweet. I guess we're doing this." Why not? I don't know anyone except Cole here, and maybe a party will lead to something more unexpected than falling asleep as I scroll through social media late into the night. I pull off my dirty hoodie and t-shirt and pull on the tight tank top. In the circle of the mirror I've wiped clean of dust, I survey myself and glance at Cole over my shoulder. She's checking her phone. I scratch my wrist absentmindedly as I look myself up and down and up and down. There's nothing wrong with showing some skin. And I *do* look hot in this shirt. Today's muggy, but I know I'll get cold when the sun goes down, so I pull a black zip-up hoodie from the ground. I put it on over the blue shirt, then look back into the mirror. "Ok, I'm ready."

When I look away from the mirror, I realize I don't know how long I've been gazing at myself. I look over my shoulder to where Cole was sitting.

She's gone.

"Cole?" I turn to face the space she was in, look over to my window, then my door. She was just there. I swear. "Cole?" I say it a bit louder. Maybe she likes to play pranks or something. Inexplicably, this might be her idea of a good time. I grip the wood of the doorframe and poke my head out into the hallway. I'm sure I see a shadow of a person move across the hallway, quickly, as if running, then it's gone and I'm left wondering if I imagined it.

"Cole?" She's not out here either. Then I hear the toilet flush and the water running. I lean back against the doorframe, my heart settling back into its natural rhythm.

She appears, backlit, having forgotten the bathroom light, and says, "Ready to go?"

I smile, nod, and follow her silhouette out of the house. I even remember to tell Traci we're heading out. She's not worried by my leaving. She just says, "Have fun!" and we're off.

ॐ

I squint up at the still-blue sky. "The sun hasn't even set yet."

"Yeah, for the best. Don't want any ghosts snatching us up around your house." This is the second time she's mentioned ghosts. Is she for real worried about them? "Dyllan likes to host parties earlier."

"Do they live close?"

"She's just up on a hill across from the river. I know a shortcut."

The shortcut turns out to be more of a hike. We walk along the highway for a bit before turning off into a patch of woods well beyond the Levesque-Gerges' property. Cole chats about all the people I'm going to meet, but I'm distracted, looking at the sun setting behind the trees and listening for sounds in the underbrush. There are some chipmunks out and lots of birds, getting their last socialization in before sunset. It smells like hay here even though there's no hay to be seen. Lichen hangs like beards from the trees. I get so sucked into observing the forest, I almost bump into Cole when she stops ahead of me. I accidentally knock the joint she's holding into the dirt.

"Sorry, zoned out. Lots to look at out here." I stoop and pick it up. It's well-rolled. Not like the one Nia and I smoked in her parents' garage back in eighth grade. We rolled following some vague instructions from a stoner YouTuber. After we smoked what was left of our mangled joint, she ate all the ice cream sandwiches and I had a panic attack on the floor of her family's laundry room. I thought I was going to die. But I'm still here.

The dreaded question: "You smoke?"

"I don't know."

She pulls a lighter out. "You do or you don't. Either way is fine. No pressure. This is really chill though. I swear. If you're worried about freaking out or something, don't. I smoke it to calm down sometimes." She lights the joint. Sucks in. In the lowering light, the orange glow of the coal feels like the sun to me. Cole holds out the joint. And I take it. She doesn't have to convince me. I just want to smoke it because she offered. Is that what charisma is? Is that what she has? It's almost like I didn't move my own hand.

I inhale. I manage not to cough on the first inhale, but on the second I break and Cole's laughing at me. "It's just . . . been a while . . ." I squeeze out between coughs. She pulls a water bottle out of her bag. I take a sip.

We share the rest of the joint. And the sun stops making the trees golden. My scalp crawls, pleasantly, like a head massage. My body settles into itself, finds its own movement. Me and Cole look into each other's eyes and giggle. I feel so light, my thoughts pass by easily, forgotten.

"One more stop, come on." Cole takes my hand. Her palms are hot, full of life. We walk forward, into the dark, until we come to a knobby old tree.

"Ugh . . ." It looks like it has tumors all over.

Cole kneels and digs through the underbrush until she finds a large, plastic Tupperware container. When she opens the lid, there's a mickey of vodka inside.

"Is it ok?" I ask.

"Drinking? You don't have to ask me for permission."

"No, the tree."

"The burls. Yeah, they're probably fine. They don't look like the fungus or insect kind."

"Insect kind?" The thought of insects crawling out of the burls makes me itchy all over. "What else is hiding out here?" I ask.

She shrugs, then holds out the mickey. "You're welcome to share it."

"Cool. Thanks." The vodka burns my lips. "You're so generous." I say it like I'm surprised, but she smiles.

"'Cause you're the new kid."

Maybe I should be the new kid more often. Seems to come with a lot of benefits. And no one even really knows me.

No one even really knows me
or what happened to Dad
or how fucked-up I am or anything
no one even really knows me
it's such a relief."

"But you just told me all that, so I feel like I kind of know you." Cole takes the mickey back and brings it to her lips. "What happened to your dad?"

I barely noticed myself saying that aloud. Loose connection between my mouth and brain. As loose as it is, I don't answer Cole's question. "And I know stuff about you, like who you are, even though we just met." I don't really know what I'm trying to say, but it feels true.

Cole pulls me close and pats me on the shoulder. "Well, we're really old friends, aren't we? How much can either of us have changed since we were babies?"

We both giggle. "I like this weed."

"I thought all skaters were stoners, but you've never smoked before, have you?" She's looking at me with her big, glassy eyes. The only light left in the world is reflected in them. I can't find the words to respond. I don't think I need to either. The moment flows into something else more muffled, more silent. The wind rushes against the trees as night falls.

Then she says, "We're here. That's the place Dyllan told me we were meeting up. Supposedly a murderer lived here. Come on." We're standing on the edge of the woods at the top of a hill that slopes toward an abandoned farmhouse. A murderer? If Cole was worried about the ghosts at Aggie's place, no doubt there's more than a few hanging around here. The place is unassuming: gray and crooked. The setting sun lights the whole place up like a beacon.

She goes, I follow.

❧

I find myself on a threadbare couch with a beer in my fist in the middle of a long-abandoned cottage. I take a sip. Everyone has a beer in hand or a flask of hard liquor in their pocket. Or both. I've said hi to everyone but I barely remember anybody's names.

I should correct myself. I've said hi to everybody except for Devon and Maddie, who Cole is avoiding and pointed out to me so I could avoid them too. They're the only people whose names I remember.

Here, on the couch, I can pretend I'm back home. I don't see how a party in the city could be much different. Maybe it wouldn't be in an abandoned farming cottage like this one, more likely in some wealthy kid's basement while their parents are away on business. The dim lighting, here sourced by battery-powered lanterns and fairy lights, would've been sourced with plug-ins in the city. But the inevitable people making out in whatever corner's the most private, music blasting, someone crying in a hallway—I'm pretty sure parties are like this everywhere.

A while ago, a couple guys left to start a fire out in the backyard. I'm thinking of going to check it out. The walls might start sweating in here if it gets any hotter.

Maybe Cole would want to come out to the fire with me. Where'd she go? This is the second time she's disappeared tonight. First back home, now here. She's there and then she's gone.

I survey the crowd and grimace as I sip my beer. The mustiness sticks at the back of my tongue. Beer's gotta be an acquired taste. I look for Cole where she was when I went to sit on the couch. Last I saw her, she was losing her mind laughing at something the person across from her was saying, a guy with a buzz cut and horsey teeth who she introduced to me as Skunk. She told me his given name but I can't remember it now. Skunk's still leaning against the wall, sipping lemon gin.

I walk back over to him. He holds out his hand and we shake. His grip is firm, his palms rough like he works with his hands. We already did this a few minutes ago. He must be wasted. I save him the embarrassment and reintroduce myself. "I'm Asha."

He points to himself. "Skunk—but that's not my real name. Just got sprayed by a skunk and it stuck."

"Yeah, Cole told me about that."

"Cole?" He's confused for a minute, but his eyes light up when he remembers. "Oh, Nicky. Yeah. Prolly said I still smell too." His breath reeks of lemon gin. Even the scent of it makes me nauseous. I don't know how anybody can drink it straight out of the mickey. Apparently, it goes down easy even if it smells like furniture polish.

"Hey, Skunk, you seen Co—Nicky?"

"Think she went to give it to Devon. You hear what happened between them?"

I nod.

"It's *right* fucked. I always thought Nicky and Devon would end up together. Guess she thought that too and tried to make him jealous. Or maybe she just likes Maddie. I don't know, man—it's bad vibes. I'd stay out of it if I were you."

Shit. I catch a glimpse of Cole's head as she makes her way around the corner to the barren kitchen. She said she was going to avoid him.

Skunk's hand lands on my shoulder, and he begins to twirl one of my braids. I yank it away from him and follow Cole.

My shirt is too tight. I wish I'd brought another shirt to change into instead of the sweater I've zipped around myself. Between the tightness and the sweat accumulating underneath the hoodie, it feels like I'm being squeezed and cooked down to nothing. It's like I'm moving through the crowd semi-transparent. I can tell people don't really perceive me as one of them, like I'm not really here. But I am. I am here. I scratch at the rash on my wrist.

I turn the corner and see Cole marching toward Devon and Maddie, who are making out beneath the stairwell.

"Cole!" I try to yell over the music, but I can't even hear my own voice. She's close to them now, and I see Devon's eyes open as he detaches himself from Maddie. Cole and Devon lock eyes, and I can feel the tension from here. I'm about to run over to try to defuse the situation but someone runs in from the back door, bringing in the smell of woodsmoke and cigarettes with them.

They shout, "Cops!"

My stomach turns over. The bad vibes I've been feeling all night evaporate off me and into the air of the entire place. I'm constricted by this top. I step up next to Cole. "I'm just not feeling good. Can we get out of here?" I say. It's not a lie. My heart's burning. I can't feel my edges. I didn't drink or smoke enough to feel this bad.

"Yeah, let's split. I don't want to get caught by the cops anyway." Cole glares Devon's way as we step out the back door. Neither of us looks back as we bolt toward the woods. The music cuts mid-rap-country mix and behind us the chatter quiets. We get closer to the woods. When we're behind the trees, I vomit. It's a near miss from Cole's shoes.

"I'm sorry. I'm so sorry. Oh my God."

Cole swears. "Did you drink too much?"

"No. I'm fine. I swear I didn't."

"That pile of vomit says different. If your mum tells my mum about this, I'm never going to leave my house again." I can tell she's still charged up from her near encounter with Devon and she's taking it out on me.

"It's not that. I think I might be sick or something." I lean back against the tree, wipe my mouth on my sleeve. Then I'm sitting, holding my hands and trying to breathe deep. I count each inhale and exhale. *Two, four. Two, four.* When that pace feels good, I move on to *three, six* . . . I read online that this can help when you can't breathe. It sounds crazy, but I think I'm dying.

"I think something's wrong with me."

Cole sits down next to me. We're still close enough to Dyllan's party that the blue and red lights flash through the foliage.

She sighs, letting out the tension. "Look, I don't know you well enough to tell you that, but what I can tell you is that party sucked. Sorry for bringing you along for all of that. I'm sure where you used to live parties were way better. Probably like in the movies or whatever."

I let out a weak laugh.

"What?"

"I've never been to a party before."

"You're kidding me."

"Never."

"Here I was thinking you were cool."

"I *am* cool. That's why I've never been to a party."

"That's such bull." Her tone is cool, but I catch a flash of a grin. She blows out a big breath. "I used to come to these parties with Devon and Maddie. I don't think they expected me to show up tonight."

"So, you didn't bring me to introduce me to people?"

"I wanted that too! I don't know. I just . . . I guess I miss hanging out with Devon. I used to go over to his place all the time or shoot hoops with him behind the school. I'd tell him *everything*. He knows stuff about me even God doesn't know. And he ruined it. Now I'm stuck with Millie and my mum all day, every fucking day." Cole's really upset about it. I get her anger and her disappointment in Devon. If Nia ever did something like that to me, I'd be heartbroken.

"What about Skunk?"

"We don't have anything in common."

"What about me?"

"I mean, yeah. I guess I'm stuck with you now too."

I've managed to catch my breath. "I'm over this night. Can we just go home?"

"Yeah." She rubs my shoulder and helps me up. I appreciate that she didn't make me feel awkward about panicking. "I'm sorry things got so intense in there for me, too. I forgot about you. As soon as I saw him, I couldn't help it. I wanted to confront him about how he messed with my trust."

"Probably better to do it when you're not faded."

Cole nods slowly, her face colored by the tiny checks of red and blue that make it through the branches. "Pretty terrible introduction to the town, eh?"

"The absolute worst. I had such a bad time." It's true, but I'm smiling when I say it and I can tell it makes Cole feel better for me not to insist I had a good time when she didn't either.

As the last of the party goers clear out into the woods or onto the road, into designated driver's cars, and the cops head out too, Cole asks, "You good to walk home now?"

"Mhm." Vomiting did make me feel a lot better. It's weird how that can happen. It's so gross but I feel at peace after emptying my guts. Like whatever was bad in me is all out in the open now. I don't have to hide it anymore. Maybe that's messed up.

When it's safe to come out of the woods, we walk back the way we came. If I was on my own, I'd be terrified to make the journey in the dark, but with Cole I know I'm safe. Safe like how I felt with Nia, back home. Or on Nan's couch, watching TV and eating snacks. Cole walks me all the way to the end of the driveway. She says she doesn't want to leave me stranded but I know she's worried I just won't find my way.

Right before she leaves, I blurt out, "You want to sleep over?" I don't want to be alone tonight.

"Are you kidding? Our parents will know we were lying if I don't wake up in my own bed tomorrow. Take care of yourself. Go to sleep. Wash the vomit off."

"Please? I just don't know what my mum is going to say if she finds out I'm drunk."

"I don't know what *my* mum will say if I'm on your haunted property after sundown."

"You believe in ghosts? Like, for real?"

She shrugs. "No. My mum does, though. And I don't want to cross her. She's told me there'll be *severe consequences* if I go to Aggie's house after dark. Which means she'll take my keys to the truck." She pulls her hand out of her pocket, her ring of keys dangling from her middle finger. "Do you believe in ghosts, Asha?"

I shake my head. "Nah. Not at all."

Cole steps back, turns and trudges toward the Levesque-Gerges property, waving as she walks away. "Then I hope you don't get proven wrong. Later!"

And she's gone. Disappeared again into the dark. I pass over the wooden bridge beside the moat and trudge up the driveway. None of the lights are on in the house. Everything's pretty much dark. I look up to see where the moon is, but it's not around. Instead, I'm stunned by the sky. I can see the milky way spilled across it. The more I move my eyes, the more I see. Even if this night didn't turn out the best, at least there's this patch of—

HONK!

I shriek. The car's lights come on and I see it: Jeff's slate Tesla SUV, parked diagonally across the driveway, blocking Traci's station wagon in. I hear the click of the door and he comes out on the driver's side. He's chuckling long and loud—the type of chuckle that pats itself on the back and fills a board room with assurance that everyone there is making the *exact right decision.*

I thought he was supposed to arrive Saturday morning, not Friday night. He's early.

"What the hell!" I yell toward him. My voice cracks, betraying my fright. I know fright is exactly what he wants. Always playing his little power games.

"I got you good!" he says in the glow of the car's interior lights.

"What if I got hurt?"

"How would you get hurt? There's nothing around here and I'm parked."

"I don't know—I could've fallen or something." I rub my fingers over the still tender bump at the back of my head. He's right. The driveway's barren after the moat. If it was anyone but Jeff, I would've assumed it was nothing but a prank. "I thought you were supposed to come tomorrow."

"I wanted to surprise your mother. I hear it's been a big week." Did Traci tell him that? We'd barely even started on the cleaning. Mostly we just moved a bunch of junk to the spare room to clear out space. Maybe it's been hard for Traci, being in the same space as me all the time. I thought we were getting along pretty well, fashion choices aside. "What are you doing out here anyway?"

He walks closer, eyes my tight blue shirt underneath my hoodie suspiciously. I wonder if he recognizes it from that trip with Traci. I cross my arms. Jeff is the same height as me. I'm always grateful for this when we're in a fight because I know it bothers him. I stand a little taller to try to establish dominance. I read somewhere that this works but doing it now it makes me feel silly. He's not trying to threaten me. He probably wasn't even planning on pranking me until he saw me at the end of the driveway. Did he see Cole too? Hear me say I was drunk? Shit.

Jeff sniffs the air, leans closer to me.

"Board games at the neighbor's."

"You've been drinking."

"What?" I scoff.

"You've been drinking. I can smell it on you."

"Cole's mum's beer spilled on my sleeve."

He reaches out and pulls at my sleeve. "Did she vomit on your sleeve too? Pretty sloppy. Though I have heard alcoholism is a real issue out here . . ." I pull my arm away a little too hard. I'm not interested in delving into Jeff's class anxiety right now. He clearly thinks the fact I have vomit on my sleeve is just as funny as his prank. If Traci were here, he'd frown and make serious about it but since we're alone, he takes the opportunity to laugh condescendingly.

"I haven't been drinking."

His playful tone deadens. "Lying always has worse conse-quences than telling the truth." I know he's not really interested in giving me fatherly advice. I bristle. He just wants me to feel guilty. So maybe it's that I'm still not totally sober, because I full on snort at him.

"Excuse me?" He cocks one eyebrow up, inviting me to continue. So I do.

"What, you wanna play daddy and pretend I never caught you talking to her?" Something lights behind his eyes. They give off a dangerous glint in the moonlight. I shouldn't have gone there. But something's alight in me too, in my chest, and I don't care if he writes me off as a lost cause. I'll never forget that night. As much as he says it was a mistake, that the woman he was talking to got the wrong idea, I know what I heard. I know he wasn't talking to Traci, and it wasn't just a minor flirtation.

Keeping that secret made it impossible for me to live in our house with Jeff. At Dad's, I didn't have to hide anything.

"I thought I made it clear. That was a misunderstanding. I don't know what else I can do to convince you otherwise. I've been good to your mother. I'm good to you. I told you then and I'll say it again now—when you're ready to accept me as a part of this family, I'll be here for you."

"I know what I heard." I manage to say it with a steady voice. It almost sounds adult. He knows it's a threat, and that gets under his skin. He can't stand the thought of being cast in a bad light.

"I'm a good man. It's fine if you can't accept me, but don't put your delusions on your mother. That's my reputation on the line." He clenches his fists and adds, maybe as an afterthought, "There's no way she'll believe you."

I know he's right and whatever composure I had leaks out onto the muddy ground. "Maybe I'm not talking about my mother. Maybe I'm talking about your workplace. I could make things sound even worse than they are."

He leans in closer. I can smell fresh breath strips on his tongue. I don't break eye contact with him. Jeff's so close now our noses almost touch. "You think anyone at my work would care what a little girl has to say about an affair that *allegedly* happened years ago?" There's malice behind his eyes. Does he take pleasure in knowing no one would believe me if I told them how his whole façade as a family man rescuing his wife and stepdaughter from a hard life is as crumbly as the country roads?

I've never seen Jeff this furious. He's been angry, sure, but never like this. An icy fury sloughs off him into the air around us. We don't move for several long seconds. It's as if our feet are frozen to the ground.

I've broken his trust. I promised never to mention his affair. I can see how happy Jeff makes Traci. He takes good care of her, brings her on trips and out to eat at expensive restaurants, he even helped when she fell behind on the mortgage. He convinced me it was no big deal, a mistake. I was younger so I fell for his act, momentarily. And I kept my promise for two years. But the secret drifted deep and sank its teeth into me. It hasn't let go. I haven't become a better daughter, I've lied about more— my grades, skipping school, shoplifting, my fights with Traci, now about going to the party with Cole . . . Meanwhile, Jeff has only solidified his image as this savior, this good man, this white knight. All the chinks in his armor began to melt together until he became this solid figure in our lives. No matter where he tightens his control, he explains it away with his perceived interest in me and Traci's wellbeing. He is immoveable.

Something rustles in the woods and we both strain our necks to see what it is. Whatever's out there brings warmth back into me. Coyotes? Adrenaline hits my system. When I look back to Jeff, his head is bowed in what I think is shame. He sighs, and his face softens. "If you don't tell your mother about my mistake, I won't tell her about yours."

"Fine." I hope I don't regret this. Decked out in golf pants, a polo, and boat shoes, he's the image of a perfect dad to the kids he never had. I'll do my part to keep the peace and pretend happiness. At least we're not all living together full time anymore. Pretending on weekends is manageable.

I let out my tension in a sigh. "I'll show you the way in."

He grabs a long triangular paper package out of the front seat and a sweet scent cuts the thick air between us, lets it mellow. It looks like he brought flowers for Traci. The burning anger in my chest cools slightly. She'll love that. Dad never did anything romantic for her—he was never really capable of loving her the way she needed. As much as Jeff and I don't get along, there are moments when I do see how much he cares for Traci and how much she needs his care. I know it's hard on her being a single mother and unemployed, not because of me, she insists, but because it's lonely.

I head up the porch steps, Jeff following with his brown canvas bags. A chill washes over me, as if the house is putting off a force field of cold.

"Careful of the—" I begin to say, but before I can finish with "rotting step," Jeff's foot crashes through the mushy wood and he cries out, dropping the flowers.

I swear I hear the pop and crack of bone. The whites of his eyes glow against the pitch of night as they widen in fear. One time I saw someone break their leg at the skate park. Their bone shard cut its way out of their skin. For a moment, I'm as scared as him—I don't like Jeff but I don't want to see him hurt. His yells escape his throat with animal force. I want to slap my hands over my ears like a little kid, convinced if I don't hear his screams, his pain won't infect me. The flowers spill loose red petals across the porch, and his leg reaches down into the black hole beneath the steps.

I rush to his side and throw his bags to the left so I can help him up. He winces and hisses through his teeth. As his foot resurfaces from the hole, he gulps down another cry. I don't know what I expect to see, but it looks like nothing. There are no bloodstains on the beige of his pants. The leg looks normal and, as he hoists himself to his feet, he can stand.

"Probably sprained," he grunts.

I was sure I heard a bone snap. I can tell he's confused too, the way he keeps glancing back down at his leg.

"I'll help you in." I wrap his arm over my shoulder, carry him over the threshold.

I feel nauseous and dizzy as we cross into the house. Maybe I am sick. I pass Jeff one of Great Aunt Aggie's canes, the one with the crow's head handle, and he uses it to get the rest of the way inside. He thanks me. I pull his luggage in and up the stairs and get some ice for his ankle as he wakes Traci to say hi, tell her what happened out front—omitting the details of our confrontation. I can't believe she slept through his screams. She's always talking about how she's such a light sleeper. Maybe the dark of the country really does help her.

While Jeff settles in and shuffles around downstairs, I lie on my bed shivering at the new cold that's settled over the house like a blanket. When Jeff finally turns off the lights and closes the door to his and Traci's room, I get up and take a hot shower. As the steam swirls into the cold night air, I consider the evening, how I had so much hope for this town and new friendships and this house. But with how the party ended with me vomiting, my chest tight, crouched behind the shelter of the trees, I didn't think I'd made a great first impression. But when I thought about it more . . . me and Cole were really able to connect when we were away from everyone. I want to get to know her better. I wish we'd stayed in, played board games, or watched a movie.

Jeff's arrival was a second blow to my hope. Until he'd arrived, I was able to forget most of how I was, the things I hated about how others thought of me in the city, and focus on who I want to be moving forward. Someone better who can heal her broken relationship with her mother. Someone who can go to parties and have fun without consequence. Jeff's arrival reminded me that all those hopes were just the same as playing pretend. I have no control over people's perceptions of me here. They've all decided who I am already. Even when I haven't.

I flick the bathroom light off and walk down the hall on the edges of the carpet where it's remained soft after all these years. My hand trails against the unfamiliar cracks and crevices of these walls. In the dark of my room, I pull on my pajamas and fall into bed.

The ceiling spins above me until it takes the shape of a woman's face, vaguely familiar.

I squeeze my eyes shut, wondering if this is some delayed side-effect from Cole's joint and all the beer. The face stays firmly in place.

"Who are you?" I can barely hear myself over the thumping of my pulse in my ears.

The woman floats down. Her long blond hair tickles my nose. She leans in with her cheeks dimpled, lips pursed, and kisses me on the forehead, soft as a butterfly. As my mother did. As Aggie did for my mother. As if bequeathing a spell of protection. I don't need to be scared. My heartbeat slows.

I don't want to fight. Maybe if I'd had a different night, I would question this presence more. Maybe I would be lying here in terror instead of surrender. But I let it hold me. Before the past can come rushing back, I let it all go and let the woman pull me into a peaceful dream of walking through the forest, holding my hand out for the birds to land on, just like I used to with Aggie when I was little.

CHAPTER FIVE

*T*raci sighs as she watches the taillights of Jeff's Tesla disappear beyond the moat. She's leaning against the layer of dust on the kitchen windowsill with the wistfulness of a nineteenth century widow. I'm warming my phone in my hand as I search for the right words to text Nia back—after Cole came by for the party last night, I completely forgot about our conversation. Maybe I wanted to forget about it. Her last message to me read:

What's new?

It should be easy enough to answer. I let my eyes wander over the cupboards hanging on by their ornate brass hinges and the scuffs scarred onto the floor by routine in front of the stove. Nothing is new out here. I know that's not what Nia meant. What could I tell her about, though? The party? Maybe with distance last night will become more embarrassing. I'm not ready to joke about it yet. Cole? What if this new friendship makes her feel replaced?

Veins twang in my temples. I lean my head against the peeling eggshell to soothe the headache that is last night's souvenir. Endless content scrolls across my screen as I hop through every app on my phone, all of it useless information, just something to look at other than Traci. Then, I refresh my feed and see Nia's bright face. She posted a selfie with her family against the busy background of Pearson airport with text that reads "peace out canada xoxo."

Shit. I do the math. She was supposed to leave on the ninth. The ninth was Friday. Yesterday, while I was out with Cole, she was getting ready to leave the country. She was probably texting me from the car to the airport. My heart sinks into a slimy pool of guilt. By now, Nia's probably close to landing in Sierra Leone or else in some middle-European country on a layover, where she doesn't have a phone plan. I've been so caught up in my own world, I forgot to care for the best friend I've already got. I hope she's stepping out into the sun now, with her parents and Jamal behind her, ready to walk into the arms of her mother's extended family, who they haven't seen for years.

Knowing Nia, she'll forgive me for going silent. Also knowing Nia, she won't tell me she was sad I didn't show up for her. How could I have let her slip my mind? Nia and I promised each other we'd stay committed to our friendship no matter what, and I couldn't even remember to wish her safe travels a week after leaving the city. I toss my phone onto the table. The clatter turns Traci's head.

"I hope Jeff doesn't take too long at the hardware store," she says. "He really shouldn't be on that ankle for long. You know how he gets stuck looking at power tools."

I snort. "Not that he even knows how to use them."

Traci lets out a long sigh and I lean back on the feet of my chair, waiting for her to lecture me. "Don't start with that again, Asha."

"I'm not starting anything!" I say, but my tone's already off and Traci has hypersensitive ears for when I'm giving her tone.

"That was a dig at Jeff. Sit properly on your chair."

"I swear it wasn't." I let the two legs fall back to the floor. They crush stray crumbs from breakfast. "I'm just saying, he likes looking at those tools because he has masculinity issues, not because he knows how to use them."

"How is that not a dig?" Traci's tone is becoming more severe too. If I want to keep the peace, I'd better back off.

I take a deep breath, and just like when I let the presence in the ceiling hold me last night, I surrender. "All I'm saying is—he'll be fine." It's cold, but my annoyance is not because of Jeff, really, despite his threat last night. I'm cranky more because I'm kicking myself about forgetting my best friend. Plus, I'm hungover. So I follow up: "Besides, this means we get some time alone." It's a positive spin, which is what moving here is supposed to be all about.

Traci's shoulders relax from where they've crept up by her neck. I can tell she's pleased at the suggestion of one-on-one time with her kid. She lets my comment about Jeff go. I'm finally taking an interest in our relationship! It makes her happy. And admittedly, I'm looking forward to time just the two of us together too. Jeff can take as long as he wants at the store.

"I still can't believe his foot's okay," Traci mutters, half to herself. I showed her the hole Jeff made this morning while he was taking a shower. In daylight, the jagged gape of the hole makes even more of a dramatic contrast with the rest of the deck. He almost took the entire third step down with him. "The state of that step and you would've thought he'd have broken a bone at least. But he's healthy, his body's reliable."

The word *reliable* sticks in my brain, and I remember that phone call I overheard, his voice low, strained, sinuous with sexual intentions . . . and I think of Traci, the only woman he's (allegedly) been with since the end of his relationship with his ex-wife.

Reliable. Is he as reliable as he's made himself out to be since then? With all his good deeds and showing up a day early for extra time with his wife? Or is all this do-good behavior a cover-up? All his newfound alone time in the city—he must get lonely without Traci around. Hell, I'm lonely *with* Traci around.

What does Traci mean to him? She loves him, keeps him fed, watered, held. And he does the same for her. I just hope Jeff isn't using her to feed his savior complex, to make him feel like a good man while he gives the ok for another old-growth forest to be chopped down.

He loves her for who she is, right? After all, Jeff drove all the way out here just to see us. He's going to do a bunch of work on the exterior of the house, which means I won't have to climb up the rickety ladders we found in the garden shed to replace shingles—which I don't even know how to do anyway. All this work is on his weekend, too. He won't get a real break until the house is fixed up. Meanwhile, me and Traci can take our time and don't have to drive back to the city late at night. It's really generous of him.

Then again, his secret sits festering in my stomach. I don't know how to feel about Jeff, is the truth. And I don't want to mess things up with Traci. She thinks I'm doing well here. She trusted me to go out last night. *And look how that turned out.* Embarrassment simmers beneath my skin when I remember crouching in the bushes with Cole.

"Well, we'd better get started on cleaning." Traci's already tying her hair back in a ponytail and stretching her arms like she's about to run a race. Maybe I should stretch too; from the list she's pasted up, the length of the refrigerator door, it looks like cleaning will be at least a week-long marathon. Traci wants to take it room by room, so today we're starting with the mustiest, dustiest room of them all; the living room.

I pull all the new cleaning supplies from where they've been languishing on the counter for the past few days. We had more pressing issues to attend to, like washing the sheets so that the small, itchy red bumps that have continued to rise on my wrist and Traci's sneezing fits might dissipate. She thought it might be mites in the pillows, but her allergies have continued to take us both by surprise as she scream-sneezes at the least opportune moments: over the pasta we ate last night, while she was brushing her teeth, in the dead of night . . . and the bumps on my wrist are still there. They've started leaking a clear fluid. Traci says we should go to a clinic on Main if it gets any worse. I try not to scratch, but as well as I do at avoiding digging my nails into the rash during the day, I end up scratching it in my sleep. This morning I woke up with a scrape of blood on my fresh white sheets. After that, I clipped all my nails so short my fingertips stung when I washed the breakfast dishes. If that doesn't solve the problem, I don't know what will.

"Stop itching at that rash and come help me carry these supplies to the living room." Traci swats my hand away from my wrist.

I examine a bottle of extra strength disinfectant she found in the back of the cramped town hardware store. From the faded and minimalist packaging, it looks like it's been sitting on the shelf at least ten years. A skull and crossbones leers ominously from the back label. "Should we wear masks? Looks deadly."

Traci snaps her new purple rubber gloves on. "God, I hope it's as lethal as they say. For pests at least. The current ecosystem in this house is *not* conducive to human life *at all*." She slaps a fresh rag over her shoulder. She realizes she hasn't answered my question and adds on, "I think there are some masks in my suitcase if we need them."

Moments like these, when we're doing mundane things, are when I feel closest to the mother-child relationship I idealized as a kid. That relationship, once a warm, living, breathing thing, folded itself down into a paper-doll version of what we had. Cleaning, cooking, sitting together reading . . . those are the times when I am most comfortable in a room with her. When our differences in opinion and misunderstandings hibernate for a while, our focus is off of each other's flaws and we can just *be*. The accumulation of arguments and disagreements about which parent I want to live with, who's the better parent, where I'm going, what I'm doing, if I'm doing enough, if she's a good mother, if I'm a good kid, if I care about school enough, whether she cares about me, and the biggest irritant of all in our relationship, Jeff, all dissolve. I feel safe.

I want that safety back so bad I would cut this house up and put it back together a thousand times if it meant I could feel it again. To not have to worry anymore. I used to feel something like what I felt last night when that apparition held me: true peace, even against logic.

The woman in the ceiling is just another thing I have to keep to myself. Like when I finally told her, with all my bags packed, that I'd made the decision to stay with Dad, and she shouted at me that all he'd do was hurt me like he hurt her. Living with the idea of a protective apparition brings me a sense of reassurance. Whether this is real or in my head, Traci would only sense danger if I told her about it.

Then again, Traci wasn't exactly wrong about Dad. But she wasn't exactly right either.

∿

Aggie's house has a living room and a den, which was confusing to me growing up. The living room was "for company" but whenever family was visiting, we only hung out in the den. I'd ask Traci why we weren't considered company. She'd answer that family isn't company, that this was our home too. That confused me more.

In my eyes, this house was, when Aggie was alive, unequivocally hers. There was nothing about it that felt like home. Everything inside these walls was old and strange, from another time and world than I lived in. That sentiment was drilled home even more by Aggie herself. She treated my mum like a daughter most of the time, and Mum treated her like a parent most of the time too. But there were times I picked up on a frustration between them. It surfaced mostly when Aggie insisted we keep the doors closed to rooms that weren't being used, or didn't move any of the books or photos or paintings around, or that Mum should stop trying to buy her new cooking gear or throw out any of seemingly useless artifacts that wouldn't have any value at an antique market, let alone a flea market. The excuse for having things her old-fashioned way was always the same, *the house likes it that way*.

Those frustrations with the house made them both into stubborn children playing an endless game of tug of war that often ended in injured feelings. I could understand now where they were both coming from: Mum trying desperately to pull Aggie into a future where she was cared for, and Aggie trying desperately to preserve this house to the point that it felt like a museum for the dead and we were just ghosts passing through on a vacation from haunting. Why couldn't Aggie let Mum change a few things in the interest of caring for her? Did something happen in her past to make her so set in her ways?

All I have are speculations based on tidbits of Aggie's life that Mum dropped over the years. The truth is, I never really got to know her. She wasn't too curious about anything that happened after 1975. Our interactions all happened with my parents' legs between us, or between the stiff hugs that marked the beginnings and ends of our stays. We never got deeper than a surface conversation about her garden, and that one time she showed me the birds. That time was nice. But it was only one time. All in all, I sensed I had to tread carefully in her space, make sure I didn't cross a line that would draw her judgement; I think she liked her house better when it was empty.

Mum swings the tall oak door to the living room open. Inside, the living room reflects the same grandeur that's present at first glance of the house's exterior. The curtains are still drawn, as Aggie liked them, blocking out the sun except for a thin strip at the center where the drapes connect. They're so coated in dust I think they're gray, before realizing they are more of a minty green that makes the rest of the stiff furniture appear sickly and frail.

Great Aunt Aggie was secluded in her last years and didn't have visitors who weren't being paid to be here. Nurses or Kelly Levesque-Gerges or someone to cook. I suppose those people probably spent as little time here as possible. Other than those few townies who ventured onto her property to earn their living, it seems she only had the portrait of her and her late husband Ellis on the mantelpiece to keep her company. Must have been a lonely life.

With a strong grip on the curtains, Mum wrenches them apart. Midway she lets out a shriek and drops them. I gasp as thousands of baby spiders scramble to find their nests at the corners of the window. Coughing up the dust clouds swirling in our lungs, we check ourselves over with panicked hands to see if any spiders have found their way onto our clothes. When we're both satisfied we're not covered in creepy crawlies, we move an antique chair with roses engraved on its joints. I climb up on it and try to get a good grip on the curtains. I feel something tickling my hand and pull it back quickly in case it's some type of bug or mite. When I glance at my palm, I see I was mistaken. It's actually a tangled clump of white hairs that could only have accumulated after falling from Aggie's head. I shake it onto the floor, feeling equally disgusted and impressed that the clump of hair managed to get up there on the curtain. Once the hair clump is settled on the floor, I give my hands a thorough wipe on my pants. They leave dusty white prints behind. "Can we wash these curtains?"

Mum must be thinking the same thing. She's staring them down like an enemy to defeat. "If that ball of thread you just dropped is any indication, they may not survive the washing machine. We could just get new ones . . ." she considers. I don't mention the ball of thread was actually human hair. "Maybe we should just get new ones? God knows how long these moth-eaten rags have blocked out the sun. What do you think?"

I shrug. It's nice to be asked my opinion, even if I don't have an answer. Despite the inheritance from Aggie, I know Traci's been worried about money since she lost her job. "Let's wash 'em and see." I unhook the curtains from the long brass rod that supports them.

With the curtains off, sunlight streams into the room. The dilapidated grandeur of the Victorian style living room is even clearer now. I can imagine men gathering for scotch and cigars and discussing long-past wars. The sunlight catches on the dust motes swirling in the air currents. Light suddenly becomes tangible. I watch as the dust reconstitutes itself in places, becoming more solid. Does dust miss being part of something larger when it's set loose on the air?

The swirls fall against some current in the air that remains solid, forming a pattern, what looks like a hand, reaching . . . reaching toward Traci's shoulder as if to gently—

"Asha! Careful!"

The antique chair wobbles beneath me. I regain my footing on the navy cushion. When I look back toward Traci, the dust hand is gone. I must be imagining things. Like the woman who emerged from my ceiling last night.

My heart jolts as my eyes find the apparition's face again. Why hadn't I noticed it before? That portrait of Aggie and Ellis on the peeling mantelpiece. I look closer at the younger version of Aggie in the arms of her husband, with her dimples fresh in her plump cheeks and long, blond hair falling from its bun. I'm so used to imagining Aggie as her old self that I didn't connect the dots when I saw her face in the ceiling. It took something about the blurriness of it coming through the corner of my eye for me to recognize her younger self as the woman in the ceiling. I must've caught a glimpse of this photo some other day and fallen into a half dream. I was still buzzed and rattled from the party.

I move to begin cleaning up the spider nests. A teacher once told me dust is eighty percent dead skin. Does that make dust motes the closest thing to ghosts? If so, this house is as haunted as the Levesque-Gergeses seem to think it is. I'll have to tell Cole. I wonder if she'd think it was funny that I thought I saw a ghost. Or concerning. Can't believe I'm considering this ghost stuff Cole got me on.

"Why are you smiling?"

"I don't know."

"A boy?"

"No! Mum—" it slips out. Both of us are surprised to hear me say the word. I haven't called her "Mum" for years. My ears redden. Hers do just the same. "We've only been here for, like, a week."

"Aunt Aggie used to ask me that all the time and I'd be so embarrassed. Of course, there usually was a boy. But I know that's not your thing. At least not yet. You're so much better behaved than I was at your age. I know I get on your back about some stuff, but overall, you're much easier to deal with than I was."

I think back to how Cole's uncle called Traci "fun" when I said I was her daughter, how it seems like some men in this town think Traci sleeps around and judge her for it. It makes me mad to think about them talking about her like an object. But it makes me even angrier that Traci would ask me about boys just because I was smiling.

I rub my rag vigorously in the spider-infested corner of the window. The harder I rub, the more I direct my anger away from

Traci. A tiny brown spider crawls over the back of my hand. I let it go free, watch it climb into a safe crack on the other side of the windowpane. I open my rag to see its siblings ground to pulp in my hands. I almost feel bad leaving it as a lone survivor. I don't know if spiders have a concept of family. If they do, maybe the survivor will find some other spider family to support it.

"Aggie would say I should be careful with the boys around here," Traci continues. "She didn't like most of them. She really didn't like most folks around here."

"Why not?" I can think of a few reasons based on my encounters with Joe. But he's a man, not a boy, and he's RCMP, which doesn't add to his likeability as far as I'm concerned. I'm not sure police would've been an issue for Aggie, though.

Traci turns from me and kneels to rub the baseboard with her disinfectant-dampened cloth. Beneath the gray grime is a slightly lighter color of yellow, which I think is supposed to be white. "She was more radical than most of the women around here."

"Radical?" I have to laugh. Looking around this old house and knowing Aggie as a nice, but eccentric and rigid old woman, it's hard to imagine her ever being "radical." She kept all her riches locked away in these walls. I can't remember her ever making any comments about women's rights when I was visiting.

It's as if Traci reads my mind. "Well, she was a feminist from the time she was quite young. She ran the local chapter of Women United in this room up until Ellis's death."

I imagine a group of well-dressed, white, upper-class women gathering here in the '60s, driving over in bright cars, smoking cigarettes and laughing at jokes they could only make when men weren't around. The town was doing well back then. For those women, it was probably a good time to think about the future, even their futures in this town. By the time Traci was living here, everyone's idea of success had flipped. If you wanted to be anybody, you had to leave. That's how she ended up in the city. Nan too, in a way. Traci spent her whole childhood in small New Brunswick towns. Her whole life after Aggie's, she'd lived in cities. Until now.

"Why'd she stop after he died?" Wouldn't that be the time she needed those women the most?

Mum takes a deep breath. She doesn't often talk about Aggie's husband. I always assumed that since he died long before she moved in with Aggie, she just didn't know much about him. "I think it had something to do with the circumstances of his death?"

"Suicide, right?" I knew that much. She nods.

"Ellis died by suicide, but because of Aggie's feminist leanings, a few people—mostly husbands of the women in the Women United group who didn't approve of feminism back then—started a rumor that Aggie was . . . responsible for his death." I can tell the thought is affecting Mum. Her anger simmers close to the surface. She often tries to push things down and pretend everything's okay, but I've learned her tells. Her shoulders and eyebrows tense up like they did earlier in the kitchen. I think that's why it's so frustrating for her to argue with me. I'm like that too: barely giving a warning sign before my anger boils over.

"You mean, like, she murdered him?"

"You know, I don't know if it matters, Asha. Did some people think she murdered him? Yes. But most people just put the blame on her. For not caring for him, for not being a good wife."

"So that's why people think this house is haunted?" I say it half-jokingly, to lighten the mood, tamp down some of that anger before it bubbles over. If even a few people thought she murdered Ellis, then that explains the rumor.

Traci half-snorts, half-laughs. "Who told you that? Kelly?"

"Cole. She said Kelly thinks this house is haunted."

"See, rumors always come back around in this town. And usually when they do, they've still got a grain of truth in them.

I'm not saying there was foul play in Ellis's death, but the ghost rumor might have some weight to it."

I'm shocked. "You think this house is haunted, too?"

Traci shrugs, turns with a slight smile to look at me. "Maybe not haunted with ghosts. Haunted by bad memories, sure."

"Have *you* ever seen any ghosts?"

"Never. But sometimes there is an energy I can sense." Traci wipes her hair out of her eyes and sits back on her feet. She stares up at the mantelpiece inquisitively.

"What kind of energy?"

"Protective, maybe?" She squints, unsure. I think of the presence—maybe Aggie?—that helped me drift to sleep last night. How Jeff's leg was uninjured after what should have been a serious accident. Then I remember the house blurring out of focus when we first arrived; the way the key I took from the rafters was unnaturally warm. And that flash of firelight in the mirror, the unnatural cool that preceded Jeff's leg dropping through the step. Was that the energy Traci was talking about? And if there's a protective presence in this house, then what are we being protected from?

Traci continues, interrupting my thoughts. "Maybe it's just growing up here with Aggie, knowing how she was. Protective of the house and all its artifacts, protective of the space as a whole. I kept telling her to fix the moat out front, but she blew me off. I think she liked that it deterred people from coming to visit. This house was like her shell. At first, when I came here after my mother died, everything looked hard and sterile. But as I got to know Aggie better, I saw how she cared for the place. There was a softness to her. She could be such a sweet old lady, but Aggie had a difficult life."

I look around at the crystal doorknobs, the vintage light fixtures, cherry wood chests, a once-scarlet crushed velvet chaise lounge, and I think about the farm where my dad's mother grew up, how I couldn't recognize it from the other broke down farms beside it and beside that and beside that. Aggie had it hard in this bougie house? I know privilege isn't a measure of happiness, but it's almost funny thinking about her having a hard time here, with everything paid for by generations of colonizers who came and pillaged this land before her. Aggie living in this house having a hard time with all this land, with all these people coming in to care for her, with running water, with everything, *everything* she could want. And Nan, Dad's mother: working with horses into her late teens until her parents decided they needed to get away from this town. All of them left together to move someplace closer to their idea of freedom.

It's like Traci reads my mind: "Asha, I know what this house looks like. What Aggie's life looked like. There *is* wealth in these walls, nobody could deny that, but Aggie, personally, had a very hard life. She lost her husband. They were very close. I don't know if she loved him, but they were very close until he died."

"Why do you think she didn't love him?"

"The way she'd talk about him, mostly. She'd tell stories about the hijinks they used to get up to when she was young, that they were really partners in crime. She'd tell me stories about how they'd break into the town swimming pool on summer nights, make prank phone calls . . . all sorts of fun." *Fun.* Maybe for them. If they got caught by the police, all their parents would've got was a stern phone call. Meanwhile, my great grandfather was wrongfully arrested and got his leg broken by the same cops who let their hijinks slide. "But Aggie never said she loved Ellis. I think she felt a lot of anger toward him for leaving her here alone in this house. I'd hear her yelling his name sometimes in the night, worse than the way she'd yell at me if she found me smoking in the backyard. Even when I asked her if she loved him, when I was marrying your father, she wouldn't answer straight."

"Did you—?"

"Love your father?" She stops scrubbing, sits, and turns to me. She's all the way at the far side of the baseboard now. Traci looks me in the eye, so I know she's telling the truth. "I loved your father very much. And I think a part of me will always love him, even if he didn't pull his weight when we were together. It was like I was raising two kids."

She's said this before. I asked her again hoping she'd say something different, something more callous, or tell me something awful he did—anything to confirm he's the bad man the courts think he is. Anything to confirm he isn't the man I know: kind, generous, loving, and present.

I wish I could be mad at him for leaving me. But I know it wasn't his choice. His imprisonment has felt like a replay of their agonizingly slow split.

"I believe you," I say.

"I know." I want to ask her about how Dad compares to Jeff. If she really loves Jeff as much as she loved my dad. But I'm scared of what she might say: that Jeff is the love of her life, her soulmate, that she wants to spend the rest of her days with him. I can't bring myself to broach the topic.

Traci goes back to scrubbing. "Asha, I'm not making things up about Aunt Aggie. I saw how hard she worked to regain her reputation after people started those rumors. She was still working at it when I came to live here. People were not kind to her. They were scared of her, and the men were not interested in becoming her next victim, never mind she never had a first. The women weren't much better. They'd invite her to their fundraisers and parties, hoping to get enough drinks in her that she'd tell the truth—or the truth they wanted to hear. But she never did. I think she was glad to have me here. She was deeply lonely, and I gave her some entertainment at least."

"Do you think she ever loved anyone?"

"I don't know. I don't know if she loved who she was supposed to love."

What does that mean? Mum sighs now, folds her cloth over and refills it with disinfectant.

I can't believe we've gotten through a conversation without fighting. I don't want to ruin things by asking Traci if she means what I think she did. She's implied it before, after a few glasses of wine with girlfriends when they start talking about their fucked-up childhoods: *Aggie was queer.* Whether or not it's true, I don't know. But I get uncomfortable with the way Traci talks about it, like it's a family secret, like it's still something shameful even if it's not. So what if she was?

"You know, Asha, it's ok if you don't like boys."

"What? Why would you say that?" I drop the rag and turn back to face Traci. All I did was smile and she's invading my privacy. Heat rises in my chest.

"I just want you to know—"

"Just because you think Aggie was queer doesn't mean I am. Just 'cause I don't want to talk about boys with you doesn't mean I don't like them. Maybe I'm bi. Maybe I'm ace. Maybe I'm not even a girl. Whatever, it doesn't matter. I still wouldn't want to talk to you about it." I realize my voice is rising, my fist is clenched. The words hanging in the air sink in somewhere deep in my stomach. I wanted our time together to be as free of conflict as possible. But she had to bring up sexuality because she always wants to know everything about me. We've had this conversation so many times before. My sexuality is something Traci keeps picking at like a scab. I'm not ready to have a conversation with myself about what I want, let alone her. She wants to know everything about me. It's suffocating.

I wish I had Cole's confidence and certainty to know who I am and to be that person with my family. Traci keeps hinting that she'd be accepting if I wasn't straight. I'm not worried about acceptance. I just don't *know*.

I can tell I hit a nerve. I was harsh, but I said what I meant. I don't want to apologize, but seeing her face turned away from me and reddening with embarrassment, I want to make up for it somehow, too. It feels like someone is pushing against my chest, crushing all the air out of me. This is the way hurt has grown between us unchecked for the past few years: Traci tries to get close to me and I push her away. I can see that. But I don't know how to stop this cycle when she pressures to me to answer questions that I haven't even fully thought through myself.

Before I can gather the right words for an apology, Traci says, "Oh, damn. I think this might be black mold. It's one thing after another here. The mites, the mice, the spiders . . . now mold?" Traci pulls back from the corner where she's now seated, looking worried about the dark patches creeping up from below the baseboard.

The words roll around in my stomach and I feel like puking again. "I think I need to go to the bathroom."

"Ok, sweetie. I love you." She says it without looking back, so reflexive it might've been one of her big sneezes. For a second, everything is just the same as when I was a little kid, like I never got frustrated with her. But those words didn't make my eyes sting so much then. Those words made me feel safe, not like I had anything to lose.

"I love you too."

As I leave, a breeze bends a tree outside so the sunlight streams in brighter. The light reflects off the frame on the mantelpiece, obscuring Ellis's face. Aggie remains visible. Separate from him, her smile is even brighter, her dimples deeper, her eyes knowledgeable, obscuring any chance of truly knowing of her.

୬୧

Upstairs, in the bathroom, I pop a pimple and press the goop out until there's blood. Then I dab at it with a piece of toilet paper and wash my hands. The water rushes out, too hot. It almost burns my hands.

I don't know how long I've been in here.

It's hot on the top floor. Hotter than outside. It's suffocating with all this dust. I pull open the bathroom window first, dislodging leaves and dirt from last fall (and possibly many other falls before). Next, I open the windows in my room. A breeze wafts out into the hall, where I open a window that's higher than I think Traci would be able to reach.

I pause outside Traci and Jeff's room by the head of the stairs because I'm used to their door being shut. This is a new thing since Jeff started hanging around more. I used to spend a lot of time in Traci's room before he was in her life. When I was younger, I often had night terrors or trouble falling asleep, so I'd crawl into Traci's bed. It was the only way I could sleep soundly until I was embarrassingly old. Even after I started being able to sleep on my own more, I'd still sleep better in Traci's bed. But Jeff doesn't like me hanging out where he and Traci bang, I guess.

But today, the door is slightly ajar. Just enough that I think it would be believable to say I'd opened the window because the door was left open and it was so hot in there. Any curiosity I feel at entering a space I haven't felt comfortable in since his arrival in our lives is secondary. Besides, I'm doing them a favor. If they want to sleep in a hot sticky mess tonight, that's up to them. But I know Traci likes sleeping with a cool breeze touching her skin. Back home, in the summer, she used to position the air conditioner so it blasted her face while she slept. Her skin felt like ice whenever she touched my shoulder to wake me up for school.

The door creaks a bit when I open it, but I hear Traci running the tap and singing to herself in the kitchen. I step inside. Having the door shut has only concentrated the heat. Sweat pearls on my upper lip. In contrast to my room with clothes and books tossed around the floor, Traci and Jeff's room is unnatural in its neatness. Jeff's beige canvas weekend bag is folded neatly in one corner, his polos and golf pants hung in the closet, I suppose so he feels at home for the few days he's here.

It still smells like Great Aunt Aggie in here. Her rosewater and mothballs. It smells like Traci too, that warm spiced scent, almost like apple cider, and even a bit like Jeff's sweat. But as I walk toward the window, tiptoeing on the creaky hardwood, noticing the lavender sheets Traci brought from home, her jewelry tree with all her heavy necklaces, the rosewater and mothball scent becomes overpowering. It's one of those smells that gets behind your eyes and takes up all your brain space. I think this is what people mean when they say "heady." I don't know if I'll be able to wash it out of my brain when I leave. I dig my nose into my elbow and hurry to the window, pull it open, and let the wind rush over me.

Across the room, the door slams.

I jump, then let out a giddy laugh. It was just the change in air pressure with all the open windows up here. I look around for something to prop the door open and decide on Jeff's canvas bag because . . . well . . . because it's the only option available. I swear it's not out of spite. I try to reach for it without letting go of the door, which wants to shut again.

"Asha?" Traci calls from downstairs, "Is everything ok up there?"

"Yes! Coming!" I shout back, peeking my head into the hall so she doesn't think I'm in her room. I hope the muffled acoustics of this house will cover for me.

I twist the crystal doorknob, but it's unnaturally cold and slick as ice. It slips from my hand. The door slams again with the force of someone pulling from the other side, someone a lot stronger than me. I can't reach Jeff's bag. I turn the doorknob in its socket. It's useless; it won't catch. A lot of the doors in this house are like this. They're loose or something and won't catch in their rusted mechanisms. The fear I felt when the door slammed earlier crashes back into me like a wave. What if it's not just a broken knob? I try not to think of the apparition, Aggie. She was so strict about keeping the doors shut.

As I pull harder on the door, my eyes are drawn to a dark spot in behind the doorframe. At first, I think it's a fly, or more black mold, but then I realize it's something else: the corner of something, maybe dark paper. I abandon my struggle and look more closely. Even with fear lapping at my ankles, I'm too curious to ignore whatever's revealed a corner of itself to me. It must be a picture or card. It's bent, creased, old for sure. And it looks like the only reason it's begun to fall out is because the paint on that side of the door has cracked. When the door slammed, a bunch of paint flakes fell to the ground to reveal it.

God, I wish I hadn't cut my fingernails so short this morning. I dig the pads of my fingers into the tiny crack as deep as I can and carefully pull at the corner. A photo begins to emerge, covered in paint chips and dust, but there.

When I get the whole thing in my hands, it's as supple as leather. The paper that backs the photo is thick. The photo itself is black and white. At first, I wonder if it's a photo of Ellis that Aggie hid away, but that doesn't make sense, because the man, in his wide pants, vest, and tie has his hair pulled back in a bun. Eyeing the bun, I second guess myself. Maybe he is not a he. Maybe Traci was right about Aunt Aggie being queer. Why else would this person be hidden behind a doorframe and a layer of paint?

The person in the photo looks directly into the camera, with a wide smile that shows crooked teeth. They're freckly, probably a redhead. And the way their eyes crease is familiar. It reminds me of Cole, the first day I saw her, squinting in the sun. In more than that, too. The way the person in the photo is leaning against the wall reminds me of Cole too, as I watched her at the party talking to Skunk, far away and totally involved in conversation, but looking back at me every once in a while, like we had some secret. Like we would be talking about whatever happened that night afterwards, alone, sharing our observations and maybe even—

"Asha?" Traci's close, maybe at the bottom of the stairs. I pocket the photo to show Cole and turn the knob. The door opens immediately this time, and I step out.

"What were you doing in my room?"

"Just opening the windows. It's hot up here."

"Oh. Thank you. That's thoughtful." She sounds surprised but I'll take it over accusations of trespassing.

I meet her at the bottom of the stairs. For the rest of the day, whenever we're not cleaning, my hand finds its way into my pocket to pass my fingers over the rough edges of the photo. Maybe Aggie wanted me to find this. As I remember her protective presence holding me last night, the peace I sank into, how good it was, how I'd do anything to feel safe that way again, the terror I felt when I was stuck in Traci's room retreats then surges back like a rogue wave. Aggie's protection was so powerful. Why would she need such a strong ability to protect unless there was something else in this house? Something that's more of a threat. Something bent on harming her—or us all.

CHAPTER SIX

I'm elbow deep in the toilet when I hear the phone ring. Traci is in a back and forth with contractors and exterminators for each of the unique and specialized issues this house presents, so the phone's been ringing off the hook. Since we arrived a couple weeks ago, she's made an astounding amount of headway on pest control. Traci and the exterminators closed up all the holes. They set traps in every room. It's working, which means that unfortunately, I've become very familiar with the sickly sweet smell of rotting mouse.

For today's cleanup, I've taken on the upstairs bathroom while Jeff works on the shingles and Traci works on the den. It's quiet up here. The bathroom is my cocoon. I could spend hours in here locked up doing my hair, taking a bath, reading, or scrolling social media. It's rare that I get the chance, since it's the only bathroom in the house and it needs to be shared.

As if he's aware that I'm enjoying the peace and quiet of the bathroom, Jeff appears at the door and gives a sharp rap on the frame. "You up for lunch? Tomato sandwiches."

"No thanks." I'd rather eat just about anything else. Besides, working in the toilet isn't exactly whetting my appetite.

"You should take a break, come back with fresh eyes. I always find that helpful." He's been on my back all morning about making sure the bathroom's spotless, standing over me on his breaks from fixing the shingles to guarantee I didn't miss a single clump of limescale or mildew. Even though I know he means well, his presence is invasive and controlling. If I wasn't using so many chemicals, I'd lock myself in so I could be completely alone. "Your mother would love to see you at lunch."

I roll my eyes at the wall. "I'm not hungry yet." He clicks his ongue in annoyance, then disappears back down the stairs. Since Traci brought up my sexuality yesterday, things have been weird between us. It wouldn't take a ton of emotional intelligence to notice the discomfort, hence Jeff picking up on it. On top of that, I still don't feel my best. I didn't sleep well again last night. When I went to bed, I spent a long time staring at the ceiling, hoping the woman would appear again so I could be sure it was Aggie, then flip-flopping back to panicky self-reflection whenever it occurred to me that waiting to see Aggie appear in my ceiling might mean something is very wrong with me.

If Traci's glimpsed anything supernatural around the house, she's keeping it to herself. I complained about being tired at breakfast this morning to see if she saw anything unusual the past few nights, but Traci's in such an intensely cheerful mood from getting work done on the house that she just said, "Takes a while to get used to a new bed." The heavy bags that lay beneath her eyes for the past few years have finally started to lighten, while mine, for the first time, have started to darken.

Aggie's not the only thing keeping me up. Last night, I'd barely drifted off when I woke up to the sound of Jeff coming in the back door and clomping up the stairs. I checked my phone; it was past midnight. When had he even gone out? I listened as his footsteps led right to my door. He paused there. I think he was checking to see if I had snuck out to a party again. My heart was beating so loud that in my semi-conscious state, I thought he might hear it. He's not a predator; I wasn't worried about him coming into my room, but it was hard to imagine any situation in which his presence outside my door so late at night was a good omen. I turned on my lamp and dropped a book on the floor to make sure he knew I was there. Soon his footsteps wandered back down the hall to his room.

Since I was fully awake, I pulled the photo I found from the book I dropped on the floor, where I'd tucked it for safekeeping. I've kept the photo near me since I found it—something about it feels precious. It's in my pocket now. I'm constantly aware of where it is in relation to me. Looking into the eyes of the person photographed makes me lose my sense of location. The photo immerses me in the world of its subject. I can almost smell the dusty curtain that's hanging behind them, feel the rough fabric of their pants as they lift their leg onto the stool where it's perched.

I tune out the phone ringing until I hear Jeff grunt, "For Christ's sake!" and clomp over to the landline. Jeff calls to me, "Asha, it's for you!"

It must be Cole. I remove the extra-long rubber glove and wash my arm vigorously. The prospect of talking to someone other than Jeff and Traci after a couple days of intense scrubbing is thrilling. Talking to someone outside this house will get my mind off this haunting stuff.

Jeff's silhouetted in the downstairs hallway, holding the corded phone out for me to grab in one of his unnaturally clean hands. The whole of him is unnaturally clean, now that I notice it, as though the shingles are fixing themselves. I've seen him working. It's as if the house doesn't rub off on him the way it does on me and Traci. At the end of the day, we're both beat and filthy, but he doesn't so much as have a paint chip in his hair.

Despite his frustration with me upstairs, his smile is warm as he hands me the phone, an overcompensation. As our hands brush and he passes me the receiver, I remember his ear hot against his iPhone, his hand on his lap beneath his desk, the words he spoke to the woman on the other end of the line—

"Asha? It's for you." He seems concerned at my hesitation. I push any thoughts of his infidelity out of my mind and take the phone from his hand and he waits a beat for me to thank him. When I don't, he heads back to the kitchen to finish his sandwich.

"Hello?"

"Hey, it's Cole!" I smile at the crackle of her voice over this retro phone. A warmth to counter Jeff's coolness hovers around me.

"Who's the dude who answered the phone?"

"My stepdad."

"I thought it was just you and your mum over there."

"He's here for the weekend. Brought some of our stuff from the city. What's up?"

"Just wanted to see if everything's ok on your end. It's been dead silence from you since the other night."

I should've let her know how I was doing the day after, but I just got so wrapped up in cleaning. Plus, I was embarrassed as hell. "Oh. Yeah. No, I'm good. Busy. You?"

"I'm good. Bored." Wish I could say the same. But I'm not prepared to talk ghosts with Cole yet, even if she does keep bringing up the subject.

There's an extended period of awkward silence before Cole clears her throat and says, "Want to come over for dinner to-night? My dad's back from the oil sands and we're going camping 'til next weekend, so last chance to see this guy!" I don't respond fast enough. Cole laughs awkwardly and follows up, "Mum always cooks way too much when he comes home. She thinks he doesn't eat out there."

"Uh . . . I don't know. It's kind of intense over here with the cleaning and stuff." I don't know why I hesitate. There's nothing I want more than to get out from under this partially shingled roof.

"Come on! We can watch scary movies or something after."

"Sure, yeah. That sounds fun. I'll just check with my mum." I really want to go. The pull of her bright voice affects me like the gravity of the moon on the tide. I can't imagine turning her down. I find myself smiling at the thought of getting out of the house for a few hours.

"Ok. Sweet! See you later, Asha! I'll come pick you up around five thirty."

Before I can say bye, she's already hung up. The exhaustion of cleaning and getting no sleep lifts a bit. Dinner and a movie with Cole's family sounds a whole lot better than falling asleep over another can of chicken soup and discussion about investments.

In the kitchen, I find Traci and Jeff deep in conversation. He says, "I just don't like the way your social media reflects on me. It's about good optics. If I want this promotion, then—"

Traci glances up and sees me. "Asha!" I watch her face perform the kind of gymnastics she's become good at over the duration of her relationship with Jeff: flipping from a deep frown to a soft smile effortlessly. Jeff keeps his back turned toward me.

"I'm going to Cole's for dinner tonight."

"Oh, honey, we were going to get fried chicken from that joint on Main, though." She's disappointed. I would be too if I had to spend the night listening to Jeff tell me what I can or can't post on my social media. They've had this talk many times before. It boils over into an argument without fail.

"I really want to go," I plead, "Cole says her dad's home right now and her mum made a huge feast—"

Jeff sighs, then turns to me in a way that would seem casual if it wasn't so stiff. He's still annoyed at me for not wanting to eat lunch with them. "I thought we were having this meal as a *family* tonight." He's smiling like he was earlier, when he handed me the phone, his eyes hint at threat.

Traci clicks her tongue. "Jeff, Asha should go. The neighbors invited her. It would be rude." Her smile widens impossibly farther as she tells me, "Plus, good for you for already making a new friend, Ash!"

"You're right, Trace," Jeff agrees as he turns his cold gaze from me to her, "It would be rude of her not to go. I just want to make sure we're all taking this family seriously now that we're in a new home. We have to be a *united front.*"

Traci's face flickers between that eerie fake smile and a frown. I take a deep breath to stop my temper from rising, remember to keep my mental distance. We are living in different worlds. I manage to keep my exterior calm even while my brain runs the numbers on his hypocrisy: he's talking about us being a united front and he doesn't even live in this house yet. He's the one who's new to this space and he continues to assume I don't want to be here. It's always the same: if I just acted a little different this family could be perfect. Maybe we could even get a golden retriever and a picket fence. But if I want me and Traci to heal our relationship, I have to let Jeff's comment go. Somehow, I manage to keep my façade intact. "It's ok, I can stay home tonight." If this is what it takes to make peace with Jeff, so be it. It's not that big a cost. Me and Cole could always reschedule.

"What? No! Go to Kelly's place," Traci insists. "You should be out with friends, not with your boring parents."

I want to say, "He's not my parent." But I know it would sound childish, so I manage to keep that to myself too. I focus on rubbing the edge of the photo in my pocket.

Traci waves her hand as though it will waft the tension in this kitchen away. "And when you go, say hi to Hassan—Cole's dad—for me. It's been years."

Her eyes flick to Jeff's face and her smile wavers a bit. Shit. I hope they don't have one of their big fights over this while I'm out. I can sense the pressure building. Everything in the house stops when it's about to happen, the fridge stops whirring, clocks stop their ticking, floors don't creak. Their big fights are hushed, whispered over the table full of dagger-sharp gestures and white-hot burns that could take weeks to heal.

"Ok, well it's still in a few hours so let me know if you change your mind."

"Asha, you're going." Traci has this ability to get staunch about the most trivial things. Sometimes it works in my favor. I know even if a fire consumed this house, Traci would still make it a priority to get me over to Cole's for dinner tonight.

♪♪

If Aggie's house is representative of neglect, Kelly and Hassan's is representative of overattention. As I emerge from the woods, I lay eyes on what was once a modest homestead that has received addition after addition until the place became a patchwork of shingles and yellowing vinyl. Cole's waiting for me on the stoop to let me in. She beckons me inside.

The inside of the house is, like the outside, a patchwork. It's cute verging on hoarder. Bookshelves are disorganized messes of novels and National Geographic magazines. I imagine removing one would be like playing a game of Jenga. The stairs have beige carpeting that's starting to look more like gray. I can already imagine Traci commenting on the state of their house. But I think it's charming. The walls are all warm colors, deep reds, sunny yellows, and the crowdedness of the place makes this house look lived in, unlike Great Aunt Aggie's place, which, the more we clean it, the starker and colder and less familiar it becomes.

We sit at their round kitchen table. Me next to Cole, her sister Millie on my other side, and then Kelly and Hassan across from us. There's a mountain of food in front of us. There's lobster and butter just in time for the start of summer, fish cakes, a salad with greens from Kelly's garden, and warak enab, stuffed vine leaves, that Hassan's mother taught Kelly to make to satisfy his craving whenever he came home from Alberta.

"How d'you like everything?" Kelly asks me just as I stuff another piece of lobster in my mouth.

I nod vigorously, and Hassan answers for me with a grin. "I'd say it's right good, hey, Asha?" I nod even harder, smiling with full cheeks. "See, Kel, everything turned out. You're amazing."

He and Kelly beam at each other, then he kisses her on the cheek. Millie and Cole make gagging noises at the same time, but I can tell they're just as happy to see their dad home and their parents in love. It must be hard living without him for so much of the year.

A wave of sadness hits me as I imagine eating dinner with Dad after he gets out of prison. Then I push the thoughts down. I don't want to cry at their dinner table. I count my breaths and run my fingers over the edge of the photo a few times, and the thought of Dad is out of my mind.

We all eat until our stomachs are bursting. When I can't possibly take another bite, I wait for a lull in the family's conversation and say, "Thanks for inviting me for dinner. My mum says hi to you both."

"No problem, Asha, I'm happy you could join us. We're practically family, after all. Traci knows that." Kelly is so genuine it makes me wonder if what Traci told me about the resentment between them is just her perception of things. It's weird being treated as family by this group of lovely people who I don't even really remember from my childhood. It's almost as if I'd lived next door the whole time.

"Good to see a young person in that old house, too," Hassan adds. "Place needed upkeep a long time ago. Would've helped Aggie myself if I wasn't gone more than half the time. When I'm back home, I just want to spend time with my kids." He winks at Cole and Millie. I wonder what it's like for him to be away from his family in northern Alberta most of the year. I've heard people sometimes work over twelve-hour shifts and that there are a lot of substance use issues in Fort Mac because of the way people are forced to stay on to make enough for their families to survive. Coming back home to New Brunswick must seem like returning to a totally different world.

"Can me and Asha go down and watch a movie now?" Cole asks Kelly.

Millie scoffs and glares at Cole. "What? No fair! I did the dishes yesterday!" She's twelve and still has some whiny kid left in her tone. She looks a lot like Cole, same big brown eyes and round face, but younger, and with her black hair in one long braid that reaches halfway down her back, tied with a pink scrunchie.

"Barely," Cole replies. "I had to do them all again in the morning because you left gunk on everything."

"*Girls.*" Kelly's tone is firm. Cole's face reddens and I can tell she's biting back words. Kelly notices too and corrects herself softly, "Sorry, kids." Cole is appeased. I can't imagine Traci noticing my discomfort the way Kelly just noticed Cole's.

Kelly says, "I'll do the dishes tonight. Cole, include your sister in the movie."

"Fine," Cole surrenders, "Is that okay with you, Asha?"

"Yeah, sure."

Millie's grinning. I always wished I had a sibling. Someone to hang with me while my parents lived their adult lives. Instead, it was just me, my books, and my imagination. Whenever Jamal would hang out with me and Nia, she'd get annoyed at him. I'd be happy to have him around. Little siblings are goofier and usually excited to be included.

The three of us kids get up and Cole leads us through a dark hallway and down a rickety stairwell to their basement. They have an old department store couch with a '90s era flower pattern that would have made Aggie break out in hives if she saw it. It's well broken in and as we all flop down, Cole in the middle of us, the after-dinner food coma hits me and I can barely keep my eyes open.

Cole and Millie bicker over the remote and the streaming selection. It really does feel like I've been coming over for years. Maybe some part of me remembers hanging out here as a toddler. From the decorations, it doesn't look like too much has changed in this basement since at latest the early 2000s. When the movie's finally playing, Cole nestles in next to me and drapes a blanket over the both of us. Our bare legs touch and I worry I'm too close, but she doesn't seem to mind. We share our warmth. Before the movie even begins, my eyes are drooping shut as the endless cars on endless concrete overpasses dissolve to bees and Tony Todd's voice leads us into the story of the Candyman.

In and out of consciousness, I half keep track of the narrative. I understand this all has something to do with gentrification and the system killing Black people but the details are fuzzy. Laid over the screen and Cole and Millie's gasps, is a curtain just like the ones I pulled back yesterday. We took them to the basement to throw in the washing machine but I watch as hands pull them shut over the screen, then open again, then shut, then between them, another hand emerges, one that is thicker, more masculine, white and clammy looking, opening, the arm lengthening, as if ready to find its way to the person from the photo's silhouette against the blue of the screen, reaching for their neck . . . and—

"Asha, wake up! We have to walk back to your place now."

At first, I mistake Cole for the person in the photograph I found yesterday. In the dark, her features are blurred. Then, I catch a whiff of her garlic breath. It's warm on my face. I rub my eyes and sit up. Millie's fallen asleep on the other side of the couch too. The credits are paused. I guess Cole's the only one who made it to the end.

"How was the movie?" I whisper before we head out the door.

"*So* good. You really missed out."

"What happened in the end?"

"Sweet revenge." Cole laughs. "Or maybe justice? Sometimes it's hard to tell the difference."

I gather myself up, make sure I have the hoodie I brought with me, and that my shoes are tied tight, and we head out. Cole leads the way through the woods. I can't help but notice how fragile and pale her neck is in the blue light of the moon.

CHAPTER SEVEN

*T*he back door slams behind me when I walk into the kitchen. I jump at the sound and hear a yelp in the dark. I flick the light switch on. It's Traci, sitting alone at the dinner table.

"You scared me," I tell her.

"*You* scared me. You have to be careful with that door. It's heavy."

"Sorry." I notice the red rawness around her eyes. "You and Jeff fought."

She nods. I take a seat next to her. "Was it bad?"

Traci doesn't seem to hear my question, which means it was bad and she's still upset. "How're our neighbors?"

"Good. I'm still full." I show Traci my big belly. She sticks a finger in my belly button, trying to lighten the mood. I swat it away. "What did you and Jeff end up eating?"

Traci glances at the wall clock. "Jesus, time really slipped by. I'll have to whip something up quick."

"It's ten thirty and you still haven't eaten?"

"No." Traci gets up and pulls a can of soup out of the cupboard. She flicks on the element and it sparks. She yelps again, then slams the can of soup on the counter in frustration. "Everything in this house is a fucking mess." As she cranks open the container of soup, she seethes. "Go get Jeff and tell him it's time to eat."

Jeff's sitting on the edge of his and Traci's bed scrolling on his phone. Blue light is sharp against his chin. He's lit from beneath like how me and Nia used to light our faces when we were telling scary stories as kids. I knock on the doorframe. "Traci says dinner's ready."

"Not hungry." Sometimes I wonder who the teenager is in this house.

"Traci's making soup for you."

"You can have mine."

"I don't want it. I'm stuffed from the neighbor's place."

"Did that woman spill beer on your sleeve again?" He lets out a hearty laugh. I don't find his comment funny. Why won't he just go eat with Traci?

"No. Traci said to get you to come down for supper. Are you going down or not?"

"I hate that you call her Traci." Sometimes he'll bring this up. In his perfect vision of our perfect family, I call Traci Mum and Jeff Dad and none of us ever pose a threat to our "united front." We're so far from that version of a family I can't even imagine *imagining* it. Jeff's delusional if he thinks it's ever going to happen.

"She's my mother, I can call her what I want."

"She hates it. It feels disrespectful. She won't tell you, because she doesn't want to hurt you, but it pains her. And that pains me." He looks up from his phone and places it neatly back in his pocket.

"If you're so worried about hurting her, why don't you go downstairs and eat the soup before she thinks you hate her cooking?"

"It's canned soup." He chuckles. Then adds, more seriously, "It's good to see you thinking about other people's feelings, Asha. You're really growing up."

I'm starting to lose my temper now. Whenever he says he's doing anything on behalf of Traci or comments patronizingly on how empathetic I'm becoming, it makes me furious. He knows he hits a nerve. He stands up and stretches casually, then brushes past me in the doorway.

"Good talk, kid," he says, then heads downstairs.

All the sleepiness has left me. I'm too frustrated with Jeff to go to bed. My head's all hot. I go across the hall to the spare room instead. It's stuffed with all the junk we plan to get rid of. I step over the furniture, avoid the allergen filled linens, and seat myself in front of the bookshelf that hosts all the paper that isn't just loose on the floor. Between the shelf taken up entirely by disintegrating birdwatching paperbacks and the bottom shelf, which hosts what seems to be forty years' worth of bills, are stacked a couple of flaky leather photo albums.

I put my hand in my pocket and feel for the photo from the wall. When my fingers catch on its border, a warm surge travels from one arm to the other, and I find myself instinctively reaching for the gold embossed *Album* label of the least damaged looking spine. I take my hand out of my pocket so I can flip through as many warped, brown, mildewy pages as possible. Close to the center of the book, I stumble upon the period when Aggie started living in this house. It's the mid-late '60s. There are a lot of marriage photographs, all blurry with damage, then some group portraits of "Women United." Those ones are clearer.

I slip the last photo, from 1969, out of its plastic casing. I can see Aggie at the center of the group, smiling wide. All her teeth are exposed. I can even see her crooked bottom teeth. The closer I look, the surer I become that the woman in the ceiling was some version of Aggie. She has her arms around two women on either side of her, spread out, like she's gathering them all into a protective hug. It's the same protection she held me with when I came back from the party. Am I seeing things? How could I have recognized her energy in this photo if her . . . what? . . . aura? . . .

ghost? hadn't become visible to me? My heart rushes and the same warmth that made me reach for the album flows across my entire body, my earlier anger at Jeff replaced with a fear that I'm seeing things. Do I feel so unsafe in this house that I had to make up an imaginary friend to protect me?

She seems benign, whatever the vision of Aggie is. I'll just have to keep quiet for now and see if anything else happens. I don't want to worry Traci. She has enough to deal with between the house and Jeff.

I place the photo back in its spot in the album and wipe my hands on my pants to get all the dust from the album off. I'm about to close it back up when I spot another familiar face in the group of women.

It's the woman from the photo in the wall. She's at the edge of the group, almost cut out of the photograph, leaning against a bookshelf with a cool smirk. She's dressed way more femme than in the photograph in my pocket, so at first I don't make the connection because I thought the person in the photo might be a man. But her hair's the same here, pulled back, with loose strands popping out. I'm sure it's the same person. It's another connection between her and Aggie, but I'm no closer to understanding what that connection is.

"You're not in bed yet?" This time I yelp. Traci's standing in the doorway. "What are you doing in here?"

"Just looking through some old photos."

The hallway is dim. Backlit, Traci appears extra grim. She steps forward a bit. "Jeff told me you talked back to him."

That snake. He pushed me to talk back. "I didn't mean to."

Traci rakes a hand through her hair. It's starting to gray at the roots. "I'm exhausted. I don't know what to say. Can you just apologize to him?"

It's classic Jeff to tattle on me to Traci after he upset me. He uses it as proof that I think he's an invader in our house. I mean, I *do* think that, but I'm not maliciously attacking him the way he makes it sound to Traci. He's manipulating us both, but Traci can't see it.

"Fine," I say. Jeff appears around the corner. Was he waiting there this whole time, just to get the satisfaction of Traci telling me off for talking back? "Sorry, Jeff."

"Don't worry about it, Asha. I told your mother not to get worked up about it. I understand how it is to be a teen. The hormones take over sometimes . . ."

I fake smile at him, play along. At least it makes Traci feel better. It gives me acid reflux.

I rush through my bedtime routine so I can just shut myself in my room and ignore Traci and Jeff for the rest of the night. Everything at Cole's was so nice. The meal, the movie, her parents.

With the photo in my hand, I begin to drift off, the woman in the ceiling floating down for a second time. It's definitely Aggie. It's impossible to feel scared in her presence, although I know tomorrow I might be disturbed by whatever her presence might mean. Why has she chosen me to protect? Aggie's face is as gentle as it is unexpected. My body relaxes completely. She leads me into sleep again.

⁂

I wake in the pitch black in a pool of sweat. I try to reach up to my neck to pull the hands I dreamed a moment before away, but I can't move. My heart feels as though it's being squished by the weight of a full-grown adult. I manage to kick and scrabble free from whatever was holding me down. I sit up, consumed with terror, gasping. My body is vibrating so hard I struggle to make it to the wall to flick on the light.

It's the same nightmare I was having at Cole's place, only this time, more vivid, and I was the one getting choked. Nan always says dreams mean something, but what could this possibly mean?

After seeing Aggie for a second time, I have to wonder whether it was a dream at all or a supernatural attack. I look up to the ceiling to see if Aggie's there to provide any protection, but she's vanished. I turn off the light again and lie on the side of my bed that's not soaked. If she's not in the ceiling, was she the one who squeezed her hands around my neck? Was her protective appearance just a cover for something more sinister?

Still vibrating, and reluctant to stay in the space where I was just attacked, I go to the bathroom and lock the door. The air in here is still chemical. When I've sat on the toilet for long enough to convince myself I won't see any faces in the mirror behind me, I check out my neck to see if there are any marks. As close as I can get to the mirror, I don't see anything to indicate the grip of two strong, meaty hands squeezing the life out of me. It was only a dream. I'm fine. Unscathed. But if Nan's right and dreams mean something, the only thing I can think is that this means I'm not welcome in this house.

CHAPTER EIGHT

"Asha?"

"Hm?" I look up from the photo's gray scale, surprised at the morning light streaming through my window. I don't know how long I've been staring at the person in the photograph, running my eyes over their face, considering just exactly how much their stance reminds me of Cole's. Down to the way her hair moves in tendrils rather than fluffs or strands where it sticks out from its otherwise tight-pulled bun.

"Did you put the curtains in the parlor back up?" Traci is standing with her arms crossed tight around her ribs as if she's holding her stress in. Contractors and exterminators were in and out all week. The bills are starting to pile up on the kitchen table. I take note to tread lightly today.

"Uhh, no?" I say, glancing back at the photo. It's tucked inside the spine of one of my books so she can't tell what I'm looking at. I don't know why, but I get the sense this photo isn't something I should share with Traci. If it had wanted to reveal itself to her, wouldn't it have done so when she was in the room with it? Why did the photo reveal itself to me? The mischievous gaze of the woman in the photo makes me feel like her co-conspirator.

"Uhh, well neither did I?" Traci mocks my tone. I do my absolute best not to roll my eyes.

"No. I didn't." There's something so eerie about the background too; it's blurred and unfocused. If I stare at it long enough, it's almost as if I can make something else out . . . some other exposure, maybe?

"I thought I told you I wanted to throw them out."

"Yeah . . ." My eyes land back on the photo. Why was Aggie keeping this hidden in the walls? Was it a friend? A lover? Maybe a rival? I've looked over the photo a million times since I woke up at dawn and couldn't get back to sleep. It's become even more of a fixation since the movie night at Cole's, when I mistook Cole for the person in this photo coming out of that dream where a hand reached around her neck. The same hands that later reached around my neck . . .

Now I start each morning staring at the photo. It's not as though the woman will tell me who she is. I'll have to ask Cole about this when she gets back from camping. Even if she doesn't see the resemblance between them, she might know more about the history of the town and how this woman could fit into it. Or she could ask Kelly. One of them has to have some idea of who this person might be, even if it's just someone they glimpsed coming in and out of the house many years ago.

"*Asha!* How many times do I have to say your name before you pay attention?"

"Sorry." I hadn't heard Traci calling me.

"It's time to get out of bed and start your day. There's breakfast downstairs. Books aren't going to fill your stomach."

"Fine," I say, and make sure Traci sees me swing my legs off the side of my bed so she'll leave me in privacy. Once I'm alone, I take my time going downstairs.

Since our last tense weekend with Jeff, Traci's insomnia is back, and the lack of unconscious hours is really starting to irritate our old conflicts. She won't admit it, but I hear her up in the early hours of the morning making tea and shuffling to the den, where she's curled into a threadbare armchair when I come downstairs around nine. I haven't been resting well, either. I fall asleep fine, more immediately than usual because all we do all day is clean, and that's hard work. Plus, Aggie's been coming down from the ceiling every night. I focus on her face, trying to make its lines clearer in the dark. If I can see her, and if I can just feel her presence, imagining details that were only visible in the photographs I unearthed in the junk room—a mole above her right eyebrow, a strand of hair dropping from her ear—it's kind of silly, but deep in the night, knowing Aggie could appear to protect me, keeps me from running into Traci's bed like a little kid.

Even with her protection, I'm forced awake later in the night with that same sense that a weight is pressing down on my chest. My blankets are usually tossed to the floor and my skin clammy in the cool night air.

At night, in my half-asleep state, I'm sure she's a protective figure. In the daylight, when I'm fully conscious, I have more doubts. If she's trying to protect me, then why can't she stop whatever settles onto my chest in the deep hours of the night? Is it her doing? If not, what else could be causing it? I don't want to think about it but if none of this is supernatural, could I just be experiencing some sort of breakdown? Isn't that usually triggered by something specific?

Like moving, like Dad being locked up, like living with Jeff? Some voice in my head nags. I breathe deep and push those thoughts down.

Today is Friday. Jeff's driving in again. I don't want to see him, but at least Traci will be distracted enough by him that I'll be able to go out without her bugging me about all the chores we still need to complete. That is, unless Jeff has another hissy fit about "family time." When they're together, they aren't usually interested in my presence, no matter what Jeff preaches about making this family a cohesive unit. And I'm not interested in listening to Jeff whine about how whatever marginalized community his company is trying to steal land from isn't giving it up. If I can get out of the house before he shows up, it will be a win-win.

"Asha!" Traci calls again.

I pull my shorts on and place the photo in my back pocket.

♪

It's a relief when Cole shows up at the front door, just after lunch, her face glowing with sunburn. She clomps onto the porch in the muddiest sneakers I've ever seen.

"You're here. I was just going to call you to meet up." All the muscles in my body relax. The tension in the air of this house dissolves to nothing.

"Are you coming?" Coming? Coming where? I didn't even know she was going to show up. I figured I'd have to call over since they were supposed to get back from camping this morning.

When I don't answer, she clarifies: "I texted you about going hiking. You didn't see?"

"Haven't been checking." To be honest, when my phone ran out of batteries a few days ago, I didn't bother charging it again until last night when I figured I should probably plug it in in case Dad was trying to call. Minus the farmers' market call, which I don't really count, I haven't heard from him in weeks. I hope nothing happened to him. Or maybe he just doesn't want to talk to me. I try not to dwell on it.

"Your mum told mine that she wanted you out of the house as soon as I came back. Sounds like you two are going stir crazy in this old, haunted house."

Traci went behind my back to call Kelly? It's one of our old fights: she doesn't trust me to make my own decisions. She always thinks she knows what's best for me. I'm too happy to see Cole to be mad at Traci for long, though.

"Yeah, we're getting pretty tired of each other. Let me just grab some stuff before we head out." I think about cracking a joke about haunting, but I can't bring myself to infuse humor into my now very real nightly experience.

Cole follows me into the kitchen. I look out the window over the sink and see Traci weeding the garden. From what I inferred, she decided to go outside because she didn't like the way I was washing the windows. I could sense her watching over my shoulder, itching to correct my technique.

Weeding is arguably the most difficult task to accomplish on this property. It might take all summer, it's so overrun. Traci's out in the bushes wearing jeans and a long-sleeved shirt, gloves, a hat, and rubber boots. She must be cooking in her skin. I lift open the window and yell out, "Cole's here."

She gives us the thumbs up, then goes back to digging.

"I'm going out," I continue.

"Have fun!" she yells back without looking up from her work. I'll take it. Maybe she'll be in a better mood when I come home.

I open the fridge and pull out a box of fresh strawberries we picked up at the side of the road a couple days ago and a bag of potato chips emblazoned with a covered bridge from the cupboard and squish it all into my ripped-up knapsack. Snacks are essential to any hiking trip. Plus, I'm not hoping to be back any sooner than dinner.

With our supplies packed, Cole and I cross the street and head deeper into the woods on a path I never would've seen without her. Beneath the tall evergreens the air is cool and sweet, the floor soft with moss and old pine needles. Being out here is such a contrast to the dust and mold and vermin of Aggie's. It's hard to believe all those harbingers of death live so close to this green expanse of life. Living here only a couple weeks has already taught me that a backyard and a forest are two very different versions of outside. I'm coming to appreciate the forest's proximity, especially with Cole as a nature guide. She points out different kinds of trees and lichen, hangs her head so close to the forest floor that her hair trails on the moss next to the mushrooms, contrasting copper against the dark green.

As much as this landscape is foreign to me when compared with the concrete and jungle gyms of my childhood, some part of it lingers familiar on my palate as I inhale. My ancestors on both sides must have walked these same forests. And although I can't remember it very clearly, I've walked these paths before too, in what resembles a dream but was actually childhood.

"You're quiet today," Cole remarks as we climb a steep incline.

"Tired, I guess."

"Your mum's a talker, huh? But not you?"

"Not really. You are, though."

Cole laughs, her burnt red face shining and crinkling. "Like my mother."

"Do you two get along?" It's a question that feels like it might be too much, but I want to know. I want to know if I'm the only one who finds their relationship with their mother hard.

"Yeah, we do now. We used to fight when I was younger."

"Me and Traci too."

"*Traci*? First name basis. That's never a good sign. Something happen?"

Not something. Many small things added up over time. I shrug and deflect. "What happened between you and your mum?" And how did they fix whatever was broken between them?

We're both breathing heavily now. I can see the trail plateaus up ahead.

"Not much. We just grew apart since my older brother passed."

My heart jolts like it wants to be close to her and far from me. She mentioned it once before, but I didn't want to pry. I don't like to think about losing someone close to me so permanently. "I'm sorry. When?"

"It's fine . . . I mean, it's not . . . but it was a long time ago. Five years." I don't know what to say in response. The silence between us stretches out. Cole walks up ahead. We can't speak between the huff of our breaths anyway. I take the time to consider what to say next. But nothing comes. I don't know how to speak around death. I haven't lost anyone I'm close to yet. Not permanently. I'm suddenly aware of my own innocence. At least Dad can call. It's a privilege to still be able to talk to him, even if it will be hard, if he does.

We reach the top of the plateau. I turn back and see the entire river valley set up like a toy town below. The trees little broccolis, the houses intricate miniatures. Toy cars riding the roads that are smoothed out by our vantage point. Me and Cole sit side by side. Heat radiates off our skins and meets in the air, sweaty, salty, covering us like auras, pulsating. I want to take a picture of Cole in the dappled light because she looks so effortless and comfortable in this space, but I didn't bring my phone. I want to take a picture of town too, but I don't want to be a tourist in the place I live. We share water from Cole's canteen. Her leg brushes against mine, the little hairs invisible and sharp.

"My parents just got super religious after my brother died, but I was kind of too old to get into it, you know? I was twelve, and we hadn't gone to church since I was pretty much a baby. I tried really hard to believe, but I couldn't . . . I think partly because of who I am . . . no one ever said anything overtly homophobic and people were generally accepting, but I just couldn't shake the feeling that if I was part of this big organized religion, then my identity would always be up for debate for some people." She sighs.

I can tell it was hard for her to make that choice. This town's population is only three thousand, but I've seen at least four churches on drives through town. Christian belief seems like a big part of the town's identity. It must be isolating not to be a part of that.

Cole goes on, "I liked youth group though, so I stuck with it for a while."

"Do you still go?"

"No. Do you believe in God?" She says it with such innocence it almost sounds like a child's question. I can remember asking my parents the same thing. And both of their answers were the same as mine now.

"No."

"Why not?"

"I don't know." Why not believe in some higher power? Science? But science feels close to God too, in a way that I can't place. Maybe in its vast incomprehensibility. So why not? "Just never got into it, I guess. My grandmother's kind of Christian but she never goes to church." I only ever picked up on that fact because of the cross on Nan's dining room wall.

"Ok, so tell me something else about you. I feel like I barely know anything about you."

"How about a secret?"

Cole flashes a mischievous grin; her front teeth spill over her top lip. I smile back, but I'm nervous. I reach into my back pocket and pull out the photo. "I found this picture in one of the walls at Aggie's house." I pass it to Cole gently and watch her give it a once over.

Her expression changes from neutral to confused.

"She looks like you, right?"

Cole's face drains of blood. Even with her sunburn, her skin is unnaturally pale. She brings the photo closer to her face. "Where did you find this?"

"I told you, in the house. Behind a door frame. It was hidden." I don't tell her about the strange presence that directed me there. We're not at the stage of our friendship when I can share anything about *feeling presences* and *seeing women in the ceiling*. Besides, she's laughed off any mention of ghosts since day one. Maybe next time.

"She does look like me." Cole looks up from the photo to me, still confused. It wasn't my intention to blindside her with this. I just wanted answers. And in a few more seconds, Cole supplies one. "I think . . . I think this is my grandmother."

"What? No way!" I thought it was just a coincidence they looked similar, but this makes sense. That same warmth rushes over me. Aggie and Cole's grandmother were probably next-door neighbors, just like we are. "This picture's been driving me up the wall all week. I can't believe all I had to do was show it to you and—it's your grandmother. Case closed." I laugh and snatch the picture back from Cole's hands. "Why do you think she was in the wall at Aggie's place?"

"I don't know. Don't close the case just yet. I want to make sure this is her." Some color is returning to Cole's cheeks. She's looking down at her hands, where the picture was a second ago. She doesn't look up when she asks me, "Can I keep it?"

I want to say no. Selfishly. Because I haven't been able to stop staring at it, and even now that Cole told me who it is, I can't help wanting to find out more. More that Cole might know, that I suspect she *does* know, from the way she won't meet my eyes. "Yeah, of course," I say, smiling a smile that doesn't feel my own. I scratch at the rash on my wrist. It's moved up my forearm now.

Cole slips the photo into the pocket of her athletic shorts. It makes me anxious knowing the loose fabric could twist the wrong way at any time and the picture might fall out.

"Were Aggie and your grandmother friends?"

"I don't know," Cole replies flatly. "I mean, I'm sure they knew each other."

"Well, do you think there's something else going on here? It's weird, right?"

"Yeah, it's pretty weird."

I can take a hint. She doesn't want to talk about it anymore. It takes all of what I have to bite my tongue and not ask any more questions about Cole's grandmother. I let it go. For now.

There's a long silence between us, filled only with the crunch of chips.

"Sorry if I, uh, was asking too many questions," I tell Cole after a bit. The birds are twittering above and the trees around us creak as they blow in the breeze.

"It's fine. Don't worry about it. I never knew her." I wish I had just dropped it from the clear discomfort Cole is experiencing right now. Both our hands find their way to the strawberries. Then she says, "These strawberries are really good." And balance starts to restore itself.

"Right?" I pop one in my mouth and let the juices flow over my tongue.

She stands to stretch, then points out at the valley. "You see our houses over there?"

I stand too and follow the line her finger is drawing over the town far below. "They look so close together from up here. You can barely tell Aggie's house is falling apart."

"We should keep going. We're almost there!"

"Almost where?" I hadn't realized we had a specific destination.

"It's a surprise!" Cole skips up ahead and I run to catch up. We keep walking as the heat rises. In the summer, I want to roast like a turkey. Save up vitamin D for the winter to come.

"How was that trip with your dad?"

"So nice. Perfect. It was our first time in years; you know." The longing in her voice is as palpable as the longing I feel to spend time with my dad.

"Must be weird only having your dad around for a couple weeks every few months."

Cole smiles. "It's all right. When he comes back, he spoils me and Millie rotten. And Mum's happy. Your stepdad lives with you?"

"Kind of."

She laughs. "You sound jazzed about it."

"I mean, he's *fine*."

"Oh, ok, I'll step off, then." She's being sarcastic. I laugh at the goofy face she pulls.

"He's just . . ." I search for the right word. ". . . insecure. My mum likes him. But he only lives with us part time. He's, like, trying to become the CEO of some evil energy corporation." I remember too late that Cole's dad works in the oil sands. "Shit, sorry, your dad—"

"I'm not offended. Not like my dad works in the oil sands because he's obsessed with crude oil. More 'cause Mum hasn't worked since Ben, except to check on Aggie. But now that's not happening either, obviously . . . He's supporting us all, you know? He couldn't make that kind of money anywhere around here. Soon he won't be able to make that kind of money there either, which is good for the world. But he'll have to look for something else or Mum will have to go back to working at the salon." I nod. Cole stops in her tracks and spins around. "Wait. Is your stepdad that dude that looks like he's from a yacht catalogue I've seen wandering around town looking lost?"

"*Stop!*" I'm losing my shit laughing. "That's the perfect way to describe him. Yeah, you probably caught a rare glimpse of Jeff."

"Seems like an asshole."

"He sucks."

"Huh—but a minute ago you were all like, 'he's insecure,' 'he's fine!'"

"He is! He's fine! Just a boring and insecure white man. I just think Traci can do better than him."

"Hell, yeah! Your mum's hot! I mean, for a lady her age . . ."

"Ew! Cole!" I slap my hands over my ears.

She's clearly getting a rise out of my discomfort. Thankfully, she raises her arm to point ahead and changes the subject. "We're almost there. Can you hear that?"

I strain my ears, trying to separate all the noise into identifiable categories: birds, bugs, our feet, the creaking trees, and something up ahead, rushing. Cole asked if I could hear it, but I can smell it too: the scent of water on the air. Traci always says it's the ozone from the water but I don't know if that's scientific. I like the thought of breathing in pure tripleted air, though. And the smell does lift me up, tethers me, pulls me toward it.

"Is there a waterfall coming up?" I ask Cole.

She grins and I know my senses are right. I'm smiling too and before I know it, we're both dropping our stuff and running toward the falls. We step into the stream that runs off it. The water is frigid but refreshing. Little minnows nibble our toes. We splash each other until we're halfway submerged anyway, in the little pool by the falls. I forget all about the photo. Tie my hair up and wade around, checking out the crags in the rocks and mosses. Cole naming off everything she sees. I let myself live, for the first time since arriving, entirely in the present.

⌀

It's late afternoon when we get back. My entire body moves like melted chocolate. I'm more relaxed than I've been in weeks. Cole and I spent all day in the woods. We could've stayed out there forever if we hadn't run out of snacks. The whole day was a cliff notes catchup on our lives since we last hung out as babies. Favorites and least favorites. What foods we like. I said baked beans, and Cole splashed me in the face. I splashed her back when she said meatloaf.

I don't want today to end. When we reach the end of the driveway, I ask if she wants to come in for a few minutes.

I yell my hellos to Traci and Jeff as we race upstairs to my room and strip out of our still damp clothes. I throw Cole a t-shirt and shorts, and get dressed myself. All my clothes are too big on her smaller frame. The soccer shorts I lend her almost touch her knees. She's lying on my bed flipping through a copy of a zine Nia gave me as a goodbye present.

"I make comics, you know," she says, waving it around.

"Oh yeah? Are they good?"

"I don't know. What kind of question is that? I haven't shown them to anyone." All of a sudden she's shy, on the defensive.

"Can I read one?"

"Maybe."

I flop down next to her. "I like this page." I point out a full spread Nia drew called "places to go when you're bored as fuck." A lot of the places are abandoned and eroded from World War II and filled with graffiti. They were nice, private places to hang for an afternoon or evening as the tide dribbled in and out on the nearby beaches. Nia did a sketch of me in one of them that's photocopied in high contrast black and white.

"That's you?" Cole asks, pointing at the sketch.

"Yeah. My best friend Nia did these pages."

"Cute."

My ears turn red. I flip my braids over the side Cole's lying on so she won't see.

"So, how's the move been going? Like, for real. Don't just say 'fine' 'cause I know you want to."

She's right. I would've just said "fine." Instead, I take my time and think about it. "It's kind of a new thing living with Traci. I was living with my dad before, but he can't be around anymore." I don't follow up. Cole must be curious; I can see it in the crinkle that forms between her eyebrows. But I think she can also see this is a boundary for me. I'm not ready to talk about him. I can feel the words drowning in my throat as I force myself not to be pulled into memories of the past. The blue and red lights.

I'd never seen him cry like that before. My eyes stayed dry. Everything happened too fast to react.

She doesn't push further. Instead, she says, "It's nice to talk to somebody else about their messy family. Everyone's been telling the same lies about their perfect families for so long. Here there's only the stories we tell left and none of the truth. My mum says that's cynical."

After going over to Cole's house for dinner, I thought her family was perfect. But hearing about her brother and the way she got quiet when I tried to ask about her grandmother, I wonder if there's more to her family than the first image I was exposed to.

"Do you want to stay here? Like, after you graduate?" I ask.

"Maybe I'll live here one day, when I have a family and stuff. I loved living here as a kid. But I want to get out first and see somewhere else. Go to university in someplace with people I didn't do baby group with."

"Oof, yeah. That's history here."

"Oh, come on!" She teases, pushing me to the side. "It's not like you don't have history here too."

She's not wrong. It's a history I'm still discovering.

The rest of the afternoon slips away. When it's time for dinner, I see Cole out the door. I watch her walk away, into the woods, flies swarming her damp head, and the back of her neck just as red as her sunburnt cheeks. The warmth of our day together settles in my chest. Even with Jeff present, dinner is easy to get through. I even manage to laugh at his awful jokes.

∾

It happens again. I wake, gasping for breath and clawing at my chest like there's someone sitting on top of me. I'm shivering. I can't stop it. Something grips my neck with frosty hands.

And then whatever presence was gripping me is banished as the hallway light snaps on and screams pierce my eardrums, followed by quick, heavy footsteps. My door bangs open so hard the doorknob leaves a dent in the wall. Jeff stands in the doorway, breathing heavy in his boxers. I rub my eyes to try to get rid of the double image I have of him. Another man sways beside him, as if he's backup in whatever fight Jeff believes we're in. My laptop slips off my bed from where I left it as I fell asleep watching TV. I don't know what he's saying. I stare at him blankly, trying to blink away the second Jeff until his rising volume starts to help hammer his words into my skull.

"—*dead rabbits? And babies at that? Are you a fucking psychopath? You want me and your mother's relationship to end that bad, huh? How could you do this to your mother? What kind of sick prank are you playing on her? She's already been through enough. And if she even knew what you were up to when she wasn't paying attention—*"

"What exactly is she up to when I'm not paying attention?" Traci is standing behind him. Her bathrobe has a rosy streak of blood up the side. Jeff's neck bulges, pink and sweaty. He turns to Traci. I know before he opens his mouth that he's going to tell her about the party. That traitor.

"I don't know what you're talking about." I'm distant, this doesn't feel real. Shivers run up and down my frame.

He turns back to me. "And you're lying. Again. Unbelievable."

"Lying about *what?*" Traci asks, her volume rising to match his. She's getting worked up too. "Asha, what is he talking about?"

"I don't know!"

"She was drinking last weekend."

Traci's lips flatten into a neutral line. This is when I really get scared. When her face no longer conveys emotion, it's time to get out of the way. "Jeff, I want to talk to my daughter alone."

"Traci, she shouldn't be treating you this way—"

"*Jeff*." Her voice is sharp, and he listens to her. He stomps back to their room.

Traci sits on the edge of my bed and picks up my laptop. "You shouldn't watch TV in bed." Her voice is tight. But then she sighs and puts a hand on my knee. "Asha, did you put those dead baby rabbits in our bed?"

"Why do you think it was me?" Rage fills me up and takes over.

"I know you don't like Jeff—"

"So what if I don't? I'm not a psychopath—"

"You don't have to be a psy—"

"To kill baby rabbits? Are you serious? Jeff just wants to blame it on me because he doesn't like *me*. Jeff probably did this to prove I'm a shitty kid."

"He likes you. He's trying."

He's trying. As if I'm not. There's silence between us.

"Maybe a wild animal broke in . . ." Traci trails off. Seems unlikely if they were *in* the bed like Jeff said. "I want to believe you, Asha, but there's just no other explanation. I can't believe you would do something like this."

Obviously, she can believe I did it if she's accusing me. My head pounds with fury.

"Were you drinking last weekend?"

"Yes." I admit it. Can't be worse than lying to Traci and her finding out.

"At least you're not lying about one thing here. Why didn't you tell me? I would've picked you up." Traci's face softens to concern.

Her softness takes me completely aback. "What?" I thought she'd ream me out for drinking.

"I would've picked you up, Asha! I don't want you getting in an accident. Lots of kids around here die. Kelly's son . . ."

"We walked."

"We?"

"Me and Cole. It was that night I went over to her place."

"Ok. I'm glad you went with a friend. You can tell me if you're drinking. It's normal at your age to want to experiment. As long as you're safe . . ." She takes a deep, stabilizing breath. "I don't know if it was you or some . . . barn cat or . . . who knows what that left the rabbits in the bed, but just please, *please* try to get along with Jeff. He's really trying hard. And I'm trying really hard too. You just make it so *difficult* sometimes, Ash. This passive-aggressive behavior toward Jeff needs to stop."

I want to say *I'm trying too.* But I know that even if I told her two truths just now, she'll flag it as a lie. I've been trying. I've been trying hard. I don't want to lose her. I don't want things to be cold and distant between us forever. This is supposed to be a fresh start for us, a way to heal the emotional mistrust between us, and if that means tolerating Jeff, then I'm doing the best I can. I wish Traci could see that. And I wish I could understand why she would believe Jeff's interpretation of me over my own. I'm angry at him for putting this wedge between us, for making it impossible for Traci to believe me when I say I'm trying. And that's what really takes my anger to the next level. If she hadn't made any comments about my behavior toward Jeff, I'd be totally fine. But she's taken his word over mine. Again.

This is just like it used to be before we moved here. If I did anything slightly off—forgetting to load the dishwasher after school, staying out past curfew at Nia's, not talking or smiling enough around Jeff—he'd make it into more than it was. He'd convince Traci I was shirking my responsibilities around the house because I resented him. Anything Jeff tells her I've done wrong, she believes, even when I beg her to believe me. I don't know what I did for her to stop trusting me. Maybe it was choosing to live with Dad over her. Maybe it was something I don't even know I did. Jeff whispers in her ear and she takes his side *without fail.* When I even begin to suggest Jeff might be at fault, I get made out to be a threat to the blended family dynamic. I thought things were changing. But with Jeff here, it's just the same.

She gets up to go and flicks the light off. I can sense she wants to say one more thing, but she holds back.

"What were you going to say?" I shout after her. But Traci doesn't answer. She doesn't say what I think she would: that she doesn't want me to turn out like my father. Immature and vengeful. Reckless. Mean. Whichever words she wanted to choose this time, she chokes back and holds down in her silence. But as soon as the door clicks shut behind her, their ghosts burst into the air, and I'm left empty. If a truck hit me right now, my rage wouldn't let me feel a thing.

Jeff is the one who's been walking around in the night, creaking floorboards, trying to catch me sneaking out. Maybe he did this to prove once and for all that I'm the reason our little family isn't perfect. But even in my rage, I have a hard time imagining Jeff snapping the necks of baby rabbits in his white polo and khakis. Who could've done something this awful?

"Where are you?" I ask the ceiling. Aggie's face doesn't emerge. The crack remains dark and empty against the blue of the rest of the ceiling. I want to scream. Rage is pounding against my skull. I can't fall asleep without Aggie's comfort, so I throw off my sheets and walk over to my wall to turn the light on. I lie in bed attempting to recreate the person in the photo from the wall in my head until I drift off to the sound of Traci and Jeff whisper-yelling behind their bedroom door.

I dream the person in the photo is holding me, whispering to me: "It's not your fault."

Even if it isn't my fault, it doesn't matter. Jeff's going to be on my case from here on out. We're back to where we started before this pointless move.

CHAPTER NINE

The next morning, I'm still fuming. When I go downstairs to eat breakfast, Traci is rifling through the cupboards with the frantic energy of someone held at gunpoint. Jeff's shoulders are hunched as he holds his head in his palms; the pure antithesis of Traci, monumental in this kitchen. In contrast to his bulging red complexion last night, today he's pale. He winces as I slam the freezer door closed and toss my waffles violently into the toaster.

"What are you looking for?" I ask Traci coldly. I already know she won't answer. That's how she is when she's this angry. Completely silent. She doesn't want to look at me, let alone speak to me. I'm too disgusting to behold or whatever. It's childish, even from my standpoint as her child. I got used to this a long time ago. So I pretend innocence, like I'm the bigger person and nothing ever happened. It drives her up the wall. Which I suppose is equally vindictive and childish. Like mother, like daughter, I guess.

"What are you looking for?" I ask, louder this time.

Jeff winces, pinches the bridge of his nose. "Asha, can you please quiet down?"

I turn to him and whisper, "What's for breakfast? Rabbit soup?"

This brings some color back to his face for a minute before it all rushes out again and he white-knuckles the edge of the mint green melamine table. Traci turns to glare at me. I can't help but smile. I know I'm being awful. There's something inside me that wills me to push things to the edge until someone else explodes. It's terrible, but if that explosion is finally achieved, a wave of relief will wash over me. Sometimes, I'll even smile. There's nothing more unbearable to me than pent up resentment.

Traci's lips form a long thin slash across her face. The fire in her eyes scares me because in it I recognize my own potential for violence.

"Out," she says firmly.

"But who's going to help you clean up all the toxic mold and dust today? Doesn't look like Jeff is up to it." In fact, Jeff looks like he needs to lie down and take a few Aspirin. He gets headaches that put him in what Traci calls "moods" when he gets too stressed. That means he gets sulky and whiny and mean, and Traci can chalk up his bad behavior to headaches when really, the way I see it, he's just being a blatant asshole.

"Quiet. Or. Out." Her voice draws a line that I decide not to cross for now.

"Fine." I grab a sweater from one of the hooks on the kitchen door and smush my sneakers onto my feet.

I take one last opportunity to show them both how angry I am by slamming the door as Jeff mutters, "Jesus," behind me.

Outside, it's so hot I regret bringing the sweater. It's like living in that frozen tomb so close to Jeff just chills me to the bone.

∽

It takes me thirty minutes to make it to Cole's through the woods. I get hopelessly lost and realize I'm walking in circles when I spot the lightning tree a second time. According to Cole, her house is a straight shot east of our house and should only take ten minutes tops. When I finally emerge from the woods, frustrated and devoured alive by mosquitoes, Kelly waves to me from an Adirondack chair where she's tanning in her sunflower-yellow bikini.

"Asha!" she yells, raising her cup of coffee in welcome as she slips on her baby-pink flip-flops. Her toes are painted to match. "Glad to see you here. Cole won't stop talking about you two and how much fun you had at the falls yesterday."

"Mum! Leave her alone!" Cole's leaning out one of the second-floor windows, exasperated with her mother. She's been talking about me. My ears warm.

"I knew you girls would get along from the start. Always did as babies. You're both right firecrackers. Brings me back to me and Traci. Don't you go getting into trouble now." Her smile freezes.

"We won't." I wonder if Joe's been telling her I'm trouble too. "It's nice to have a friend," I say to soften myself in her eyes. It sounds flat, though, fake, like something someone who's never had friends would say. It's a struggle to muster any emotion except rage right now. The anger's clenched between my back teeth.

Kelly seems to pick up on the fact that something's going on with me by the way her usually expressive face stiffens. "Well, don't be a stranger, just head on in. I'm going to stay out here and get some more sun. Vitamin D helps with the blues. Help yourself to anything in the kitchen." I guess I look surprised because Kelly starts laughing loud and long. "You really are from the city, hey? We just call that hospitality out here."

"Thanks."

I look to the upstairs window, but Cole's disappeared. She reappears at the front door and beckons me in.

"You talked about me to your mum? That's cute." My face relaxes into a smile easily when I see her roll her eyes. I really mean it. I wish I could talk to Traci about Cole, how waiting to see her next is almost impossible, how when I catch a glimpse of her in the distance, I want to run toward her, but it seems like we won't be talking about much of anything for the next little while.

"Come up to my room." I follow Cole up the stairs, pausing to look at the photos lining the floral wallpaper: portraits of the Levesque-Gerges kids, interspersed with a sprawling array of family members.

"Wow, are these all your cousins?" I point at the diagonal line of faces that all relate to each other in different ways—the overbite, rosy cheeks, auburn hair like Cole's, narrow shoulders, dimples, her mother's long nose, sticking-out ears like Millie's.

"Mum likes to keep a wall devoted to our family. All her siblings have, like, nine kids. The family reunions are nuts. Mum didn't have as many kids because of Dad's work schedule. But she's kept a whole area free surrounding me and Millie in case we ever have a million kids too." Cole points to the two highest portraits on the stairs: two awkward school pictures. One is of Cole, maybe a few years ago. Her cheeks are rounder, and she has braces. The other is of Millie from the past year. She's wearing a t-shirt with a face printed on it. The words above the face are crumbling off from over washing, but I'm pretty sure I make out the MADD logo.

It's only when I reach the top of the stairs and nearly walk into what I would describe best as a shrine for Cole's older brother that I recognize the face on Milly's shirt as his. Portraits of her older brother at all ages stand gathered beneath a cross nailed to the wall. A funeral booklet lies underneath what looks like a kindergarten photo of him. The booklet reads, *In Memory of Benjamin Hassan Levesque-Gerges.* Below is his birth year and death year. He was only seventeen, the same age as we are now.

"Sorry," I say, glad nothing fell off the wobbly table and smashed.

"Don't worry about it, just hurry up!" Cole sounds blasé, but I saw the fear in her eyes as my leg almost took the whole shrine down. Before I can mumble any more apologies or ask any questions, she pulls me along the hall into her room.

Cole's room: baby-pink walls are pasted over with dark metal and experimental electronic posters squeezed between layers of what looks like Cole's original artwork and comics. "Your room is sick."

"Thanks. I like it in here." She's rooting around in the upper drawer of a mirrored vanity table that looks like it would fit in well at Aggie's except that it has My Little Pony and Power Rangers stickers pasted all over it. Aggie never would've stood for that.

Cole pulls the photo out of her drawer, then leans against her dresser and looks at her feet. "Promise not to be mad at me."

My heart drops. "What happened to her?" I'm not mad but my heart is beating the drum line from one of the dark metal bands' songs. So far, this day's been nothing but cursed.

She pulls out the photo I gave her. "It got wet when we were at the waterfall." She holds it out and I take it. Cole said "wet." Looks more like soaked. The paper's yellowed and the picture's even more blurred, like the cloudy background is taking over the whole image.

"I tried my best to salvage it. You can take it back now if you want. I don't want Mum to see it. She's been going through my drawers looking for my weed. She caught me smoking last week and she was furious. I mean, ballistic. I thought she was going to ground me."

"Oh, that sucks," I say, but I'm distracted. There's something strange about the way the water patterns accumulated. Another, separate presence in the image is surfacing.

"If you put that any closer to your face, you might fall in," Cole jokes. She laughs awkwardly. When I don't laugh along, she joins me in looking at the photo. "Probably better that you'll have to throw it out. I don't think you want to fall into old Sabrina's world."

"Sabrina?"

"Yeah, my grandmother's name was Sabrina."

"Why wouldn't I want to fall in?" Falling in would give me more answers about what's going on with this picture than Cole, that's for sure.

"Your mum didn't tell you?" I shake my head no. "Sabrina was murdered. At least that's what my grandfather said. They never found the body."

Why did Aggie have a photo of a murder victim in her walls?

"How long ago?"

"I think my mum was five? Sometime in the late '70s. We don't talk about her much."

Now it makes sense that Cole was so tight-lipped when it came to Sabrina before. "I'm really sorry." I think about how my great grandfather's leg getting broken by the cops here is a story that's constantly at the back of my mind. How it's affected the way Nan's, Dad's, and my life have gone. I can't imagine what a grandmother's disappearance and possible murder has done to this family, even to Cole, who never knew her.

"It actually took me a while to be sure it was her because in all the other photos, she's wearing dresses or riding gear." Cole looks back down at the photo with her eyebrows pulled together. In this photo, she's wearing men's clothes. "I never really felt connected to her until I saw this picture. Seeing her like this messed with me, like seeing another version of myself . . . "

I'm not sure what she means by that. Before I can ask, she keeps talking faster, the words spilling out, "Her life was so different than mine. I never thought if we'd met we could've had a close relationship. Mum and Uncle Joe always talk about how she gave up her life to come live with my grandfather on his farm. She was from the city and liked it there better. Like you, I guess. And she was wealthy. She met my grandfather because of his horses. Apparently, she was always happy out here, until . . ."

"Until what?"

"Until she went missing."

I'm numb. "There weren't any warning signs?"

"My grandfather thought she was murdered, but Mum says it was suicide. Murder makes more sense. That's what Uncle Joe thinks happened. With suicide, he would've noticed something was off, right? He told me they had leads on who did it but they never properly followed through."

I think of that rumor Traci dismissed about Ellis being murdered. Now Cole's telling me Aggie's neighbor was murdered too? Maybe the rumors have more truth in them than Traci wants to let on. Could Aggie have killed Ellis *and* Sabrina? Maybe Joe was right about our family causing trouble in this town. I think about waking with that weight on my chest and my pulse speeds up.

"They never found her body. After a while, the cops stopped looking. I think that's why Uncle Joe became an RCMP officer. He wanted to solve his mother's case and thought becoming a cop would do it."

"Shit." I'm sweating and jittery, learning all this new information.

"You ok?"

"He didn't do it? He got let out, right?"

"Who?"

"The guy who got arrested?"

Cole shifts away from me, pulls the photo out of my hand and places it beside her, where I can no longer see it. "Yeah, I'm pretty sure he got let out . . . why?"

"I don't know, I just . . ."

"Your hands are shaking."

"What?"

"Your hands—" She takes one of my hands in hers and lifts it up so I can see. I pull it away and sit on it to stop its vibrations.

"Do you think Aggie murdered her?" I say it so she'll stop looking at me like that, all concerned, like I'm going to puke on her again.

"Sabrina?" Cole seems to think this is ridiculous. She cackles outright. When she sees my face is still serious, she continues, "No, I mean, do you see the way she's dressed? Maybe they were fucking. But you know Aggie, she's uptight but sweet."

"My mum did say there were rumors that Aggie was gay—"

"For the record, everyone knows Aggie was gay. It's common knowledge in this town. Maybe your mum said it was rumors, but the old birds talk about it all the time. Say she killed her husband. I don't know if that part's true. Whatever. She was good to our family and so we're good to yours."

I sit down on the edge of the bed. My body feels like it's on the last leg of a marathon. My mind is still running. Was it possible they *were* lovers, and something went wrong? Something ended badly? If Aggie didn't do it, maybe someone caught them together or something? A hate crime? Fuck.

Cole sits down next to me, still studying the photo. "I never had any reason to think about it before seeing this photo, but maybe Sabrina was bi. Lots of people like people of all genders, right? She and my grandfather were definitely in love. Why do you care about all this, anyway?"

"I don't know, I just do." I'm frustrated and it comes through. Up until now, I haven't given much thought to why this is important to me. But now . . . if Sabrina was murdered out of hate and Aggie was queer, I feel differently. This hurts more. Before, I didn't know why it mattered if Aggie was queer or why it mattered if I was. I didn't know if it mattered that I don't look at Cole the way I look at my other friends. But suddenly all these loose connections are tightening. All of it has started to matter much more. Especially, it matters that someone was wrongfully accused of Sabrina's murder.

Since I found the photo, I've just wanted something to distract me. Dead baby rabbits and no calls from Dad. Not one call from him since the day at the market. And it feels like it's all my fault. It feels like it was me who did all this, because I didn't do anything about him getting taken away. I didn't protest. I didn't know if I should trust Dad when he said he didn't do it. I just let it happen. And now we're out here. We're supposed to be far away from the messiness he left behind, but now that mess feels closer than ever.

I just wanted one thing to not be about the living. Because the living are shitty people. But all this distraction has shown me is the dead were shitty too. I don't want to think about any of this. Holding it all in isn't working either. I have to let something out. "Do you promise not to think I'm crazy if I tell you something?"

Cole sighs, bracing herself for whatever she thinks I'm about to tell her. "Sure." Her touch is soft on my damp t-shirt. I want to pull away, but I barely feel connected to my body.

"I think your mum's right about the house being haunted." I can't look at Cole's face. I don't want to watch as she potentially loses all respect for me. "It sounds bananas, I know, but there was this . . . presence . . . that guided me to find this photo in the wall. Otherwise, I never would've found it."

"You saw a ghost? You're sure it wasn't just a dream or reflected light or something?" I can tell she's struggling to take in what I'm saying seriously.

"I didn't see one." That's not true, but it seems easier to wade into supernatural waters rather than jump right in.

Relief flutters over Cole's face. "My mum says 'you don't always see them. Doesn't mean they aren't there.' She's always saying how it's unnaturally cold in that house, too. You should talk to her about it. I don't really know anything about that stuff." She sniffs disapprovingly of her mum's beliefs. "There's probably some other explanation. When you arrived, the place was a death trap."

I can tell she doesn't really want me to talk to Kelly. I don't really want to talk to Kelly about it either. She'll tell Traci as soon as I'm out the door and then Traci will freak out and do who knows what. "The house has good airflow," Cole suggests.

But Kelly is right. The house is cold. And colder whenever Jeff is there too. Jeff, whose foot went through the step and was better the next day. It's unseasonably cold, except for when it's scorching. I think of the sweater I carried all the way here on my arm. I thought it was cool outside, but when I stepped out of the shadow of the house a thick, wet heat coated my skin. There's rash on my wrist that keeps growing. I've bandaged it up because it's embarrassing, and so I don't wake up scratching it until it bleeds on my sheets anymore. Band-Aids draw crosses and lines on my lower left arm. The nightmares. Aggie in the ceiling leaning down, kissing me goodnight like I'm her very own. Waking up with the weight of a full-grown person on my chest, the cold hands reaching around my neck . . . would believing the house is haunted be better than any alternatives? That I'm losing it? That I can't handle Dad being in prison, can't handle Jeff and Traci's relationship?

"Just come back to my house with me and help me find something else. Something more than this one photograph. I just want to know what's happening with the house. *Please*."

"Ok," Cole says, "But all that aside, why'd you come over? You showed up all jumpy. Don't tell me it's ghosts or this photo either."

So, I tell her about the baby rabbits.

ʃɾ

After we check the nest and find it empty, she cries.

"I'm sorry," I tell her, and pull her close, even though it wasn't me who did it. Sorry isn't near enough. How could anyone murder a whole nest of baby bunnies?

"A human did this. Some sick fuck did this and I'm going to find out who." She breaks out of our hug and spits her words out into the luscious, sunny forest that looks like it couldn't know such violent deaths. The moss and ferns stretch out, nothing marring them. No footprints, nothing we could use to track down whoever did this if we were the type of people who knew how to track someone down. I don't. Maybe Cole would. She's outdoorsy. Besides. I already suspect I know who did this.

Something catches my eye just behind a layer of ferns. I think it's a splash of blood at first, but it's too pink. And the white that surrounds it is too stark to be anything natural. I leave Cole and walk over, pick it up. It's a receipt from Fen, one of the fancier restaurants in the city. That's where Jeff took Traci on their first date. On the back of the receipt is a perfect puckered lip mark that could be used for marketing whatever brand of lipstick this is. I read the receipt. They got oysters and wine and steak and quail and chocolate mousse, tiramisu . . . the total comes to well over a hundred dollars. Jeff couldn't have eaten this all alone. The date is for July fifth. Last week.

I crumple the thing in my hand and I'm about to throw it when I stop. Careful as I can, I smooth the receipt and fold it neatly. This isn't my mother's lipstick color. Why would Jeff have been out here if he wasn't slaughtering baby rabbits? I fold the receipt neatly and walk back over to Cole.

"What did you find?" she asks, wiping the last of the tears from her eyes.

"Proof Jeff did it." I don't know whether I'm talking about the rabbits, or his affair, or both. This is proof Jeff isn't the man he appears to be. Proof he's been using me as a tool to distract from his own sins. I thought I would feel triumphant if I ever found anything that incriminated Jeff. Instead, my heart sinks. How could I ever show this to Traci? I would be the one breaking her heart.

"That yachting catalogue motherfucker . . ." she continues to curse under her breath. It's satisfying to see someone else so alight with disdain for Jeff.

I hear the sporadic buzzing of my phone and pull it out of my pocket. I have two missed calls and a text. All from Traci. The text says:

emerg, come home.

⁂

When we cross onto Aggie's property, I sprint toward Traci's car. Cole follows. Traci is packing Jeff into the front seat. He's glassy eyed, and it takes me a moment to realize the liquid spilled down his shirt is not water, it's drool. "*Sssssss* . . ." Saliva seeps from his mouth as he gasps wetly for air, like a drowning man.

"What's happening?" I ask. Whether I like Jeff or not, the panic in Traci's eyes gets my heart racing.

"I don't know. He's having trouble breathing."

"*Liihh—lihhh*"

"Sh, baby. We're going to the hospital." Traci pushes his hair back. It sticks to the pate of his skull it's so wet with sweat.

"*Ss—Liiih—*" He chokes on his own spit.

"What's he trying to say?"

"Nothing—what does it matter? We have to go—"

Cole interjects, "The nearest hospital—"

"Isn't for forty kilometers, I know. We're driving; the ambulance will meet us on the way."

"Is he going to be ok?" I lock eyes with Jeff and he gives me a hateful glare.

"*Ssss*," he says again.

"What's he trying to say?" No one answers, but Jeff's fixated on me with an eerie clarity.

This is your fault, his eyes say. And then his eyes close and it looks like he's passed out. But the corners of his mouth curl up to reveal a sinister grin. He starts laughing. More spit gurgles out of his mouth onto his chin.

"He's delusional," Traci says. She isn't crying, but there's a tremble in her voice. "He was seeing things. I don't know what to—"

"Seeing things? Like what?" Aggie? "I should come with you," I tell her, but she shakes her head.

"No, Asha, you stay here."

"I want to come with you."

"No. I don't want you to be there if . . ." She bites her lip. If what? If he dies? "I don't understand," she says instead. Her tears are falling now, but I'm not sure she's aware. Mascara streaks her cheeks. "He was fine and then he wasn't."

"Get going now." Cole speaks with urgency and the stability of someone much older than us. "I'll stay with Asha until you can come home."

"Thank you," Traci says, and she gets in the car. She stares at me with sad, watery eyes, throws the car into reverse, and then they're gone.

I hold the receipt that could end their relationship in my pocket. It's just a useless, petty piece of paper.

CHAPTER TEN

As soon as the kitchen door closes behind us, I turn to Cole. "You can go home if you want."

"What?"

"You can go back home. I'm fine." I want to be alone. Today's been too much. I can't get over the way Jeff looked at me, like he knew every dirty corner of my insides, like it was me who caused his illness. I scour my memories for anything I could've done to make him so sick, but come up blank.

What else could have caused it? The rabbits? Maybe they were diseased. But he put them in the bed, didn't he? What if he didn't know they were contagious?

That night a couple weekends ago when I heard Jeff come in late and walk by my door—where had he been? Was that the first sign of his illness? Maybe he didn't even know what he was doing. This whole time, something could've been sowing disease in his brain: a clot, a tumor, some environmental toxin from all his years working to implement pesticide dispersal on forests . . .

That could be it. I'm just paranoid. It was a stressful situation; maybe I misread his glare. How could this be my fault? Should I have said something about Aggie, warned them about the strangling hands in the night? If she did murder two people in her lifetime, what's to stop her from killing one more invader in her space, even after death? If she did this, then I'm partially to blame for not saying anything—not that they would've believed me. Even if it wasn't Aggie, something's not right here. Whenever Jeff's around, the house feels off. It gets cold, dead rabbits appear in beds, he takes strange midnight walks, he falls through the porch and doesn't get a scratch. And then there's the weight on my ribcage every night and Traci's insomnia, worse than ever. I'm starting to wonder if the house is uneasy with all our presences.

I just want to go to bed and wake up tomorrow morning when all of this is resolved. If he dies—

"It's not like I'm babysitting you," Cole says. "I'm confused. I thought you'd want to find out more about this house—about Aggie and Sabrina? Is this 'cause I was weird about it earlier? I didn't mean to react like that. Why don't we go up and look for clues about what happened to them?" She starts toward the hallway.

I don't follow. Cole's question and the concern in her voice make me feel even worse. Is she just pandering to me? What I really want right now is to ask Aggie why all of this is happening. I can't start asking questions to the ceiling with Cole here though. Anyway, how can I play detective when Jeff's so sick? If he dies, how will Traci ever get over him? Will she spend the rest of her life in mourning? Then he'd haunt us wherever Traci ends up living. The thought of living with his ghost in the room for the rest of my time with Traci on this earth leaves a bitter taste in my mouth. I know if she loses Jeff right after we had such a big fight, we'll never be able to heal our relationship.

"Sun's setting anyway. Shouldn't you be getting back home?" I pull a can of chicken soup out of the cupboard and begin wrenching the can opener around the lid.

"No, I don't care. I'll stay." Cole's quiet and firm. "I don't care about sunset. I told you. I don't believe in any of that stuff. I just want to know you're ok after—"

"I told you, I'm fine. Jeff will be fine. I'll find a way to fix it."

Cole raises her eyebrows in disbelief and pushes the stray hairs out of her face. "Fix it? How is that your responsibility?"

I don't have an answer for her. I think of that gruesome smile spread across his face, exposing his perfect veneers, coated in slimy fluid. Did anyone else see that? Did I imagine it? Why would he look at me that way, like everything about who I am is a joke to him? Like he knows I did it. But I didn't, right? I didn't make him sick.

I'm starting to come up with a plan. When Cole leaves, I can call on Aggie and ask her what's going on in this house. I don't know if she'll show up, or if she'll answer me. So far she's been passive, just appearing on my ceiling at night. But I need to do something. If I can find out why this happened, I can make it stop before it affects any of us any more than it already has.

Chicken soup splashes onto the counter and my hand. I curse and throw the can opener into the sink, splash the soup into a pot and crank the heat to high on the burner.

"Whatever. He'll be fine. Traci's with him." She didn't even say goodbye to me. She had nothing to say to me. If it was me in that car, would she be in such a rush? Would her eyes be filled with the same fear? Of course they would. Of course. She loves me. She loves me. She used to tell me all the time. I believe her. *I believe her*. She *loves* me. She's my mother. She'll be back. He'll be back with her.

She barely even looked me in the eye.

Cole walks over to the stove and turns the heat down to medium. Then she sits down at the kitchen table and puts her head in her hands. "Let's just eat something and then we can talk."

I pour the soup into two of the hexagonal bowls. We eat in silence. Eat's a strong word; mostly, we both stir our noodles around. I can tell Cole's frustrated with me. I don't care. She doesn't understand. This can't be an accident. On some level, Jeff deserves this.

Do I really believe that?

"He killed those rabbits," I say, finally. Maybe things would be better with him gone. Just me and Traci in this big old house. No one else. "He's cheating on my mum."

Cole stares at me blankly. "What if he's really sick? Like, if this isn't temporary." The confusion leaks from her eyes and a stronger force grows there. "What if he doesn't make it to the hospital on time?"

"They'll make it." I don't want him to die. But every part of me wants him gone. I want him out of this house. Jeff keeps pulling everything backwards. Me and Mum. He's pulling us all back to something unspeakable, a deep despair that I can't fully articulate. It's like things are worse, but they're also better. And things are better, but they're also worse.

I just know I can't survive with him here and maybe neither can this house. I can feel the way the cold dissipates when he's not here. The way his foot crashed through that step, now he's seeing things and in immense pain. What was he trying to say? Maybe something or someone wants him out even more than I do. Still, I can't shake the feeling that I'm somehow at fault. If I'd been nicer to him. If I could've just acted better—

"Asha, I get you don't like him. He's still on his way to the ICU, probably. Do you understand that? This is really serious. When my brother—"

"He was laughing at me. Did you see that? He was smiling this big smug smile and he was laughing at me. Or maybe I— I don't know—" my voice is rising, I realize. I cut myself off. Maybe it's this house. But I don't know how much more I can say to Cole about the ghosts when she was reluctant to talk about the possibility of a *presence* earlier.

She scoffs. "He was delirious. There's no way he was conscious enough to even—"

"What do you care? You don't know him. You don't know what he's like. He's a snake. He killed those rabbits, and he's cheating on my mum, and she's driving him to the hospital, and she won't even speak to me. Maybe he's not faking it, but this is happening for a reason. He's going to be fine. As long as he's not in this house, he's going to be fine."

Cole pushes her chair back so hard it falls over as she stands. Something inside her snaps and her voice turns sharp. "Are you serious right now? He looked like he was halfway to the grave. What's this house got to do with anything?" She pauses, leaves a space for me to interject, to protest, but I don't. Her voice is rising too. "Be realistic! You could lose him. You're lucky he's around. I'd kill for my brother to be around, even just for the weekend. Illness and death don't happen for 'a reason.' My brother didn't die for 'a reason.' I'm so tired of that bullshit." I recoil. It's like she slapped me across the face. She stomps across the room and slams the door behind her.

I got what I wanted. I'm alone at the cost of hurting my one friend in this town with my thoughtlessness.

The rash on my arm itches so bad that I rip my bandages off and tear into my own skin. When I start bleeding, I run my entire arm under the kitchen tap, watching the blood circle down the drain like paint. I shiver. It's the first time I've been in the house totally alone with the hum of the refrigerator and the pipes gurgling in the walls, the rhythmic creaks of floorboards as the earth moves below us. I sit at the kitchen table and stare at the paint peeling from the walls. I don't want to be here in this town so far away from everyone.

If Jeff survives, I will make things work. I have to make things work. I can't lose Traci. When she comes back, I'll do whatever it takes to make things right.

I lose track of myself for a while, staring into the swirls of the melamine.

♪

In the last pink minutes of sunlight, Cole comes back through the screen door. She shocks me back into my body when she touches my shoulder and holds up a jumbo bag of marshmallows and a pack of bamboo skewers.

"I still think you were selfish," she says, "but I didn't feel right leaving you."

"I'm sorry." I rise and pull Cole into a hug. We stand still for a moment before we step apart. "Thanks for coming back."

Cole nods awkwardly and pulls out a skewer and marshmallow. I can tell apologies are uncomfortable for her. She clears her throat. "I went back home and got this stuff. My brother taught me how to do this. Watch." She turns one of the elements on and it slowly brightens to orange, then she begins roasting a marshmallow on top of it. It turns golden on all sides equally, then she pulls the outside off and pops it in her mouth and continues to roast the iridescent white inner layer. I set mine on fire, then blow it out. "See, that's why my mum hates when we roast marshmallows inside. There's always someone who wants to set theirs on fire."

I pop the whole thing in my mouth. Crisp, bitter, sweet. "How did your brother like to do it?" I glance at Cole sideways to make sure it's ok I asked her. Her face opens up into a smile. I'm relieved she wants to talk about him.

"Like you. He'd burn them to a crisp."

"It's the best."

"People like you and him always say that, but the truth is you're just impatient."

I laugh. She's right. I don't have the patience for a thousand-layer golden marshmallow. I pull another out of the bag. We roast another four each before Cole talks again. "I'm sorry too."

"Why'd you come back?"

"Because I realized if I wasn't here, I'd just be thinking about you anyway, and sitting around feeling guilty I let Traci down. I like you. And I wanted you to understand where I was coming from. It was really hard for me to see Jeff like that. It scared me. I think it scared you too, but maybe you're not ready to admit that."

I nod.

"I don't want to seem like a know-it-all or anything, but I've been down this road before with my brother. It was a late winter night, he went out, and he was driving home drunk or high or whatever. My parents won't say what he was on." Cole pauses. I become a statue. Any movement or too loud a breath might rush into the space and interrupt her telling and my listening. "He slid across the road into a tree. He was in a coma for a month. We were at the hospital every day. I know it's silly now but somehow each day he was on life-support, my hope that he'd be ok again kept growing. I had hope he would pull at my hair and drive me to school and sports and to get ice cream in the summer, just the two of us. I kept hoping harder, even though the reality that he wasn't going to survive became more real every minute.

"I think my parents still believe on some level that it was his fault he died because he wasn't sober. But how can I blame him when I do the same stupid shit, make the same stupid mistakes he did? I just wish he was here to tell me how not to repeat his fuck-ups." She's not crying, but her voice is pulled tight. The marshmallow she's roasting sets aflame. "I'm just scared. I

don't want you or anyone to have to go through a loss like that."
Cole hands me the marshmallow. I blow on it, then pop it in
my mouth.

Cole seemed so self-assured when Traci was loading Jeff into
the car, but maybe that's just a result of her having experienced
abrupt loss before. Now that I've had time to sit by myself, I
can recognize she's right about me too. I am scared. For me and
Traci, but also Jeff. If he survives, this house might still want us
gone. If taking out Jeff this way was its first attempt on our lives,
what will it be pushed to do if we decide to continue to live here
despite its warnings?

"I was hurt when you told me to leave because I know what
this is like," she continues. "When Ben was at the hospital, and
I was back in my bed at night, not knowing if I'd ever see him
again, I felt so alone. Nothing could change that. So, if you don't
want me here tonight, I can leave, as long as I know you're going
to be ok." She has marshmallow on her right cheek. She won't
look me directly in the eye.

I nod. "You can stay. I want you here too." I don't tell her I
think I'm crazy half the time. Or that I'm not as scared of losing
Jeff permanently as I am of Traci having to live with that pain. It
would be like losing her too.

So Cole stays. We eat marshmallows until we feel sick. The
evening slips into night, and before we know it, we're in bed, and
Cole has her arms wrapped around me. I don't know if any of us
are going to be ok, but in her arms I feel safer than I have in years.

☙

It's the first night in days that I don't wake up gasping for breath.
Instead, it's Cole's screaming that wakes me.

Cole is lying flat on her back with her palms up, shrieking
with her eyes open wide. I don't know if she's awake or not. Her

face is blank and open in terror. The covers are twisted around me; I must have stolen them from her in the night. They tie me to myself. In the panic of trying to get out of the knots of the sheets, I'm not able to follow Cole's gaze. Whatever she's seeing is still eclipsed for me. If she can see what it is. To me, it looks like darkness. Finally, she takes a hoarse breath, then starts shaking with uncontrollable sobs.

When I get loose, I rub her shoulder softly. I still can't tell if she's awake or not. I don't know if you're supposed to disturb someone who is stuck between dreaming and waking. My hands are trembling, clammy. I follow her gaze to the exact point on the ceiling where I watch Aggie before I fall asleep.

"Did you see her too?" I ask Cole. It's strange to feel this much excitement as tears continue to pool on the pillow, in her hair, on her cheeks. Aggie's not here right now, but if Cole saw her, then that means she's real. It means Traci and I *do* live in a haunted house. "Did you see her, Cole?" I don't know if she hears me, even though I can see she's awake and aware of my physical presence beside her. Cole grabs my arm, her fingernails digging into me. I pull her closer into a hug, let go of the question. She curls into my warmth. I rub her damp back until she quiets, catches her breath, and eventually stops crying.

I stare at the space on the wall lit ice-blue this time of the morning. A perfect corner of my window reproducing our heads side by side. "Sh, it's ok." I hear myself whispering over and over again. The sound echoes back to me from the blank wall, almost like someone else is saying it, almost like it's coming from the whole house, through me, to Cole. I close my eyes and can almost feel the house as if it's an extension of my own body. I know whatever was in the room with us is now gone.

When she's been quiet for a few minutes, I release her from my arms and walk across the room to open the window, let the fresh night air in. My door, which must have swung open by itself in the night, swings shut with the air pressure. We're closed into my room with the peaceful harmony of crickets, a distant stream, the trees breathing in long yawns, the way they only do in the privacy of night. I let the outside in, and it breaks something hard that was in the room to softness. We lie side by side and Cole curls into me. It's the first time I feel she needs me as much as I've needed her.

"I saw something . . ." She trails off. I know she's searching for the right words to make herself sound sane.

So instead, I tell her, "I didn't think anyone else would be able to see her. Was she in the ceiling?"

"Her?" Cole asks. She doesn't know what I'm talking about. A chill runs through me.

"The woman in the ceiling. Aggie."

Cole's voice drops to a whisper. She holds onto me hard again, so hard I'm worried she'll leave marks. "I didn't see Aggie. It was a man. He was on my chest. With his hands around my neck. He kept saying 'you're going to hell.' Over and over. I knew it was true. I couldn't breathe. I thought I died. There were . . . colors popping, like fireworks. He was so close to my face, like he wanted to kiss me . . ."

I reach a hand up to my own neck, the place where I feel cold hands grip me each night before I wake up gasping for breath. But I've never heard those words, never woken up to a face close to mine, threatening hell.

"But I know it was just a dream. Just Mum telling me haunted house stories about this place all these years, and then all my grief stuff . . . it got dredged up earlier, seeing Jeff."

I hold her tighter. And as my discomfort rises, thinking about the man she describes sitting on her chest, Cole settles in, her breath deepens. Mine quickens. I count each in and out to try to stay calm, but this trick no longer works. My body is pumping adrenaline. Everything around us sharpens, becomes dangerous.

I don't believe it was just a dream. The way she was screaming was too real and prolonged. Aggie's not the only ghost in this house. And she's not in the ceiling right now. So where is she? Where is *he*? I stare at the thin sliver of light coming in from the moonlit hallway. Eventually, as hard as I try, my eyes begin to droop too.

And then I hear footsteps. As quietly as I can, I pull on a pair of wool socks and creep toward my door. I open it quietly and peek out into the hallway. When I see who it is, I step out in full.

"Jeff?" He's pacing back and forth at the end of the hall. I didn't expect him back from the hospital so soon. He must've been fine after all. Maybe it was just an allergic reaction. I'm angry at him for recovering so quickly, so easily, angry he would smile at me like that and then come back home the same night, fine. And I'm relieved that he's ok, despite all of his shortcomings. "You're already back? What happened?"

I rub the sandiness out of my blurry eyes. He looks taller somehow, more solid. I remember how small he looked this afternoon when he was on his way to the hospital . . . how can this be the same man who could barely breathe earlier today?

But then—Jeff never wears suspenders. And he isn't as tall as the man who is now walking back down the hallway, straight at me, staring through me as if I'm not even there. As if I'm the ghost and not him. I recognize him from somewhere. The sharp light in his blue eyes, the early signs of crow's feet at the corners of his eyes, and his hair, parted to the side and greased. His solid, muscular form shrinks me. Jeff is slight. How could I have mistaken him for this man? This other man in our home who I do recognize. I've seen him before—arms around Aggie in that photo on the mantel. And standing next to Jeff when he barged into my room after finding the rabbits, I realize suddenly. I'd thought it was sleepy double-vision. But it wasn't Jeff's double, and neither is this: it's Ellis.

He's walking fast toward me, his feet creaking the floorboards in all the right places. And I'm so stunned that I forget to move. I freeze outside my bedroom door. As he approaches, the best I can do is close it behind me so Cole is protected. That is, assuming he can't walk through walls.

He's covered half the distance between us when his eyes lock onto mine and he smiles with the same loose malice that marred Jeff's face earlier. My head spins, an itchy buzz fills my ears until I can barely hear, and I grip the wall for support, thinking I might pass out. My knees go weak and I'm on the floor, watching Ellis's patent leather shoes stomp toward my useless body.

And then she drops into me. I know it's not Aggie. Aggie's presence always comes with a gentleness, the rosewater and mothball scent. This presence is more energetic, with a damp, earthy smell that reminds me of the forest after rain.

The easiest way to explain what's happening is that I'm realigned; I'm standing, but I am looking down on my body as if it is not my own, from above. And a reassuring voice tells me, without sound, *I will care for you. Don't worry. I won't let you be hurt.* Ellis's hands grip the shoulders of my body and slam it against the wall. The house shakes like my bones. Though I can't feel it from up above, I know it. Like watching a movie, I see my mouth move—not the way I've noticed it does in the mirror, small and tight, but loosely, casually, in an accent that belongs to an older generation. How Aggie used to speak, and a little like Cole.

"What are you going to do, kill her just like you killed me? Bloody hell, Ellis."

He opens his mouth and lets out a tortured yell that could only have its roots in a combination of grief and fury. "You took my wife to hell with you. You made this place hell. *You*, Sabrina."

Sabrina. Cole's grandmother. *That's you*, I think to her.

Yes, she replies, *that's me*. Ellis's body is pulsating, coming in and out of focus. My body, below, is floating a foot off the floor. *Don't let me die*, I plead with Sabrina.

I told you. I'd never let him hurt you.

"This place has always been hell, Ellis. And you've made it so for others. You know it."

"I've never—"

"Who built this house? Whose money? Whose blood?"

Ellis's grip on my body's shoulders loosens, then flickers. My body falls to the floor, and Sabrina becomes visible. She's dressed in a flannel nightgown, her hair limp. Her body's tiny, just like Cole's except for the bruised hand prints on her neck, yet she manages to look bigger than him.

"What was it for? Your death was only Aggie's idea of justice," Sabrina yells at Ellis. And Ellis turns, begins walking down the hallway toward the head of the stairs, as he fades.

I fade too. Before I'm even aware I'm back in my body and Sabrina is gone, Aggie is floating down wordlessly from the ceiling. She kisses my forehead, and everything goes black.

৶৹

It's the slamming kitchen door that wakes me. The jingle of Traci's keys. I unglue my face from the carpet and wipe the drool from my cheek. I grip the doorframe to lift myself up. Bile rises in my throat, but somehow, I keep my vomit in. *Sabrina*. I remember what happened last night and look at my hands. I'm in my own body, but there's something of not being the driver that lingers in the dizziness and nausea that crawls all over me inside and out. I open the door and see Cole sleeping undisturbed in my bed. I close the door again and head slowly downstairs.

It must be only a bit past six. The sun's golden, just coming up and filling the kitchen with light. Traci leans over the sink. She's quiet, but I know she's crying from the shake of her shoulders.

"Mum?"

Traci turns to me, pulls me into a hug. And I'm holding her tight too, because I want to.

"Jeff, is he—?"

"He's stable. You didn't answer my call."

"Guess I slept through it. Do they know what's wrong?"

"Long night. Tests will come in over the next few days. Is Cole still here?" I nod and Traci sighs in gratitude. As if we were safer together. Maybe we were. Traci reaches out and tucks a braid behind my ear. "You're sure you're ok, sweetie? You don't look like you slept well. I should make you breakfast—"

"No, sit down. I'll make you coffee." I pull the glass pour over and a filter from the shelf. Traci sits with her face in her hands and I pull out the coffeemaker. All slumped like that she looks like an old lady. Tired, given up.

She lets out a shaky breath and runs a hand through her greasy hair, then speaks. "I don't want to ask this right now, but did you see Jeff going out to the woods? Did you hear anything before he came in that night and found the rabbits?"

"No." The receipt proving he was out there is upstairs. But looking at Traci now, I can't tell her I know it was him who brought those rabbits inside. Not after last night. "Maybe he wasn't fully *here* if he did it."

Could a ghost have dropped into him? Ellis? I can see how they would have attracted each other's presences now. If it was contact with the ghosts that caused Jeff's illness, could they have the same effect on us if they wanted us out? Like something in the water poisoning us, maybe we can only withstand exposure for so long. Maybe one of them wanted something with Jeff.

Traci doesn't respond. I pour us each a cup of coffee and we sit together in silence. Jeff will be ok. Will Mum? Will I?

PART TWO

ASHES

CHAPTER ELEVEN

"So, what are you gonna do?" Nia's tinny voice echoes in my ear. We've finally managed to connect.

"I don't know." We're not talking about the ghosts, but I wish we were. All that conviction I felt after the attack has taken a backseat to the current situation with Traci who's spent the past week on the couch, ruminating over Jeff's condition. How am I supposed to start digging for clues about the past if I'm also taking on all the responsibilities of keeping this house in order while Traci can't manage it?

Since the night Cole slept over, not even Aggie's appeared above my bed. On the other hand, that misalignment with myself, the sense of watching myself from above that came from Sabrina dropping into me, has been constant these past few days. Some days it's better or worse. It's uncomfortable and I find myself wondering if it's permanent.

There are benefits to this distance Sabrina has left me with though. The main benefit being that I haven't woken up gasping since Cole slept over. Ever since Sabrina dropped into me, I've slept a motionless, dead kind of sleep. And when I wake up, I feel I leave a part of myself behind, in bed. In between sleeps, the days slide across my field of vision like a teacher's boring PowerPoint presentation. I only retain what I want to.

"What do you think? She's not really eating, and she won't talk to me."

"Dude, I don't know. I'm sorry. I don't know. But you've been through this before. What did you do then?"

"Avoid her and spend a lot of time at your place?" Even if she doesn't know any better than me what to do when Traci's in this state, it is a comfort to hear Nia's voice again.

"I guess just keep doing what you're doing?" She doesn't sound so sure about her advice. There's a pause. I rearrange my legs on the bathroom floor. My back's against the door. "Well, how's everything else? Making any friends?"

"Yeah. Our neighbor. You?"

"Spending all my time with my cousins. They're chill. Tell me about your neighbor."

"I don't know. We haven't been talking much."

"What happened?"

If anyone else had asked, I would've just said "nothing," and been done with the conversation. But since it's Nia . . . "We kind of got close fast . . . maybe too fast? I know stuff about her that's, like, deep, you know? But I'm not sure if our ideas about the world totally align."

"Well, we don't align on everything. You don't want to be friends with a carbon copy of yourself, right?"

"True. But this is different."

"Different how?"

"It just is."

"Ok." Nia doesn't push anymore, but in a very Nia way, suggests something in the subtext of the next topic. "So, Jamal has a crush on this girl in the neighborhood."

"Oh yeah? How's it going for him?"

"So bad." We both laugh. "He keeps going up to her, then he doesn't know what to say and he kind of just stares at her and mumbles about soccer and shit. My mum is on him about moisturizing his knees. My dad's giving him crusty-ass advice. He's a disaster."

"Sounds like you in middle school."

"Come on. At least I could hold a conversation!"

"Nia, please—I seen you freak out 'cause you lost your retainer at Scott's birthday party because you didn't want to take it out in front of everyone when his parents brought out the cake—"

"Stop! It's too embarrassing!"

"—and your parents made you go back to his house to get it that night, but the next day was garbage day and you made me go through his trash with you in the middle of the night, middle of the street, we were rifling through everything like fucking raccoons and Scott's parents caught us—"

"Ok ok ok ok ok ok—enough! I was just as embarrassing as Jamal! God, why you always gotta be on his side?"

"I ride for the underdog."

"You're so annoying."

"I miss you."

"Miss you too."

"I should go make lunch."

"Alright. Don't ghost me again, ok?"

I can't help a smile from tugging at the corners of my mouth at her unintentional pun. "I won't."

And in a matter of minutes Nia's evaporated again and I'm alone on the bathroom floor, sweating in the oppressive heat that's settled over town.

The heatwave arrived the day after Jeff went to the hospital, and weather apps signal no end in sight. From now to the end of time, I will only be as sweaty and slow and tired as I am now. Even with the windows open, hoping to bring down the temperature, rotating endless ice cube trays through the freezer, drinking iced lemonade, iced tea, iced water, sucking on ice cubes, nothing cools me and Mum off.

When the heat is unbearable even for supernatural beings, it's time to call in a break.

Maybe Jeff's absence has finally let the heat into this house. I thought it would be a relief not to wear sweaters every day, but this heat is worse than the unnatural cool. It's all consuming, eating away at my motivation to do any of the chores Traci's set out for me.

I haven't found the right moment to ask her about the house's history. I haven't found the right moment to talk to her about anything at all, to be honest. The last time I heard her speak a real sentence was the morning after Cole slept over. It's so hot I can't blame her. And she's worried about Jeff, even though he's coming back from the hospital in just under a week.

The doctors suspect a benign growth on the surface of his brain got knocked in the wrong direction, probably when he took that fall on the step. They're doing all sorts of tests to rule out any other conditions, but for now, they're almost certain whatever's going on with Jeff, it's not life-threatening. It's a relief not to have to worry about losing him for Traci. For me too. Now we know he's going to be ok, I find myself dwelling on the crumpled receipt that's still in the pocket of the shorts I wore the day he got sick.

Traci's daily trip to the hospital takes about all the energy she has. Once she's back here, she sits with a yellowed circulating fan pointed at her face, sweating and nibbling on diagonal cuts of the sandwiches I make her for lunch. She doesn't touch supper, so I've stopped making it and just started eating cereal for every meal because it doesn't require turning on the stove. I think she's maybe even sleeping in the den, but I don't want to embarrass her by asking.

From the way she's acting, I thought there would be more bad news about Jeff. Every test has come back negative. He's recovering fast. Maybe it's just the stress of entering that hospital space. She's never liked hospitals. She had to spend a lot of time in them growing up with her mum sick.

Traci gets testy about me judging her when she's in a state like this. I haven't seen her so checked out since right after the divorce. That year, when I came back and stayed at her house, she didn't eat or move much from our living room or say more than "how was school" to me when I came home. I'd hear her choked sobs in the night, but I never left my room to comfort her. I don't know if she'd want me to comfort her or if she just wants me to pretend it's not happening.

Eventually, when she started dating Jeff, I heard her laugh and talk again. But she never talked with me about what was happening with her, how she felt, or how she'd left me alone in our house for a year with only a ghost of my mother to keep me company. It's when we started fighting more too. This isn't then, though. I understand her apathy, her inability to see the world moving forward. Sometimes I feel the same way. Like Dad was then, I'm just better at hiding it. Knowing how she feels and knowing what to do doesn't make it any easier to see her like this.

So I know if I asked about who built this house with what money, she wouldn't give me the kind of in-depth answer I need. All I know are the basics: our family was involved in settler-colonialism, which isn't news since they were wealthy white people who arrived pre-eighteenth century. Beyond that, I don't know what kind of violence the white people on Traci's side of the family tree perpetrated. From the way Sabrina talked, though, it seems like it was more than a minor offense.

I tried accessing the provincial archives for the town online, but all I could turn up were sensationalist articles that told me the exact same thing Traci told me when we first talked about Ellis: he died, maybe it was a murder, but no one really knows. I guess rural murders don't get much coverage.

The library might have more information, but I don't have a ride. One morning I tried to skate there but ended up having a pretty hard fall not far from our house. When I came back in to get some gauze to cover the slash on my elbow, Traci freaked out and told me to stay home. I should've known skateboarding was a bad plan from my last experience cracking my head on the road. Plus, I'd probably get heatstroke even walking. Skateboarding would've taken me down for sure.

I guess I could ask Cole to drive me, but I don't really want to. I'm not sure how she'd take me looking into the house and its history. She's been weirdly good humored about the haunting, cracking jokes about the supernatural over text. Her humor seems like some kind of avoidance. To me, that memory is vivid. When I think about it for too long, I start to feel nauseous. It's like I'm right back there, hearing Cole's screams and watching Ellis as his hand reaches out for Sabrina's—my—neck.

I'm grateful for the deep sleeps I've had since then, grateful Ellis hasn't come back to attack me. But what happens if he does return? What if it's not the heat that's keeping him away? Maybe he's just looking for Cole, Sabrina's closest living double. His attack on her was more violent than the ones I experienced. And if Ellis is after her now, I don't think I'd want her to come over here anyway.

My last resort was to call Nan and ask her about the town's history, but she's not answering. She loves this hot, humid weather. If the heat back in the city is anything like what it is here, she's probably outside sucking it all up like a reptile. She probably learned to love the heat while she was in this town as a girl. Meanwhile, Aggie and Ellis were collecting circulating fans for every room. On my third unanswered call to Nan, I finally leave a message:

"Hi Nan, it's Asha. I'm just calling to say hi. Everything's good here. Hope you're doing well. I haven't heard from Dad or you in a while, so I hope we can talk soon. Did you know this house is haunted? Keeping an eye out for your old house but haven't been able to find it yet. Call me back soon. Love you, bye."

She hasn't called me back yet.

Dealing with everything alone is crushing me. I need to talk to someone about the ghosts. I know Nia's busy, and I didn't want to bother her with the ghost stuff while she was with her family, but I just can't handle holding all of these crises on my shoulders anymore. Nia's always been there for me, and I've always been there for her. So I text her:

> **missed talking to you!! how would you react if I said I thought this house was haunted. like, hypothetically** 👻

My phone buzzes against the table just as I'm finishing up on the lunch dishes and wrapping Traci's sandwich up for tomorrow. I'm relieved Nia messaged me back so quickly. I wipe my soapy hands on my shorts and flip my phone over.

It's not Nia. It's Cole.

> **walk tonight? bring swimsuit.**

I try not to focus on the huge wall of text that I sent preceding Cole's casual message. I wish I'd had time to unsend it before she saw it. It's a long and overwrought message about how I feel she's not taking things seriously enough. I sent it late at night. I was tired. I don't know if I meant it. Still, I'm annoyed she didn't acknowledge it at all.

I send back:

> **sure.**

As much as things have felt strange and unbalanced between us, I can't help looking forward to seeing Cole tonight.

I meet Cole on the other side of the moat. The heat's thick on the air, but it doesn't reverberate the same as it does during the daytime. We hug and pretend like everything is normal. Like the last time we were together, we weren't assaulted by ghosts. It feels so natural to go on like nothing happened. I can shake off the presence that lingers around me, find some freedom in the night air, the buzzing of mosquitos and the crescendo of crickets.

Cole leads me down the road in the opposite direction from town to the Green Bridge, an old train bridge that's now used mostly by locals as a swimming hole. You can jump from the oxidized copper into the rushing river. It's a legendary spot in this town. A sacred space for youth. Traci's told me a few stories about leaping off the bridge after a big rain, when the waters in the winding river rose. Skinny dipping, playing chicken, and other '80s clichés.

"I hope it's not running too low from the heat," Cole muses as we stash our t-shirts and shorts in my backpack and look down at the river below from the bridge. We brought a couple lanterns to hang from the bridge so we can see in the water. My heart constricts as I imagine us bludgeoned to death by the rocky bottom.

"We're not going to be one of those stories they tell you in assemblies about kids who were fooling around and then died, right?"

"Hope not," Cole says, grinning, "but if we do die, maybe we can live at your place. Promise I'll haunt you if I die tonight." She laughs and dangles a leg over the edge. Her joke grates on me. It would have been better if she'd just ignored the haunting totally.

There's a wide silence between us. I lean cautiously over the edge of the gritty railing. As I gaze into the dim pool beneath us, my heart pounds. "I don't know. I was down before but this seems reckless."

"It *is* reckless. That's the point." She's leaning completely over the edge now. The light from the lanterns reflects in ripples on her face.

"Your parents—I don't know how I'd tell them if you . . . what if you—"

"You're not responsible for me. And I promise you, we'll be fine. We're not drinking or high. It's not like Ben."

She knows what I'm thinking. If her parents lost another child, I don't think I could forgive myself. But Cole's right. It's not my responsibility. Just like it isn't her responsibility to supervise me. Besides, it's not like I believe my safety is totally within my control. Ellis could show up at any moment and decide to strangle me, or my brain could get scrambled, or I could get hit by a car skateboarding. Nothing is certain. I take a deep breath, can my worries, and decide I'll follow Cole's lead.

I watch as she climbs over the barrier and hangs onto the railing with only her heels and the tips of her fingers. The empty water yawns below. "Three! Two! One!" She drops like a stone. A big splash, then ripples reflecting up and out around me. And then I see her head resurface. She shakes her hair out and laughs loud enough to cover the sound of the crickets and frogs surrounding us.

"Come on, Asha!"

I pull myself over the railing too. The metal is old and lumpy in some places but still stable enough that I don't feel like I'll lose my grip. My heels press into the concrete. *Please, let me go home safe tonight.* I drop off the bridge.

The smack of my body as it enters the cold river is such a shock I nearly gasp for air. When I resurface, I'm already grinning as I wipe water from my eyes and swim over to Cole, who is directly beneath the bridge, lit by the lanterns.

"See! It feels good!" Her voice echoes on the metal and concrete.

"Ok, ok. Maybe taking risks is sometimes good." I admit. The fresh, green-smelling river water drips from my lips into my mouth.

"Almost always."

"*Sometimes*. I said *sometimes*."

"Can't believe I'm friends with someone who's so boring." Cole splashes me. I splash her back, cackling.

Cole jumps off the bridge five more times before we find ourselves treading water, stars reflecting light and shadow around us. Silence starts to thicken between us, peacefully.

"Can I ask you something?" All the humor is gone from Cole's voice. Usually, an open-ended question like this would make me fear the worst-case scenario, a question that meant the end of our friendship. Why would she ask to ask if it wasn't something heavy? But we're here, still living, floating around in the pleasant cool of the water like lily pads, so I say: "Of course."

"What happened to your dad? You don't really talk about him."

Dad. I promised myself I'd try to stop thinking about him. I've succeeded. I could just shut Cole's question down, but I don't want to. These past few weeks, I've barely thought about him more than in passing. Guilt washes over me at the thought of so clearly succeeding in my goal. Some combination of that guilt and the peace I felt some moments before makes me want to tell Cole now. I trust her not to stereotype him or me.

"He's in prison."

"What happened?" She doesn't sound concerned, which I appreciate. When he was first convicted, most people made a big deal of telling me they were sorry and treated me delicately, like I was about to break instead of burst into flames with fury at what happened to him. Cole's tone holds only gentle curiosity.

"I don't know exactly. They say he stole a lot of money from the sports org he worked at."

"Oh. I think I heard about that." Everyone in the Maritimes probably heard about it, whether through the news or a friend of a friend.

"Yeah. It was big news."

"Is it hard?"

I watch the reflections of ripples morph on the underside of the bridge. Birds' nests and spider webs tucked into corners become visible every so often as the lamps sway. "It's really hard."

We float in the thick silence that follows. Cole's hand finds its way into mine. It's warm in all this cold water. "Thanks for telling me."

"Thanks for asking." I really mean that.

When we start shivering, we swim over to the bank and wade out. Unlike the middle of the river, the sides are mucky and apparently crawling with leeches, so Cole leads the way along what she calls the "rocky part" which feels slightly grittier than the slimy bottom to the right and left of us.

We gather our gear and head back toward home. I'm holding one of the lanterns out in front of us so we can see the dirt road. Two or three cars pass us before we make it to the road that runs in front of our houses.

As we get closer to home, I start to feel dizzy. I hadn't noticed until we got closer to my place, but tonight is the first time I've felt fully in my body since Sabrina dropped into me.

Before the magic of the Green Bridge fully wears off and I become too detached from myself again, I want to ask Cole about what she saw when she slept over. Maybe since I've opened up to her, she'll be willing to talk about Sabrina, Aggie, and Ellis without joking around. I stop in my tracks, and she stops too, confused.

"What's up?"

"I had a question for you too."

"Ask away." She's smiling, but I can tell she's nervous from the way she's rocking on her heels.

"It's about the night you stayed over . . ." I'm having trouble finding the words. Cole's cheeks flush. What does she think I'm going to ask her?

"What about it?"

"Did you see . . . the man who was on top of you, was he like, tall, muscular, light hair and eyes, in a '60s type outfit?"

"Oh . . ." Cole flushes even deeper. I try to read her face, but I can't tell what I see there. Annoyance? Embarrassment? Disappointment? "I don't know. It was just a dream." She starts walking ahead of me. I follow.

"It's just, I had that same dream. I've been having that dream since I got here." I wait for her response, but she just keeps walking in silence. My ears start to flush in embarrassment, but I need to know. I need to know I'm not the only one who can see the violence this house is doing. I want to be real with Cole. "I think your mum was right about the house being haunted. I think that was Ellis's ghost, and Sabrina . . . that night, after you fell back asleep, she took over me. She made sure we were safe from him. Hey—Cole? Are you listening?"

"Yeah, I just . . . I don't know. Are you sure you weren't dreaming too?"

The edge of judgment in her voice makes me bite my tongue. I don't want her to start telling people I'm losing my mind. And I don't want to lose her as a friend. If anything, I want this shared experience to bring us closer. She's the only person who can understand what I'm talking about because she was there. Even if Nia texts me back, even if she believes me, it's not like she saw what I saw. Cole did.

"Okay. Maybe it was a dream." I give in. I thought Cole would believe me if I talked to her about what happened to me too. If I could tell her some of the details about Ellis that she remembered but didn't tell me about before. But she doesn't want to believe it's real. I don't blame her. Why would anyone want to believe they might be in danger from forces beyond their control? If she doesn't believe me, then I'm the only one who can try to stop them. I don't want to have to go through that alone.

"I just have a hard time believing in ghosts. I think I would've seen ghosts before if there were ghosts, you know?" There's a bitterness to her voice I'm not sure I've heard before. Of course. Before Ellis strangled her, Cole said our argument about Jeff brought up her grief about her brother's death. She already brought him up once tonight. How could I not have considered Ben's death before? Guilt washes over me at my own selfishness.

"You mean Ben?"

"Yeah. Why wouldn't he be haunting our house? And don't tell me he would've moved on because I saw the wreckage. I know he couldn't have been at peace."

"I don't know why he's not a ghost, but—"

"I do." Her voice cuts where it was soft just a little earlier. "It's because they don't exist. I told you before: if you want to talk about ghosts you should talk to my mum."

"Ok." I back off.

She takes a deep breath. "Sorry. I didn't mean to be so harsh. I think I'm just tired."

"Yeah, me too." It's a lie, but we're at the edge of Cole's driveway now and I get the feeling she wants to be alone. I wish I hadn't mentioned the ghosts, or her brother, for that matter. "See you later, then?"

"Later." Her smile doesn't reach her eyes.

When I enter through the kitchen door, Traci is at the table sipping herbal tea. She nods my way, then goes back to scrolling through her phone. I head upstairs and hang up my towel. I whisper at the ceiling, hoping to call Aggie. She doesn't emerge.

Sabrina's questions ring in my mind: *Who built this house? Whose money? Whose blood?*

Without Cole as an ally, I'll have to put in double the effort to find out what happened in this place. Jeff's return looms in the distance. I need to know more before he comes back in case next time the ghosts do worse than make him sick.

CHAPTER TWELVE

All week I look for the ghosts between chores. It's hard work. The junk room is so full that each time I enter, I stare at the piles of broken, abandoned collections from the house before I can bring myself to start digging again. No matter how many nooks, crannies, cupboards, drawers, books, and piles of shoes I investigate, I can't find much more than suggestions of clues. I suspect the real reason Aggie kept this place so stuck in the past was to hide any clues of what might have happened after Sabrina and Ellis's deaths. Maybe this was her way of never moving past the period of her life when the two people she was closest to died. That theory doesn't exactly make me feel more comfortable staying in her house.

As for the ghosts themselves, none of them appear to me. All I have are their memories, and as days stretch into a week, even those become blurry. Maybe there's something about their presence that keeps the memory of the ghosts fresh when they're around and difficult to grasp when they're not.

In my spare time, me and Cole text a bit, but neither of us suggests meeting up. I want to, but it just doesn't feel right after the night of the attack. It's like we've taken a step backwards in our friendship. When we met, Cole was so confident and open, but she's started making small talk instead of sharing her feelings or opinions. When I try to ask about them, she diverts the conversation away from herself to more banal topics, like her occasional berry picking gigs.

She did send me some pictures of her art, but only because I asked her to. It's mind-bending: layered, tiny, and amazingly detailed scenes out of parallel worlds. They're like looking into kaleidoscopes of the everyday. Inside, everything's refracted and warped. I wonder how someone could open their mind to these intricate worlds while being so resistant to even the prospect of the supernatural. Whatever conversation I'm ready to have about the ghosts, Cole is not. I force myself to bite my tongue and keep my determination to unravel the history of this house to myself.

Not that I can find the motivation on my own. Today is so hot the radio says to stay inside. I can't bring myself to commit to the chores Mum set out for me. She says she wants a break before changing the interior too much. The truth is she's still depressed, even with Jeff coming back tomorrow. She keeps mumbling her ideas to herself noncommittally, picks up design magazines at the grocery store and points at celebrities' restored houses, always bringing in what Aggie would or wouldn't've liked: pendant lights and modern storage closets. She says she can't sleep at night. She can't stop thinking that Aggie would hate her idea of renovating the parlor into a more useable space, someplace guests might want to sit if they visited us way out here.

Which guests? I wonder. We don't really know anybody besides the Levesque-Gergeses, and Mum isn't exactly a pillar of the community here. Maybe she meant her friends from the city. But I haven't noticed her talking to any of them since we arrived.

We lie on the couches in the den, the both of us drifting in and out of consciousness. I flip through the same photo album I found the night after the movie, scanning for any further details. Mum pretends to be interested in her phone, and I watch as the sunlight refracts into gold strips that move like eels across the cracked ceiling. My eyes are drooping closed, in and out of focus, when I notice a familiar work boot in a photo of Aggie and Ellis sitting on a porch swing. The boot sticks into the frame, in focus. The man, who's out of focus, stands up on a stool with a hammer in one hand and a glass of lemonade or something stronger in the other. He's tall, handsome, with the same long face and sparkling eyes as Nan, still visible in the blur that comes with almost being cut out of the frame.

My eyes snap back open. Aren't those the boots Traci snatched from my hand the first night here, the pair that were too big for Aggie to ever wear? When Mum touches my shoulder lightly and holds out her phone, I sit up so fast my brain does a cartwheel. Her mouth is a long, thin line. "It's your father."

I snatch the phone from Traci's hand and say, "Dad?"

"Hey pumkin."

His voice again is a punch to the gut. One that's first impact fills me with warmth, but then fades to sadness. I know he's the same man who raised me, but it feels as if all our points of reference were shattered the day he went to prison. What should I ask him? How his cellmates are? The prison yard? The cafeteria food? This must be how he felt when I came home from school. Although he probably didn't also feel a burning pain in his gut, or the questions stewing there: *Why'd you leave me? Why don't they let you go free?*

I'm relieved he takes the lead, moves the silence further away from us. "I'm just calling to check in. How's everything at Aggie's?"

"Everything's good here. We finished cleaning. Lots of mouse droppings and mold . . ." Mum is watching me closely. She looks worried, like she wants to listen in. I leave the photo album behind on the couch, go up to my room and close the door.

"Hmm, that place has been left too long."

"Yeah."

"And Jeff?"

"He's good." I don't want to talk about the bad stuff. Jeff's going to be fine. There's no reason to worry him. This time is just for me and Dad.

"You're being respectful?"

Familiar annoyance finds its way into my teeth. They grind. "Yes. I don't want to talk about him."

"Ok, ok, I'll get off your back. You go by the old farm yet?"

Between Aggie's mystery, Jeff's illness, and the heat, I haven't made time to go look for the old farm. Guilt creeps over my skin. "No, not yet. I don't really know where it is."

"You should call your grandmother. Get her to give you the address. I know it's out past that little white church. Used to be across from a potato field. Don't know if that's still there. She'd be happy to hear from you, eh? It's been so long since you've seen her."

"Ok." Calling Nan makes me nervous, especially since she hasn't been answering lately—what if she's been avoiding my calls? She doesn't like people dropping in unannounced in person or virtually—she's a real shut-in, embarrassed for us to see her when she's not prepared—but if she won't even answer her phone how am I supposed to get in contact with her? A back and forth over snail mail? "When's a good time to call her?"

"Mornings. She's clearer in the mornings, most days. She'd be happy to hear from you. Anytime." The line crackles with a long exhale on his end. I can see him shifting on his feet, rubbing his hand against his forehead, maybe leaning against a cinder-block wall. What does it look like in there? Surely not what I've seen on TV. "Look . . . I'm sorry I haven't called. It's been hard here. Getting adjusted and all of that. I miss you, Asha."

"I miss you too." I wipe my eyes hard, try to push my tears back in with the meat of my hands. "I'll call Nan. I want to see the old farm." I do. I really do. How did I get so short-sighted? When I look out my window, I can't see past the trees on our property.

"So, how is it living in a haunted house?"

"You know about that?"

His laugh coming through the phone should comfort me, but instead it chills. "Everybody knows about that! Your mother just didn't want you getting all freaked out when we went for holidays. It's common knowledge in town. Your Nan has her own stories about it. I grew up on them—scared me so bad I peed the bed a few times. When I found out your mother lived there for a few years when she was a teenager I was like, *damn, I need to get to know this woman.*"

"And tell her you peed the bed thinking about her home?" I laugh too and it hurts.

"I only told her that later."

"You believe in ghosts?"

"Don't you?"

"Undecided." Asking Cole about ghosts didn't go so well. I'm going to play coy until I can prove they're here from now on.

"Well, there's lots more types of ghosts out there than the type you see busted in movies, Ash. Some people say the Atlantic is full of ghosts from when our people were stolen across the water. And our family's second journey from the States to the Maritimes in the 1700s left a few ghosts around too . . . our family goes back to eighteen hundred in that town, but you wouldn't know it from looking at any of the town records."

Dad doesn't often talk about the past. Usually he says it's not worth it, it's just a whole lot of pain. Maybe for him, but I'm considering now how much pain it's created for me, not even knowing these basic facts about our family, about how we got here. I'm back in a place where our family first experienced freedom after coming north, but no one can talk about any specifics now. All that history's been erased by trauma and time's ability to silence. But then again our family still shows up in the corners of photographs.

"What kind of stories would Nan tell you?"

"One story she told me after I told her I was dating your mother—she started bringing up how there was bad blood between our families and the relationship was doomed. I wasn't having any of that, but the story was good, so I let her finish."

"Well, it was kind of doomed."

"Don't say that. Doom doesn't allow for responsibility. We both did wrong by each other." I'm glad he can't see me roll my eyes. Who's he to talk about responsibility?

"I thought I saw a picture of Nan's dad in a photo album. Do you think that's possible?" My heart's thumping. All this week searching for clues and when I wasn't really looking, I finally might have something.

"It's possible." A surge of adrenaline rushes me. It's not much, but it's something to go on. "Your great grandfather, Raymond Sr., the one I'm named after, worked as a handyman on the side of his farm work, and he said the people who lived in the house were strange. Had 'strange ways,' your Nan said. I'm not sure what that means. You know how she is . . . not an expert with description. Maybe there was some deep unhappiness between the family members, who knows. He saw things when he was there late that he wouldn't talk about much. But your Nan remembers one night when he came home crying. She remembered because men in that day didn't cry much, and he was weeping. She said, her mother was holding his head in her hands. He'd seen something on the property: a woman running into the woods with bruises around her neck and your Great Aunt Aggie screaming God almighty into the night. The next day the police came for questioning, and you know how that went. I told you before."

He was taken to the RCMP station for questioning in the murder of a young woman who he had never known as more than an acquaintance. Dad had told me before, but not in this much detail; always as a cautionary tale. Not with this connection to Mum's family. Or maybe I'd forgotten. I can empathize with Nan in a way I didn't before. My dad got taken too. History repeats.

It wasn't just any house my great grandfather worked at, but this one. Which means that maybe the woman with the bruises on her neck was *Sabrina*. It must have been Sabrina. If Traci knew all this, why didn't she tell me? My head heats up with anger at her for withholding this story from me. My hands are shaking again and my heart's speeding up, just like when Cole first told me about the man who was arrested. My body must have held some knowledge about this, made the connection subconsciously. Now, having the story confirmed, my body's shuddering holds some power. I redirect that energy, refocus. I need next steps.

"Did he say anything else about what she looked like?"

"Can't remember. Why? You see her?" He laughs. I'm silent. "Well, I think those ghost stories your Nan tells are her way of making sense of all the violence in that town. Scars are a kind of ghost too, and that town left lots of scars on your Nan. Even left scars on me. A lot less, but I still ended up in this box. And I think, probably, it's left scars on you. Being Black can mean being perceived as a kind of ghost too, in some spaces."

I haven't often heard Dad talk like this, or even this much. Usually, like me, he prefers to stay quiet, listen to those around him before weighing in. But something's different. Everything's different.

"Did you do it?" I've never asked him before.

"Asha . . ."

"Did you do it?" I can't stop the tears now.

"Asha, no. I didn't do it. But they won't believe me."

"You're lying. I know you did it."

"Baby, I'm not lying, I—"

"All those people who lost money . . . was that your fault?" Tears are streaming down my face now. Hot on my hot skin. Burning. My stomach aches with the sobs I'm holding in. "I can't talk to anyone about it." Except Cole. And I couldn't cry in front of her like I am now. I couldn't say how Dad's absence is burning a hole straight through my chest.

There's a sad silence on Dad's end. "Asha, my time's almost up. I'm sorry. I love you."

"I love you too." I choke out before the line goes dead. And it's true. I love him so much. I miss him so much. I lie on my bed and cry until my face is raw, then suddenly, I stop. All this feeling is useless when I know what I need to do next. Even if I can't be with Dad and I can't know if he's innocent or guilty, I can do *something*.

Being in this house hasn't gotten me any closer to figuring out how to end the haunting. Hearing from Dad, as difficult as it was, gave me the sense that outside of this house there might be a bigger picture, more answers, a better path to justice for everyone in our family and Cole's. I have an opportunity here, no matter how much I wish none of this had ever happened. With the knowledge I have now, I'm sure I can prove my great grandfather was innocent and put the rumors that he murdered Sabrina to rest forever. Setting the record straight would mean Sabrina might be able to rest forever too. And if I could prove Ellis murdered Sabrina on top of my great grandfather's innocence, that's just desserts. But I'll need some help.

♪

"Where did you say this house is?"

I'm walking fast ahead of Cole. The sky is a thick, oceanic blue that cuts clear across the horizon until it's the faint orange of the setting sun. We're on the side of the two-lane highway into town. When there are cars, we walk single file. When there are none, Cole tries to keep up beside me. And I try to slow down to her pace. Talking to Dad slammed me back into my body. I perceive every noise around me, the chirping of crickets, birds finding their nests for the night, Cole's breathing, heavy and hot just behind me and to my right. I couldn't wait to talk to Nan. After what he told me, I have to find the place now. My shoes spray gravel as we continue.

"It's somewhere around here. My dad said it was past that church. In front of a potato field."

"What potato field?" She gestures around at the trees that surround us.

"I don't know; we're not there yet."

"Asha, can you slow down for a second?"

"It's getting dark."

"I know . . . Asha—"

"It's supposed to be somewhere around here." Headlights bump over the hills in the distance. There, not there, there, not there. Cole looks at me like I'm crazy. For the first time since the ghosts appeared, I'm sure I'm not crazy. I have clarity.

"It's hot. Come on." I keep walking. But Cole has stopped. I expect her to catch up in a few paces, but when she doesn't move, I turn around.

"Asha, I don't think it's a good idea to be out here so late." She's been thinking it for a while. She doesn't really want to be here. I had to convince her to come at all tonight. Usually, she's the one dragging me to the tops of mountains and to remote streams, but today I chose where we were going to go. Things are still weird between us, but I thought we could push past it like last time. Now that we're out here, I'm not so sure.

I wanted to see where my Nan lived. Maybe there would be some answers there about how my great grandfather was wrongfully accused, or some proof that Ellis was the real murderer.

We'll know what the circumstances leading up to Sabrina's murder were. Maybe justice for Sabrina and my great grandfather is the key to ending the haunting.

"I talked to my dad today."

Cole looks at me, confused. She doesn't know where I'm going with this. "How was it?"

"Great." I grit my teeth and smile. It's an obvious lie and I can't keep it up. "He told me something and I can't stop thinking about it."

Cole sighs. She's having difficulty pretending not to be tired. How long until she gets tired of me, goes back to hanging with her old friends? "What did he say?"

"My great grandfather on my dad's side was wrongfully arrested for the murder of a woman. That the arrest was on Aggie's property. Remember when you were telling me about the person wrongfully arrested for Sabrina's murder and I had that weird reaction? I think it was because I knew, or at least part of me knew. It's all connected. Our families, they're connected. I think I can prove my great grandfather was innocent, and Ellis killed Sabrina."

"What? He just told you that?" Disbelief crosses over her like the headlights; there, not there, there, not there. "How come you never brought this up before? Why do you think it was this Ellis dude? Uncle Joe never told me anything about him being a suspect and he's been researching Sabrina's murder pretty much his whole life." It's hard to miss the annoyance lurking in her tone.

"I didn't realize it was here. My dad told me the story a bunch of times, but this time I understood. He was arrested for Sabrina's disappearance, but he was really just a witness." *Who built this house? Whose money? Whose blood?* The answers to those questions are emerging from the landscape like a picture I'm watching develop in real time. I'm still not sure what I'm seeing, but I'm aware it's a much larger scope than I imagined.

"I don't know. My grandfather always said they let the person who did it go. And Mum said the person they arrested didn't do it. This whole time they were talking about your great grandfather, and no one mentioned he worked at the next-door neighbor's and that your mom married into his family? Don't you think that's unlikely? Especially here. Gossip moves fast."

"I guess maybe they had their reasons for not saying anything. I don't know why they didn't mention my great grandfather, but I do know he didn't do it. I don't know if they ever found proof he was involved beyond being at the house around the time of her disappearance. They just took him because he was Black, probably, and cops are racist. I can't stop thinking about Sabrina and Aggie. About . . . about the night you stayed over and Ellis was on top of you, strangling you. I *saw* him too that night in the hallway, clomping back and forth in his suspenders—he grabbed me by the neck. It was him; don't you see? It must have been him. And if it was him, maybe the rumors about Aggie are true too. That she and Sabrina were together and maybe she got revenge, right? Sabrina did this thing when you were asleep, like, she dropped into my body, and she said something to Ellis . . . what was it? 'Your death was only Aggie's idea of justice' so maybe she meant—" I'm walking fast and Cole is moving slower and slower.

"I know we can find the truth if we find my great grandparents' house. There must be things there to point us to the truth. They never hid stuff the way Aggie did. This whole time I keep trying to listen to what Sabrina's saying, but maybe she only knows the part of the story before she was killed. Maybe she doesn't know about who was charged. If we find the truth and expose Ellis, maybe she can finally rest and both our families can have closure—"

We've stopped walking completely. We stand motionless, statues at the side of the road into town. The silence out here is so loud. "I don't feel like talking about this right now. Asha, I'm tired."

"We're almost there, just a bit further, come on—"

"No."

"No? What do you mean?"

"I mean no. Whatever happened to Sabrina, when I was at your place, it was just night terrors. I used to get them after my brother died. It's all the stories my mum told me about your house being haunted and the whole thing with Jeff. It just got to me. All that's in the past now, though. Just like Sabrina and Aggie's stories. It's the past. I don't want to be in the past. I want to think about now, about who I want to be *now*."

How can she be who she is *now* if Ellis could try to end her again whenever, if ever, she decides to come over next? She's being so frustrating. How can she refuse to believe or even care about the violence that went on in this town that continues to affect us both? Whether she wants to believe or not, none of this will stop until something changes. I dig my heels in. This may be a mistake, but I say, "Cole, I'm telling you, I saw something."

"Ok, maybe you did. But I didn't and I'm tired. I want to go home."

"Just a bit further, please. I swear. We must be almost there." I hear the desperation in my voice, and it disgusts me. Why am I really out here? I should have come alone. Cole doesn't understand. I get it. She doesn't want to believe what she saw because it means her brother didn't come back for her. I didn't believe either. I'd never *want* to believe that haunting could be possible. But I can't force her to believe. I don't want to force her into anything. I didn't fully believe what I saw either, until Sabrina took over my body. I just want so badly for her to believe what she saw that night. For her to believe me, to trust me.

"Asha, I want to go home. I have my own stuff going on."

"What stuff?" How could it be more important than finding proof about the person who murdered her grandmother?

"Private stuff. My own stuff."

"Like what?"

"I don't want to talk about it, that's why it's private."

"You brought it up." I'm frustrated with her. How come she agreed to come look for the place with me if she was too busy? "Look. I'm sorry it reminds you of your brother, but don't you think it's important to make sure people know what really happened to your grandmother? And my great grandfather? I— we're so close to having enough proof to really make a case that Ellis did it."

"I'm not talking about this right now." She says it quietly, but there's a hurt beneath her words that pierces me. I have to let it go for now, even if I want to keep pressing her to find out what's so important. I'll have to ask her again when I'm less intense. For now, her overt exhaustion gets to me and the world goes dull again. Everything flattens.

"Ok," I say, "Fine. Let's go."

A car whizzes past us. The red of its taillights leads us back home.

CHAPTER THIRTEEN

*A*s soon as Jeff makes his return, Traci breaks out of her apathetic state and begins waiting on him hand and foot. His first night back, she prepares an elaborate meal of sole, green beans, and mashed potatoes that Jeff demolishes, cursing the hospital food he had to endure and praising Traci's cooking between bites.

While Jeff was gone, the silence that filled the house was heavy, molasses thick, and sticky. I was on edge watching the days pass without a word from Traci. Now, she and Jeff spend their days in the living room with the curtains closed under the watch of Ellis and Aggie on the mantelpiece. They're both occupied. This new silence is light, casual, happy almost. Happy for them. They're reunited. For me, this new quiet is a different kind of tense. There's a pressure in the air. The house, I can sense, is waiting.

For what, I don't know. With Jeff's presence, the house is cool again, so we all find it nicer to stay inside while this heat wave continues. I watch the garden wilt from my window; the grass that was so lush and tall when we arrived is yellowing, ready to catch fire if need be.

As I predicted, the ghosts returned with Jeff. It's welcome company. Nia's too busy to talk at times that would make sense for us both, with the difference across the Atlantic, and I don't want to see or speak to Cole since the night on the road. I'm embarrassed and angry in equal parts about her disinterest in finding proof of Ellis's crimes. Maybe Sabrina can feel Cole's disinterest too: her presence is stronger again and more restless. Her thoughts don't come to me in words, but as concepts, floating through the air through me. I catch some of them. Images of fire, sensations of heat prickling my skin.

I have upstairs to myself most days and spend my time in my room. I'm starting to think my message about the ghosts freaked Nia out. Maybe I shouldn't have sent it, or maybe she just didn't answer it because she didn't feel like it. Nia does that sometimes. It's annoying as hell. Instead of responding to my message, she's sent me a long email about her trip with a video of her in front of a tall tree. She said she'd explain more when she calls. I'm still waiting. Even though we haven't talked much, I still feel close to her. I'm lucky to have her, our strong friendship, to lean on. Just thinking about her existing out in the world is comforting to me. She's one of the only people in my life who's been there no matter what happened.

One line in her email is sticking in my head. She wrote:

You didn't really wanna talk about it on the phone, but I heard the way you talked about your new friend. I'm happy you found someone. I knew you would. Maybe I'm wrong, but it sounds like you're crushing.

Crushing. I didn't understand the word before. But the pressure of my feelings for Cole is all around me. It's something I never felt for Nia, as close as we are. This whole friendship is different. With Nia, I'm just happy she's out there. Cole, I want near. I'm so frustrated that things can't be easy, that I can't move past her disbelief in the ghosts, her unwillingness to pursue justice. I want her to care about what I care about. The fact that she doesn't and that she might not ever want to again because of my tactlessness is crushing my heart to pulp. What can I do to make things right? For now, until I have a better plan, I'm keeping my distance until she gives me a sign she wants to be around me.

Now that the extermination is over, we're prepping the house for painting. My job is to sift through the junk that's in the other unused rooms upstairs to sort it into a pile for donation, a pile for antique stores, and a pile for the junkyard. I already know so much about what's in the piles of junk that it's relaxing. It's quiet work, and Aggie and Sabrina will sometimes join me. Aggie takes a break from her protective role and Sabrina from her determination. She's nothing like the night Ellis attacked. For an afternoon, I can ignore that she took over my body so easily and forget the power that emanated from her when she threw her questions out into the night.

While I sort through the junk, Aggie and Sabrina take on gentle amorphous forms, giving me advice on wafts of smooth or sharp currents in the air: this moth-eaten quilt can go, these woven linens can stay . . . and so on.

If things had gone differently after Ellis's attack, and Cole had believed in the ghosts, I would have texted Cole immediately to let her know I was seeing them again. Even if I hadn't pulled her out on the road that night, I would have texted her and asked her to come over and work with us. Then I could have pleaded with Sabrina to stay present and prove to Cole that the ghosts were as real as the mice scampering through the walls. I want her to trust in them, in me, in their need to be recognized so they don't have to live here anymore.

It was so tactless of me to take her out in the night like that, when my emotions were high. I know I shouldn't have taken her with me. I should have gone alone, but I wonder what she was talking about when she said she had other stuff going on. Why couldn't I be a part of that other stuff? I let her see everything. I told her about Dad, took her with me to find Nan's place, tried to talk about the ghosts. But she couldn't tell me what was so important that she had to go home?

A particularly rough puff hits my arm as I drop an old necktie on the antiques and vintage pile.

"Donation? Are you sure? Some collector or vintage shop would probably kill for this. What is it? Silk?" It's an indigo so deep it looks like I'm holding the ocean between my palms. Probably Ellis's. A warm breeze blows the edges of the tie toward the donation pile. "Fine." I toss it on the pile. "But Traci's going to have my ass if she sees it there."

I've been working to strengthen my awareness of the ghosts. Aggie and Sabrina stay upstairs with me most of the time. When I venture downstairs, I watch Ellis as he sticks close to Jeff, almost his double. Their actions line up with each other. Often, Ellis will mimic Jeff, follow his lead as he climbs the steps, still with a tight grip on the rail, since he's not one hundred percent following his hospitalization. He lost some weight in the hospital and his feet now look like they require heavy lifting. Ellis follows Jeff closely as he sits at the kitchen table, cradling his phone to his ear as he catches up on business he's missed out on since his illness.

Other times, it's as if Jeff is following Ellis's lead. I woke up this morning to Jeff tracing Ellis's path down the hallway, shuffling his slippers over the threadbare ruts in the carpet in rhythm with his double. For now, Ellis seems content to mirror Jeff's motions without causing disruptions in the house, and vice versa. I don't know when he might decide to strike again or when Sabrina might decide it's time to confront him. Or whether she'll mistake Jeff for Ellis when she does.

I shadow Jeff and Ellis as often as possible. If he drops into Jeff, I want to know so I can make sure he doesn't harm me or Traci. Or Jeff himself. I still can't shake the feeling that Jeff's illness had something to do with the ghosts—even if the growth in his head was there all along. It's only a matter of time before something else happens.

With all my surveillance of Ellis, it's been impossible to find a moment to go out and look for Nan's farm again, but that's itching at me too. If Traci could see the ghosts, maybe this would be easier. I could leave her and Jeff alone while I went searching for the old farm so that I could find a way to release them from their haunting. But I've received no sign from her that she's able to see them, and I have no way of knowing for sure that there will be any clues to prove my great grandfather's innocence following Aggie, Sabrina, and Ellis's conflicts, at the old horse farm. I still haven't heard from Nan. I looked through all the files to see if they'd made a contract with anyone with the last name Walker to do work on the house, or really any clues or signs that point to foul play, but so far the only patterns I've found are the ones the silverfish left as they ate through the contents of the filing cabinet.

When Jeff notices me staring out of the doorway at him, he is startled enough to jump.

"You're up early." He frowns, not in judgment or anger, just confusion at finding himself in the hallway, I think.

"I thought you were coming to talk to me." I feel Sabrina behind me. And Aggie leaning down from the ceiling, watching, ever peaceful. Sabrina is charged and I pick up her energy. My muscles tense. This scene is too close to the one we first experienced together in this hall.

Jeff's frown deepens. Maybe he can't remember getting here at all. "No, I was just thinking."

"About what?" I worry for a second that he'll think I'm being nosy. But surprisingly, he smiles at my curiosity and leans against the hand-carved banister that protects us from falling down the open stairwell.

"You really want to know?" He's surprised I'm talking to him at all.

"Yeah."

"How lucky I am to have your mother in my life."

I nod. He is lucky. She'd do anything for him.

"Asha, I know we've had our differences, but would you be willing to give living with me full time a shot?" His face is open and earnest. He's really thinking of moving here full time. Maybe his near-death experience made him reevaluate what was important to him. And it would make Traci happy to have him here consistently, given how much energy she's had since he returned.

"What about your work?"

He sighs. "Well, I've been talking through some opportunities in the area. Got a few guys coming down to do some survey work in the next couple days. And if I get this CEO position, it would mean I have more freedom to work from home. I'd only have to go into the city once a month or so. The rest I can do remote."

He's seriously considering this. I nod. But I'm wary of the survey work he's talking about. "What kind of opportunities?"

"That's top secret." He taps his nose. Ellis does the same.

I bet it is top secret. The hairs on the back of my neck are rising. Sabrina's just as suspicious. I can tell she's almost ready to drop into me. Her borders prickle against mine and my ears ring. I lean against my doorframe. Ellis is prickling against Jeff too. He holds onto the railing as if he's feeling the dizzying effect of the ghost trying to enter him as well. Maybe if I ask him about Ellis now, I'll get a better idea of if he can feel anything when Ellis is nearby.

"Jeff, do you ever feel a threatening presence in this house?"

"Yeah, sometimes, when I think about my ex-wife," he lets out a belly-laugh. Even so, his knuckles tighten on the banister. How am I supposed to bring up possession? "Why would you ask something like that?"

I don't know what to say. I didn't expect him to take my question seriously enough to ask a follow up question. "Do you remember anything the day you got sick?"

He looks away from me, at his feet, almost as if he's ashamed he was so ill. "No."

"You were trying to say something to me—Mum said you were seeing things?"

"No, I don't remember."

Maybe he really doesn't remember. All the "ssss" and "ellllll" sounded a lot like Ellis's name in retrospect. What if he was aware then, just for a minute, of his own possession and was trying to warn us? Either that or he's lying and he's been aware of Ellis's presence this whole time. Maybe he's working with Ellis. Then, the rabbits, would he remember that?

"The rabbits—" I begin, then pause to see if he'll jump in and admit he was the one who placed them in the bed. Ellis smirks behind Jeff. Jeff waits patiently, earnestly, for me to go on. "I'm sorry about that," I say.

He waves his hand, casually clears the air of any serious conversation. "It's forgotten. But thank you for being honest."

Any other day I'd be furious that he assumed I was sorry because I was guilty, not because I'm empathetic to the fact that it's messed up to find dead baby animals in his bed. Right now though, I'm aware that Sabrina is hovering behind me, overlapping with my edges, asking for permission to be let in. It takes all my power to concentrate on wrapping up my conversation with Jeff. "Don't get mad at me, but are you sure you didn't take the rabbits when you were out? I found something . . ." Suddenly, I lurch forward. I grab onto the doorframe to make sure I don't fall over.

"Oh, hey, everything ok, kid?" I hate when he calls me kid, but there is real concern in his voice. I was hoping he wouldn't notice anything strange. I don't think he can see Ellis or Sabrina, or else he's doing a great job hiding it. But he can see the way the color's draining from my face and sweat's breaking out on my upper lip.

"Mhm," I assure him. He really does look concerned. "Just my period."

He recoils and digs his hands around in his khaki's pockets. "Oh, ok. Uh. Feel better soon. Don't forget, your mother is taking us for breakfast in a couple hours."

Jeff's exactly the type of guy to get uncomfortable when people mention their periods. To think this man has slept with countless cis women and still can't bear to make eye contact with me when I mention my period. What does he think will happen? He'll turn to stone?

"Yeah, I'm just gonna go lie down. It's really heavy flow." Sabrina loosens up. I feel a warmth behind my shoulder blades, which I think is maybe her laughing. I have a hard time not joining her as Jeff turns swiftly on his heel and shuffles back into his room.

I crawl back into bed with Sabrina holding me tight. It's not as good as when Cole held me, but it's still comforting. She reaches up to the ceiling and Aggie reaches down to intertwine their fingertips. It's not clear why to me yet, but Aggie's ghost is much more limited in its movements and interactions. The only place she can manifest in a solid way is here, in my ceiling. While Sabrina and Ellis are walking around waiting to drop into me and Jeff, Aggie stays up there, watching, just keeping company as if she's unaware of the violence that simmers in the household. It's as if she and Traci are somehow immune to the negative effects of this house. I can see why Ellis attached himself to Jeff. I have a suspicion they would've got along if they met. They could've gone golfing together or something. But why does Sabrina feel such a strong connection to me? Maybe it's our mutual desire for justice that links us.

I ask Sabrina and Aggie, "What kind of opportunities does Jeff mean?"

All money on this land is blood money.

Blood money. "How can I keep living here?"

Sabrina pulls me closer. Our edges overlap. *You look like him.*

"Like who?" She can't mean Ellis. He's not a blood relative. Sabrina must be talking about someone else, someone I haven't encountered yet.

The one they said did it.

"You mean my great grandfather, right?"

The one they said did it.

"I need you to tell me more. How can I prove he didn't do it?"

Enough questions. Just hold on—

☙

It's only when the car swerves that I snap back into myself. Traci curses. "Asha, isn't that Nicole? She'd better stay off the road if she doesn't want to get hit."

I look out my window and see Cole pushing through the brush into the woods between our houses. What's she doing out here? And when did we all get in the car? It's the nausea that tips me off. Sabrina dropped into me. I roll down the window and stick my head out. The thick, muggy air doesn't help much to settle my stomach, though. It's no longer sunny out. Rain's coming to break the heat.

"Where are we going?" I ask Traci and Jeff, their hands are knotted together over the stick shift.

Traci looks back toward me in the rearview mirror, concerned at my sudden forgetfulness. "Told you, we're going to the café to have a breakfast out of the house. I think we all need a break." Right. Jeff even reminded me during our chat.

It's only a ten-minute drive to the café in the little Victorian house on the far end of Main Street. When the car stops moving and we step out, I feel relief standing on solid ground. My whole body's pulsating. I don't know where my own edges are.

Why'd Sabrina drop into me and hitch a ride all the way out of the house? What kind of business did she have on the road? Or maybe she just wanted a lift out to Cole . . .

I pull my phone out to text her. Eleven sixteen? I must've lost at least an hour to Sabrina . . . The glass is slippery in my sweaty palms. It drops onto the parking lot pavement. Traci and Jeff are already up ahead of me, Jeff holding the door open for Traci, and beckoning for me to hurry up. When I pick up my phone, I see there's a crack across the screen. Probably a bad omen. I shouldn't text Cole anyway. I don't know if she'd want to hear more about the ghosts—what if Sabrina drops into her without her consent though? Would that even be possible outside of the house? Maybe Sabrina can only go out of the house in a certain radius before she's called back to home base . . . I'm thinking of this like a video game, but I'm not sure there are any set rules. If Sabrina drops into Cole, that would be worse than receiving a weird text from me. Then again, she clearly doesn't want to talk to me, especially about Sabrina. I'm embarrassed at how much it frustrates me that it's hard to talk now, how much I miss her sense of humor, her sure step through the woods ahead of me, the murky smell of her sweat, her teeth poking out over her bottom lip when she smiles—

"Asha, come on!" Jeff calls. "You can check your phone later." A couple of elderly patrons who are sitting at the tables set out on the veranda chuckle to themselves about kids today. I pocket my phone for now and follow Traci and Jeff inside.

We take seats on the veranda, next to the elderly couple. I clench my phone in my hand in my pocket. Should I warn Cole? When the server comes out, I'm surprised to see it's Devon, Cole's ex-best friend. The way he avoids eye contact as he places my fresh berry fruit salad, French toast, and home fries in front of me makes me sure he recognizes me. I guess that night at the party was memorable for him too. "Enjoy," he says

188 • A HOUSE UNSETTLED

with an awkward smile at Traci and Jeff, who bump their knees affectionately before digging in.

"He looks like he's your age, Ash. Cute," Traci smirks at me as Devon heads back inside with the elderly couple's empty plates. "You know him?"

"No, but Cole was friends with him." I knock a couple of home fries around my plate.

"Was? Uh-oh. What happened?" Jeff sips from his black coffee. Why's he so intent on making small talk with me today? I wish I could just eat my breakfast in peace.

"I don't know. It was before I was here."

"Were they dating?" Jeff presses.

"Why would you assume that? Can't people just be in platonic conflict?" There's a bit too much venom in my voice. Traci's leg presses against mine under the table. *Be nice.* "I don't think he's Cole's type." I try to save things before they get too tense.

"He's tall, dark, handsome, got a part-time job . . . isn't that what girls your age like?" Jeff's smile is fixed. I want to slam my head against the table. Why's he pursuing this like Cole and Devon's friendship is up for debate? Why's he trying to sexualize this, and every other completely platonic encounter Devon's had with kids in this town? No matter what he did to Cole, it seems like he's just trying to live his life and do his part-time job without people like Jeff making assumptions about him.

Why drag this out any longer? It's not like it's a secret. "Cole's queer."

"Oh." Jeff clams right up.

Then Traci steps in. "Well, Asha, are you and Cole—?"

I stand up. "I'm going to the bathroom." I can't believe Traci would bring that up again—and with Jeff here too!—after I explicitly told her I wasn't ready to talk about it. I just want one part of my life to myself. The space to figure out who I am without Traci butting in and asking me about every detail. I know she's well-intentioned, but I wish they would just leave me alone.

The tables are packed tightly inside. I don't know how the workers make their way between them without tripping or dropping dishes. Must take a lot of coordination. I manage to make it through the crowd without any serious accidents, but with pretty much everyone's eyes on my back. I think that's because I'm still a novelty in this town. And possibly because they all know about Dad. Or Aggie. Or my great grandfather. Jesus, there are more eyes on my back than at my old high school. I can't see where the bathroom is, so I walk up to the counter. Devon's sitting behind it on a stool by the espresso machine, munching on a stale-looking croissant.

"Hey—"

"Hey!" He smiles at me. "You're the new kid, right? The one Cole's hanging out with now." I'm surprised he's so friendly. I thought he'd want to steer clear of me, knowing that he and Cole were going through a friend break-up.

"Yeah. Asha."

"Nice to meet you. Devon."

"I know."

Neither of us really knows what to say next. He saves us from too long a pause, "You were at that party at the Walker house, right?"

Walker house? "You mean that abandoned house up on the hill?"

"Yeah . . . party kinda sucked. Glad it got stopped when it did. Saved me from getting a new one ripped. Cole was ready to destroy me."

I shrug. "I guess, from what I heard." Was the house where we went to the party the same house I've been looking for? Nan's childhood home?

He pulls at the straps of his apron nervously before he asks, "Do you think she'll talk to me when school starts up again?"

"I don't know . . . we don't really talk about you." God. He's chatty. Even though he broke Cole's trust, his eagerness makes me think he's likely willing to make it up to her. Maybe it would be best if Cole and Devon started hanging out again and I wasn't in the picture at all. I try to reroute my brain from Cole. *The Walker house.* I need to get to the bathroom so I can think more about what he just told me. Maybe do a few searches to see if it's on any maps. "Does everyone call it that?"

"What?"

"The Walker house?"

He takes another bite of his croissant. "Yeah, I think since forever. Some kids say there was a murderer who lived there, but I don't believe that." He shakes his head dismissively at the rumors. In a town this small, shared names are never a coincidence. Combined with what Devon said about an alleged murderer living there—this might be *the* farm. Was I already there are didn't know it? "Why?"

It would take too long to explain the whole story so I just say, "It's my last name."

"Oh, cool," he says, but I can tell he doesn't care much. He just wants to ask more about Cole. "Can you tell Cole I'm sorry? I tried to call her house, but she's never there and she won't answer my messages."

"Maybe she just doesn't want to talk to you." I don't want to be a messenger pigeon. What's between them should stay between them. It would be a good excuse to text Cole, though . . .

He laughs. "I see why you two get along. You don't hold back. Ok, I'll give her space."

"Is there a bathroom in this place?"

"To the left, behind that wall."

I start toward it, but he calls out behind me, "Hey, Asha, just a minute." I turn back around and he's holding out a scrap of paper with his number on it. "If you and Cole ever want to hang, I want to make things right. I have a car—I was thinking we could go to the beach or something. Even if she doesn't want to, I'm around. We could hang out too, without Cole."

Maybe he's lonely too without Cole. I take the scrap of paper from his hand. From what she said about Devon, I thought he'd be an asshole, but he seems nice and genuinely interested in making it up to her. We've got that in common. If Cole ever texts me back after the other night, maybe we could all hang out together. It would be nice to get away from here and sit by the ocean, wade through tidepools, dig in sand with some other people. Maybe we could forget about all the ghosts for a little while.

In the bathroom, I compose several apology texts to Cole to preface my warning about Sabrina. None of them feel right. Because what I really want to tell her is: I like you. I want to be a good friend. And I want to hold you and spend all my time next to you, without ghosts and without fear. But to get rid of those ghosts and fear, she has to believe me about the ghosts first. I can't see her suddenly changing her mind.

All that love and apology stuff is too corny. If I tell her all that, I risk overwhelming her and losing her friendship for real. After our excursion to find the farm, I'm not sure she wants to be in the same room as me, let alone any of the things I imagine us pursuing. So I just delete everything, flush the toilet, and send a simple warning:

Don't go near our house today. Weird chemicals.

That should be enough to keep her away, if Sabrina hasn't already gotten to her. I go back out to finish breakfast with Traci and Jeff.

Big feelings aside, I wish I could talk to Cole about how frustrating it is to live in this house with Jeff and Traci always poking their noses into my life where I don't want them. What Devon told me about the Walker house . . . I wish I could talk to her about that too. Maybe she could show me the way we took to the party. It's a much more solid lead than Dad's vague directions.

That farmhouse, still up on that hill, hosting parties, watching over town with all our secrets and conflicts held tight in its walls; it's a testament to survival. If I can go to the house again, knowing that Nan's family lived there and managed to survive, even get out of here when they needed to, maybe their history can teach me how to survive too.

CHAPTER FOURTEEN

*P*urple clouds take over the sky while we drive back home. It's as if day and night reversed while none of us were paying attention. Since our conversation at breakfast, there's a tightness at the corners of Traci's mouth that tells me she's not completely over the way I reacted to her and Jeff's comments. Jeff keeps shooting me furtive glances in the rearview mirror, as if I'm going to suddenly decide to rip him to shreds.

Back at home, I help Traci clean up a few last little things that popped up around the house after breakfast. She tries to make conversation with me as we scrub the insides of the windowpanes. I find my mind wandering to what I can remember of the Walker house. It was so dark in there, though, and my memories are all blurred from intoxication. So Traci keeps talking at me, about Aggie, about this house, about how far the place has come, how much better she feels about living here with me and Jeff. And finally, I know it's time to ask her.

"Who built this house?"

She pauses her scrubbing. "Why do you ask?"

"Can't I ask a question? I'm just curious. It's a big house, they must not have built it themselves."

Traci sighs. "Ellis's grandparents had this house built in the late 1800s."

"But who did the building?"

Traci knows what I'm asking. "You know, Ellis's family was wealthy. They made a lot off the fur trade. Asha, I hate talking about this—"

"But it's important." I'm firm. "We can't ignore it."

She lets out a big breath. It's almost as if the walls sigh with her. "They moved here for forestry and opened the pulp and paper mill off the river. They employed a lot of people. And to build this house, they hired some local Black folks. Your father's family among them, I believe."

I believe? I think that means yes. "Did they pay them?"

Traci is quiet. She won't meet my eyes. "I don't know. Ellis always said they did. But I don't know." Not knowing is not good enough. I don't want to be mad at Traci for not knowing, but anger simmers beneath my skin.

This entire house is violence. I don't want its lineage attached to mine. This house, which was supposed to be a place for me and Traci to start fresh, is built on violence preceding violence. It makes me feel sick to know my ancestors may have built this house for people who didn't even see them as people. And it hurts to know Traci has kept this information from me. When I'm here, I feel like I can't fully exist. Maybe that's how everyone I'm related to has felt in this town. Aggie couldn't be queer. Nan couldn't continue living here. They were isolated or expelled.

"Aggie never agreed with it, and it wasn't her ancestors who built the house, even though she chose to marry into that family. She tried her best, in her privilege, to help this town become a more inclusive place." With her white women's salons and sporadic involvement in town affairs . . . that's step one, but aren't there like a hundred more steps before justice? And are they even steps to justice, or more of a never-ending cycle of repair? Does it matter whether someone is blood related to the source of the violence when they live in a house so closely aligned with it?

"If she made it more inclusive like you said, then why couldn't Nan keep living here?"

"I would never deny that many people in this town are racist. Aggie knew it. I saw it myself. Your father experienced it when we were young and visiting. I thought . . . I thought things would be better now, Asha."

"Why would you think that? After what happened to my great grandfather, and now Dad—"

"That's different. You don't think I know about your great grandfather's time here?" This whole time she knew about that history, and she kept it from me? She continues, "We don't know your father was wrongfully accused."

"We don't know he was *rightfully* accused."

Traci presses into her eye socket bone with a thumb to release the pressure this conversation inevitably builds. All roads lead to this disagreement. She takes a steadying breath. "I thought working on all these rooms, making them our own . . . I thought we could make this space our own. I still do. Time passes, people change." She really believes it. I want to trust her on this, but I think I know better. I can see things she can't in this house. We have different lived experiences.

"What about action?" I ask her. "How can we just wait for people to change or for this house to change into someplace I can live?" I don't know if I believe we can make this space our own without sacrificing parts of ourselves to it. No matter how much we reform this house into a shape that looks better to us, into a place where our relationship can heal, it will never shrug off its violent history and that will continue to prevent us from loving each other in the way we need.

I don't think Traci gets that. Instead of arguing with me, which would only end up fueling my anger, she tells me she's going to the grocery store and asks if I want to come. I say no.

I go back up to my room to avoid one-on-one time with Jeff. Sabrina's lying on my unmade bed looking up at Aggie in the ceiling. It's weird to walk in on them. My imagination of their afterlives while I'm not in the room is limited. I'm aware that I don't understand their experience of the living world. When they are visible, they want to be seen, but sometimes what I see doesn't seem to serve any purpose.

"Sabrina?" I whisper so Jeff won't hear me. She slides her feet off the side of my bed. Aggie absorbs back into the ceiling.

That man shouldn't be in this house.

"Does Aggie agree?" I don't know if she's talking about Ellis or Jeff. Maybe they're the same to her.

She's not like me. She doesn't have opinions anymore.

"Why do you have opinions?"

Because I was taken.

"By Ellis. How do I stop him?"

Your friend. He wants your friend too.

"Cole?"

It's hard to have a conversation with Sabrina. I get the impression my words don't reach her and that only some of her words reach me. Maybe it's not a direct translation from the afterlife to this world.

That man shouldn't be in the house.

"Jeff?"

He will take his body and use it. He will take her body and use it. He will take your body and use it. Sabrina begins to fade. My heart bangs desperately against my ribs in panic. How much longer do we have before Ellis tries to drop into . . . who? Which "he" is she talking about, Jeff or Ellis? Or both? And *my* body too? What does he need to use us for if he already murdered Sabrina? Or is the conflict on some metaphysical level between Ellis and Sabrina and they're just using us as their pawns?

"Wait!" I need to know more. Why would she fade now? Jeff's footsteps are clomping toward the stairs. He begins up the steps. I close my door and stare at the empty space she's left. "Sabrina?" I whisper. She's gone.

I watch the sky through my open window. Look down at the grass below. The garden Traci was working so hard on through the first few weeks is now abandoned, reverting to a poison ivy patch. I can almost imagine nobody lives here. It's easy to imagine because all three of us in this house are already nobodies to this town. Traci is a memory, Jeff is an invader, and me . . . what am I? A ghost? Am I really the one haunting this house?

What if it's been me, all along, making everything up: the woman in the ceiling, Ellis and Sabrina, the coldness of the house, how I used to wake up gasping for air . . . the dizziness. What if living in this house built on blood, in this town built on blood, Traci keeping its history from me, Dad's incarceration, the isolation, all of it, is just too much? What if all this stress is making me sick? I just want things to work out. I still want that fresh start I gave up on. I can't think straight. All of it's too heavy.

I can't.

The first thick drops of the storm hit the windowpanes and spray through the open screen. I move back and sit by the mirror. Out of the corner of my eye, I catch a glimpse of my reflection. I barely recognize myself. My face is a mask; pale and dull, as if painted on, where it should be tanned and bright. My hair's growing out at the roots all frizzy. I was planning on taking my braids down tonight. I lean in closer. Press my cold cheeks and stare into my irises. A whole landscape in there. Reminds me of pictures of other planets' terrains. Up close, I don't even know my own territories. Maybe I should go to a clinic. I don't want Traci to know how close to the edge I am. How sick I feel. Like I need to vomit, but for my whole insides, not just the contents of my stomach. How I'm never really *here*. Everything is so vague and distant.

I wish Cole were here. But she doesn't want to hear about my issues anyway. She wanted a friend, not a walking Ouija board. And I want her as more than a friend. Does she want me?

The wind picks up outside and the trees thrash around like they're in this town's first mosh pit. And I hear a knock at my door. Jeff cracks it open.

"Asha? I was going to make fishcakes for your mother to give her a break. Want to help?" I search for Ellis behind him after Sabrina's warning. The ghost isn't there. It's just Jeff in his fleece and khakis wanting to do something nice for Traci. I follow him down to the kitchen.

There's a pile of dill he must have braved the poison ivy for. Next to it, a knife. "Can you chop this?"

I nod. He tends to some leftover mashed potatoes, adds the fish, eggs, breadcrumbs. The silence between us is painful. Jeff must have wanted me to help as a bonding exercise and it wouldn't kill me to talk to him, at least just to pass the time.

"How'd you learn how to make fish cakes?"

"Glad you asked." He rinses his hands under the tap, then turns to me. His confident white-toothed smile imagines an openness between us. "Dad was a fisherman and Mum worked at the processing plant. We ate fish for everything—dinner, lunch, breakfast sometimes. We were true pescatarians."

I knew he came from a family that was involved with fishing, but I never realized his parents were working class. All his obsession with class and looking perfect, it makes more sense now. He's trying to conceal his own history.

"You ever get tired of fish?"

"Sick of it. Hated fish for years after leaving home."

"So why do you like it now?"

He shrugs. "I guess I got old and nostalgic. After Mum passed, I started making fishcakes again. I found I could stomach the taste."

Last spring, Jeff's mother died. I wonder if his change in taste had anything to do with that. He disappeared for a couple weeks back to his seaside hometown in the fall. I remember because Traci and I tried to have alone time for the first time since I'd stopped living with her. The trip ended in a horrible fight about how I didn't like Jeff and didn't want to live with him. All Traci had to do was mention the possibility of me coming back a couple days a week and I snapped. After I'd heard Jeff talking to whoever was on the other end of the line, living at Traci's place just hadn't felt like an option.

"It's nice of you to want to give Mum a break," I tell him.

"Least I could do." Thunder rumbles in the distance. "We really needed the rain."

He heats up the pan and adds oil. I add the dill to the mix and flatten the fishcake patties. We make a surprisingly efficient team. The aroma of dill, mustard, onions, garlic fills the kitchen. Jeff's shoulders are relaxed. I think about Sabrina's warning earlier. As much as I don't like Jeff and completely disagree with his politics, when he does let his guard down around me, I can almost imagine all of us coexisting peacefully under the same roof. I don't know, maybe we could even get a dog, live a real traditional middle-class life.

Then I remember the way he fights with Traci about what she posts on social media and how he blackmailed me into keeping his affair a secret. The receipt by the rabbits' den. Even after he broke his promise to me, I still hold on to my end of the deal. It's moments like these that make me unsure whether I would have a better life with him and Traci broken up.

"Hey, Jeff?"

"Yeah?"

"You remember that night when you were first here, and your foot went through the porch?"

"Vividly." Tension has gathered between his shoulders again. He thinks I'm going to bring up his affair.

"Did you see anything when your foot went through?"

Instead of relief that I didn't ask him about the affair, puzzlement breaks over his face. "It was pitch black. Didn't see much. Why?"

"Some people say this house is haunted."

Jeff laughs loud and full, flips one of the fishcakes. It's honey gold on one side. Perfect. "You're listening to too many local stories. You're a smart kid, Asha. Do you really believe that bumpkin rumor?"

"Maybe," I admit. "But you should watch out for ghosts. Just in case." I know he'll dismiss my warning as childish. If Ellis appears ready to drop into him without consent, though, maybe now he'll be slightly more prepared to resist.

CHAPTER FIFTEEN

I'm just finishing unbraiding my hair, combing it out and getting rid of all the dead matter when the first flash of lightning strikes. The storm is close. It's only a couple seconds until thunder follows. My head is lighter and when I look at myself in the mirror, I recognize my younger self: the little kid who first came to visit this house and had to stand on a stool to see in the mirror.

Mum used to get her hair dyed or cut a different way whenever she and Dad had a big fight. At first, it was the only way I could tell they disagreed. Then, as years of conflict compounded and their voices rose, it was only a side effect. When the haircut was good, they'd make up. When she hated it, they'd both sulk for a week. Either way, they broke up, and it was definitely for the best. Even if I have to deal with Jeff's toxic presence now, it's a million times better than the tension of knowing my parents' days as a couple were numbered.

I'm scrunching my hair, running my hands over its softness, when my phone lights up. I stumble out of the steamy bathroom in my bathrobe, reading Cole's text:

meet me @ rabbit warren in 30 mins.

After my earlier warning not to come near our house and the long silence between us, I can't believe I still want to see her bad enough that within seconds of receiving the text, I'm ready to go out in this storm. A cocktail of worry and excitement is all shook up inside me. Either Sabrina got to Cole or Cole wants to see me. Both options make me want to rush out to see her. The overhead hallway light flickers out. I flick the switch on my bedroom wall up and down.

"Power's out!" I yell down the stairs.

"I can see that!" Jeff yells back.

"Where's Mum?" I throw back even louder.

"She went into town to run some errands. She'll be back in an hour!"

I guess it's the first alone time she's had in a while. Maybe she's out savoring it. Or maybe she's stranded in the storm. "Do you think they have power on Main Street?"

"Doubt it!"

My phone buzzes again.

i need to show you smthg

sorry for being weird the other night. i just needed some time to think about some personal stuff.

Personal stuff. Maybe she'll finally tell me what that means.

"I'm going out!"

I hear the chair that Jeff's occupied in the den since we finished making the fishcakes screech back on the hardwood and his heavy footsteps clomp to the bottom of the stairwell. He looks up at me with weary apprehension. All the closeness I felt with him while we were cooking is gone. "Asha, you can't go out now. It's practically a hurricane out there."

"Just to Cole's place. I'll be covered by the trees the whole way. It's not like I'll get struck by lightning. Don't worry, you won't have to be in the same house as me all evening. It'll be relaxing. You can just sit back and watch the storm."

Jeff sighs deep then clears his throat. "Asha, look," he begins. He draws in a breath for what feels like forever. I don't have time for another big one-on-one right now. I need to go meet Cole. She wants to make up. She's sorry. My thumbs tap at lightning speed:

don't worry ab it. see you in 30

"Asha? Are you listening?"

I don't look up from my screen in case Cole texts back. "Yes."

"I want things to be settled between us. Me and your mother talked, and she told me you've been having a difficult time adjusting to this new situation. Living here, yeah, but also living with me again. I won't lie, it's been hard on me as well." He sounds so genuine I almost feel bad for rolling my eyes. "We all do silly things when we're young, like drinking or thinking our step-parents are out to get us. We're selfish when we're young because everything seems temporary. It may be hard for you to imagine, but your mother's gone through a lot more than she's shared with you. With your father, losing her job, moving . . . She's a strong lady, but this has all been hard on her. Seeing you fight with me is even harder. I don't want to fight with you. But you need to respect my presence in this house. I just want your mother to be happy. Don't you?"

"Of course," I reply. Shouldn't he respect Traci by committing to her? Being truthful to her? It should be obvious to him that I want her happy. All I've done is care for her while he was gone. I've helped her work on her projects, tried my hardest to tolerate Jeff's presence. To me, Jeff's just another dead weight on her already emotionally overburdened shoulders. He thinks the same of me. And with him around, I kind of am dead weight. A parasite on this household. Jeff's face is open, I can tell he thinks I'm going to listen to him for once and stay home. I disappoint him again. "This is important. I'll be back before sunset."

I push past him.

Jeff will never believe me, no matter how real my needs are. He's too focused on how he's being perceived.

He lets out another exasperated breath. "Asha—"

But he doesn't try any harder because he knows it means a fight. He doesn't want to ruin all our progress. Neither do I. So, without saying another word, I layer up and grab Aggie's old, yellow fisherman's jacket from the front closet and step out into the storm. I look back and see Jeff's breath clouding the window in tiny puffs that gather like frost on the glass.

ↄ℔

"Hey!" I catch sight of Cole in her oversized, highlighter-orange raincoat from afar. It would be hard to miss her, to be honest, even with sheets of rain coming down. The canopy above protects from the downpour a little, but the woods are still static with raindrops. I've always loved the smell of rain, especially in the woods. It's a smell so fresh and green, I can envision what it was like to walk around in nature before climate change really took hold of everything. All the lichen sags off the tree branches with the added water weight. Whenever lightning strikes in the distance, everything lights up like Christmas.

Cole waves back. I can't see her face; it's shadowed by the enormous bulk of her hood. I'm grinning and springing over the moss toward her, barely holding back from telling her how huge a relief it is to see her again. "Sorry I'm late," I say instead. "Jeff didn't want me to come out in the storm." I pull her into a hug. She's stiff as a board. With her damp hair hanging all around her face, she looks more like Sabrina than ever. My heart drops. "You ok?"

"Asha, I'm sorry about the other night. I had a lot on my mind." Her voice is small, trailing off.

"I know. I'm sorry I took you out in the middle of nowhere and didn't listen when you wanted to come back. I really like you. I want to be friends, like, *really* friends, not just people who meet up and go on walks. Things are just . . . complicated. What I told you about the ghosts, I should've respected your beliefs, your needs. I should've listened—" I gulp back the fear that's rushing up my throat.

"I believe you." Her eyes lock onto mine. I can see she means it. Really means it. That scares me more than being called crazy. But it's also what I wanted. Finally. I can take a full breath. It's such a relief. Cole believes me. Then fear rushes back over me. Something must have changed her mind.

"What happened?"

"I was walking over to your place this morning. I was right close to your house and then—" Cole searches for the words but can't seem to find them. "We found something."

We. We—her and Sabrina? Did Sabrina drop into Cole when she was done with me? Was this her way of answering my question to her, the proof that Ellis killed her?

I don't have much time to think about the implications. In a motion that seems instinctual, Cole grabs my hand. There's no warmth between our palms, only clammy wetness. She leads me past the rabbit warren and through the ferns to the place where I found Jeff's incriminating receipt. But there are no more ferns. A shovel rests against a tree and in front of us is a dark, muddy chasm slowly filling with water. It's shallow. And at the bottom—

"She's down there." Cole's fingernails dig into my flesh. Her whole body is vibrating. And then the vibrations start to move up my arm, almost as if we're sharing the same electric current being poured into us from the sky. The lightning tree's split smiles at us through the forest. I pull my hand away from hers and use a nearby beech tree to support myself. The edges of my vision gray and pulse. We're standing over a grave.

"Sabrina?"

Cole turns toward me. I expect Sabrina to speak for her, and she nods her head: *yes*. "But she's letting me talk too."

Then, without warning, Cole hops into the grave. She's in as deep as her chest. It won't be easy to climb back out, especially with the slick mud that lines the sides.

"What are you doing?" The water and muck swishes around above her rubber boots, but Cole doesn't seem to mind. She reaches her arm deep into the pit, almost submerging her face. The ends of her hair splay out on the water, tangled with pieces of rotten wood. From above, at the angle I'm standing, she almost looks like a corpse floating in the grave. Then, she stands up and pulls a long, yellowed bone from the water. "Is that—"

"My bones." Sabrina speaks through Cole. Cole sways as Sabrina leaves her. I worry Cole will fall into the grave, but she stays steady. When she sees the bone in her hand, she drops it back in and the mucky water splashes all over her. The water where she dropped the bone ripples outwards as the bone sinks slowly to the bottom, where we can no longer see it.

Sabrina's bones. The whole time she was buried right here. My great grandfather taken in by the police and brutalized, and the bones were right here the whole time. I should be horrified, but I'm just angry. Suicides don't bury themselves. Missing women don't bury themselves. Murdered women are buried by their murderers.

Why had no one thought to look here on the property? *Ellis*. Still, beyond the grave, he can't let go. He continues to terrorize Sabrina, me, Cole, and use Jeff for his ill will. All of this hidden in plain sight and from what Devon and Cole have said about the Walker house being a murder house, people in town *still* choose to blame my great grandfather? There's nothing here that disproves the rumor. I'll need better evidence to prove my great grandfather had nothing to do with Sabrina's death and to prove it was Ellis who killed her.

"And we found this." Cole climbs out of the grave and taps a warped metal box. She rubs the top and hands it to me. It's decorated with the vague remnants of engraved violets. I open it up. Inside is a locket. On the inside frame is etched: *To S. Love, A.* Cole watches me to see my reaction. I can't bring myself to express anything openly. To tell the truth, I'm disappointed there's so much evidence here, but nothing to clear my great grandfather's name.

"I think they were partners. You were right," she says.

I nod. So, that's confirmed. I thought Sabrina was going to give us something more to work with. Real proof that Ellis did it. "Do you think Ellis murdered Sabrina for loving Aggie?" How could somebody do something so vile in the face of what, from the little evidence we had, was a romance? My stomach turns. Maybe Ellis hid this box here to eliminate the shame of his wife's queerness from his life. I remember what Traci said about Aggie and Ellis: *She never said she loved him.* But maybe she did until this happened. Or maybe she did until she met Sabrina. And now that we've found her grave, will Sabrina finally feel peace? Is this her idea of justice? Passing the knowledge of what happened to her on to Cole, to me? What about my great grandfather?

Cole either doesn't hear or ignores me. "We need to call the police."

"No." Calling the police is not an option.

"Asha, we have to. We uncovered a dead body."

"We can't call the police."

"Why not? Not even my uncle?" Her edges sharpen, she steps closer, gains height.

My great grandfather's broken leg. My dad behind bars. *Never call the police.* At first, I think it's anger; the hotness, the feverish broil that steams the rain off my skin. But it's not just anger. It's also fear. The red and blue lights. The cops won't fix anything. All they know how to do is break people apart. "We just can't." I'm firm, manage to steady my voice, sound rational. *I am rational.*

"It's my grandmother." It rings out around us like a trump card. "Just 'cause you're scared—"

"Scared?" My hood whips off and loose curls paste to my forehead. I didn't know I was capable of such bitter laughter. I try to stop it, but I can't. It just keeps pouring out my mouth, a slow, sickly sweet trickle of molasses. "I *should* be scared."

"You don't know the police here. It's not like in the city. They're good guys. My uncle works with them." I can't believe I thought she looked sharp and tall only a moment ago. Now all that seems like framing. I like Cole. I like her so much and she just doesn't understand.

"Do you know how many people died from police brutality in this province in the last year? What do you think they might do when they see me at this murder scene? Doesn't matter it's old. Even your uncle still thinks my great grandfather did it when there's zero proof he was involved!" My rage is growing so fast I can't keep up. It's pouring out of me, hot and vile. She has the audacity to scoff and avert her eyes.

"You know what? I was so happy to hear from you today. I thought you hated me because I took you out on that road the other night. Now I know you just don't care when it comes to the more difficult stuff. Maybe I didn't grow up here, but my great grandparents and grandmother did, and they were exiled just for being Black. They were pushed out by this—this mess. But you don't get it, and you've never had to get it. We don't live in the same world. I can't believe I thought I liked you. You don't know what the fuck you're doing when you call the cops. You're white passing and your uncle's a cop, so you don't know. You don't get it."

"You're serious? You think I don't know what living in this place is like? I'm not a visitor. I grew up here with shitty people calling my dad a terrorist until he left to work five thousand kilometers away, where he's also called a terrorist but gets a bigger cheque at the end of his week. And what about this hate crime we just uncovered? You think I don't know anything about how homophobic and transphobic people are in this town? Why do you want to do this all yourself? This is your entire problem, Asha. You're so focused on yourself you can't see what the people around you are dealing with. If you'd just take a second to look around, you'd see you're not the only one this place has harmed. There're *real live people* who are affected by these losses. This isn't some mystery I've been dropped into from some suburb. Sabrina was family. She was my mother's mother and my mother never really got to know her. Aggie was like a relative to us and you're not even mourning her because you didn't really know her. You get all the benefits of her status, *your* family's whiteness. Don't pretend I'm the only one with privilege here. After everything's done, who's going to end up inheriting that fucked-up haunted house when your mum dies? You."

She's right and I'm furious. The rain comes down harder between us, drowning out any human noise. In the midst of the downpour, I'm sure she's going to leave it at that, but she keeps going. "So you're going through some personal shit? Well, good for you. So is everyone else in this shitty town. Sabrina deserves justice."

And what kind of justice could the cops bring? Shouldn't Sabrina weigh in on this? They're her remains.

"You don't know what the fuck you're doing when you call the cops." I repeat it low, with the tenor of a threat. We hold eye contact for a moment until something like disgust lurches in me. Betrayal. That's the word for what's happening inside of me right now. Cole betrayed me and I've never been so angry. "Call your uncle if you want. But if you do, don't call me."

I want to spit at her. And I can tell she's seconds from laying hands on me. I want to push her in the grave and watch her scramble through the muck. Or throw myself down there, let the police come and bury me with Sabrina. But I don't do any of these things. Instead, I throw the locket at her feet. I don't stop to watch her stoop to pick it up. She mumbles something low that I don't want to hear. I don't care. I've already turned around. I'm already running home so fast I forget my body behind me.

CHAPTER SIXTEEN

*E*verything around me is glowing slightly. The trees drop water onto my face; the tiny, buffed jewels falling toward me like I'm gravity. Sabrina pulls herself out of me and I drop back into my body. She stands, glowing across from me, the only source of light in the wooded vicinity. Without her in my skin, I begin to feel again. I'm too dizzy and exhausted to stand up. My arms are weak and achy, like I've been doing push-ups or . . .

Digging.

My eyes track Sabrina's silent form as it passes through the ferns to the shovel. To a pile of dirt. She lies on top of it, curls into the fetal position. She looks vulnerable, even though all possible harm has already found its way into her physical form.

This is when I know I'm not dreaming: Sabrina sits up. I mirror her, hoisting myself up on shaking arms. *Thank you. This one is deep enough.*

"I can't remember—"

You gave me your permission to use your body to dig a proper grave.

"I don't remember—"

You will soon. Her voice is soft but urgent. *They're looking for you.*

"Who?" A flashlight beam cuts through the side of her head, splitting her face diagonally. "Asha?" It's Mum calling into the dark.

"Asha Walker?" Another voice. Not Mum's. Deep and authoritative. Not Jeff.

"What about Ellis?" If Sabrina is going to rest now, who will protect the house? Is she going to rest now? Is this closure? How did I get here? I'm not even wearing shoes.

He won't find peace. He doesn't even know who he is. No matter how much you try to make this house safe, it's built on blood-soaked soil. More than my blood.

"What do I do?"

Burn it down. Sabrina's fading in pulses now. She lays back down. The beam cuts through the clearing and I hear Mum calling my name again.

"I can't do that—"

Then get out. This house is death. Without Aggie alive, this house is just death.

"Why can't you do it yourself?"

He's always in the way. Watching. I need you to help me. Burn it down. Please.

And she's gone. Doesn't Sabrina know I'm a teenager? Doesn't she know I can't just burn it all to the ground without hurting everyone? Without hurting myself?

A gunshot rings out in the woods, and I hear a scream. Something heavy hits the forest floor.

I lie down and curl into myself, just like Sabrina. I can feel my core trying to light a fire to keep me warm. I lose track of everything, and then Mum is over top of me, laying her coat down, lifting me up and holding me. I'm so small and so big in her arms. Once I was just an egg. How did I get here? How did I get here? I didn't ask for this. I didn't ask for this I didn't ask for this I didn't ask for this I didn't—

And I'm in bed, and Mum is patting my head. I'm warm again. Her eyebrows are so tight together it splits her forehead in two.

"Was it real?" I know it was real for me. What was it for her? Who was shot?

She can barely bring herself to speak. Her bottom lip trembles. "I found you in the woods."

It was real for her too.

"What were you doing there?"

I can't say.

"Asha, how did you end up there?"

I can't say.

"I woke up and your bed was empty. Do you know how terrifying that is? As your mother?"

I can't say.

"I had to call Joe Levesque to help search for you out there. He was off duty. There's a history of women disappearing in this town."

"Sabrina." I'm calling to her, not answering Traci, but Traci's face blanches.

"Sabrina? How do you know about that?"

Sabrina's nowhere nearby. How could she put me in this situation where Traci would call the cops on me, even if Cole didn't.

"I called the Levesque-Gergeses, but they hadn't seen you either. The door downstairs was open, and you were—" Her tears drop heavily onto the pillow beside me. So different from the jewels of the rain. These drops are messy. They sink into the fabric, make it heavy.

"I don't want to be here—" It's all I can get out before I start crying and Mum holds me, whispers, "I know. I know. I know," until I fall asleep again.

CHAPTER SEVENTEEN

Now, I remember. I remember running home after me and Cole fought in the rain, past Jeff, upstairs. I remember calling on Sabrina loud enough for him to hear. Locking my door and shouting at Sabrina to let herself into my body so I could understand. How could Sabrina put me in this position with Cole? Her bones, unearthed by her own grandchild, more than half-decomposed. No real proof my great grandfather was innocent. No real proof Ellis was guilty. How could she do this to us? How could she put us in this impossible position? At the moment when Cole finally believed me, I had thought her belief would fix everything.

I remember the lock on my bedroom door rattling. Jeff, and Ellis behind him, closing in, mirroring him, doubling the strength on the handle. I was safe inside. Sabrina leaned against the door to protect me.

I remember when Mum came home, and I wouldn't let her in. Sabrina told her I didn't want to come out for dinner. Mum insisted I let her in. I did, in the end. I was packing a suitcase. I told her I couldn't keep living here. With *him*. She thought I meant Jeff. By the time Mum got into my room, I'd already left a message for Nan telling her I'd be in the city tomorrow. I'd booked my Maritime Bus ticket out of this town. The Jiffy-Mart where I'd be picked up was within walking distance.

I remember Mum grabbing my suitcase, unpacking it, throwing clothes on the floor and refusing to let me leave. She said I couldn't go out in this state, when she didn't know if I'd be safe. Sabrina dropped back into me and promised her over and over again I was safe. And I was, in a haze so thick, so soft, and heavy as a cloud. I remember not remembering from moment to moment. I remember floating. Floating away from myself more fully than I ever had before.

I remember slipping out my window onto the roof and climbing down the freshly painted gingerbread and running off into the forest as the rain barreled down. Ellis's body tried to break itself away from Jeff's back in the house, but found itself tied too tight to his form to make it after us before we disappeared through the tree line. He didn't know where we were going. Unlike Sabrina, he didn't have anything tying him to the world outside of the house. Only Sabrina could take me to where she wanted to be laid to rest. *I need this*, she said.

And what about what I need?

CHAPTER EIGHTEEN

My eyes crack open an hour before sunrise. My phone's buzzing.

"Hello?" I mumble, balancing it on my ear.

"Hey! Didn't think you'd pick up, it's so early. Was gonna leave a message." Nia.

"I'm grounded. Not that Traci will admit it."

"Grounded?" Nia sounds shocked. She knows my parents aren't the grounding type. "Shit, what did you do?"

"Don't want to talk about it. Why are you calling me?"

"Just wanted to get away from everyone for a minute." I can sense her frantic energy, the opposite of the heaviness I feel anchoring me to my bed. Talking to her gives me a distraction from that weight.

"You miss home?"

She sighs. "Ever since we got here, it's like this side of my mum I never knew just came out. It's cool most of the time. She's telling all these stories she never told us. But it's also like . . . who is she? I feel like I don't know her. Shit's weird."

I nod, then realize Nia can't see me. "You know her."

"I know. I still want the home version of her back." It sounds like it's really bothering Nia. Her voice is going flat, like it does when she doesn't want to get emotional.

"Maybe I know what she feels like," I say. "Not exactly, just a little bit."

"What do you mean?"

"Ever since we came here, I feel different. Like a different Asha." Who was I before? I can barely remember the person I was in the city. I can feel that softer version of me somewhere nested inside this version, stirring as I talk to Nia. She can't fully surface. The new skin I've grown on top of the old is thicker. Maybe that's how Nia's mum feels too. "At first I thought it was an opportunity to be anyone I wanted . . . but then, I realized that people already had an idea of who they expected me to be, I guess, because of my family and stuff. And I've been so angry— it's hard to explain—it's not the same as your mum . . ."

"No, sounds hard. I think for my mum it's joyful. But maybe people expect her to act a certain way here."

"You ever feel that way?" I hear expectation wavering in my voice.

"Feel what way?"

"Like people expect you to act a certain way?"

Nia snorts. "Yeah, but I don't care. I'm just gonna act like me."

"Of course you'd say that."

"I just can't help being myself!" I laugh for the first time in four days. Nia is so herself sometimes it's frustrating. She doesn't compromise her identity for anything or anyone. "So what are you grounded for? Last time I'll ask, if you don't want to talk about it." I roll onto my stomach and take a big breath in. Nia's probably the only person in the world who I could talk to about this. I don't know when we're going to get a chance to talk again, so I tell her.

"You know that person I was telling you I was friends with? Cole? We had a fight. It was big. I've never fought with a friend in that way before. We haven't talked since."

"The one you have a crush on?"

Have. Had? I grit my teeth. "Yes."

"Why?"

"I said some shit about her family I shouldn't have."

"That got you grounded?"

"No, it wasn't that. It was . . ." It's hard to talk about without bringing the ghosts into things. "I tried to leave. I packed up my things and I was going to leave. Traci called the cops."

"Jesus."

"Yeah. I mean, fuck, I don't know what I was thinking." I don't know what Traci was thinking.

"Did that girl hurt you? Like, did it get physical?"

"No." But I've never felt so betrayed. The betrayal feels physical, part of that heaviness pressing down on me. I want Cole to apologize. I can't believe she wanted to call the cops, that Traci *did* call the cops. The fury that took over me at Cole's suggestion and Traci's actions hits me again. I know we could have found justice for Sabrina on her own terms if only Cole hadn't brought up the cops. Maybe Sabrina would've even given me enough proof that Ellis did it that it would put my great grandfather's memory and the rumors in the town to rest. On terms that didn't risk repeating the harm policing might do. We could have fixed things ourselves, me, Cole, and Sabrina. We could have figured everything out. But I went ahead and lost my temper.

It turns out when Traci and Joe were looking for me in the woods, Joe was startled by a deer and, thinking it was my abductor, shot at it. He killed it. What if that had been me? What if I had scared him in the woods? Would he have shot me?

"This whole summer is a disaster, Nia. Remember when we used to skate and go to beaches and eat ice cream? Why can't we have that?" I was happy, wasn't I? Or maybe that's a lie too. Things weren't perfect. When I finally leave here, will things get better? I'm beginning to suspect the problem is me.

There's silence on the other end of the line for a few minutes before I check to see where Nia went. I don't know how long we've been disconnected. I toss my phone onto the floor and bury my head in the pillows.

"Asha? What's going on up there?" Every little noise and she thinks I'm up to something dangerous.

I pull my head out of the sheets to yell back, "Nothing, dropped my phone."

Traci thinks I'm going to hurt myself. And I can't explain that the danger is coming from the house, not me. The truth of the situation that got me out by the grave in the middle of the night sounds even more worrisome than the story I told her, that I couldn't remember how I got out there. She heard me talking to Sabrina, saw the suitcase I'd packed, and freaked. Then, even worse, she saw the grave I'd dug, and made her own connections. She thinks I was hallucinating because I'd found human remains in the woods and had a mental break. I haven't corrected her.

Joe keeps bringing cops out to comb through the woods. From my window, I watch him lean against his car and smoke endless cigarettes with his stubby yellowed fingers. They haven't found anything yet. Is Sabrina making sure he doesn't find her gravesites because she doesn't want her son's version of justice? Or maybe she's protecting him from having to see his own mother's bones? Whatever Sabrina really wants, I don't think it extends beyond her being to others.

Joe came up to the house and talked with Traci yesterday. I didn't realize he was in the room when I shuffled into the kitchen in my pajamas. When I saw her talking to him, my rage came over the room like a tsunami.

"How're you doin' Asha?" Joe asked with a smile that didn't reach his nose let alone his eyes. I didn't answer.

"Answer Joe, honey," Traci prompted.

I slammed my waffles into the toaster in silence.

"Now, don't feel any pressure to answer this question," Joe jumped in, even though my back was turned. "But I'm asking as Sabrina's son and as your mother's friend, not a cop: where are the bones?"

I know the two burial sites are somewhere out there in the overgrowth, the first one by the rabbit warren Cole showed me, but I don't think I could find my way back to either even if I were allowed out of the house. I'd need Cole to help me find the spots, and I can't ask after what I said to her. Even if I still had Cole to help me find the reburial site, I wouldn't tell Joe. It's some comfort to me that even though she did want to call the cops when we found the bones, she hasn't told him what she knows about the first grave site. There's a possibility that it's not clear to her either. Sabrina might be the only one who could truly lead us there and if she hasn't trusted Joe to find the bones before now, why would I betray her trust and my own morals by telling him the first time he asks?

"So now you and Traci are friends?" I asked in response.

He was baffled, and possibly a bit offended.

Traci got up and placed my waffles on a plate for me, then pushed me softly out of the room. "Why don't you take your breakfast upstairs?" From there, I let them be.

Jeff's barely around. He says he's going out to give me and Traci space, but I wonder if that's the truth. Traci booked an appointment for me with the town doctor. I'm not supposed to leave the house without supervision until after a doctor approves, according to her rules. Like I'm seven years old. Like I did something wrong. Like it wasn't someone else puppeteering my body. Traci's treating me so softly, being so careful around me, keeping the noise down in the rest of the house and letting me stay in bed as long as I want. Suddenly, she's showing me she cares. It's all I wanted this whole time. But her carefulness grates, makes me resentful because I'm fine. Or ok. I'm not going to crumble. My anger at all this injustice keeps me glued together.

I can't sleep because I'm scared Sabrina will take over and burn the house down. Before the night of her reburial, she always asked permission. I don't remember if I gave her my consent when she took me back out into the woods that night. Even so, I thought the reburial would be the end of things, that it would bring closure. Sabrina has bigger ideas. This was just step one. She lurks, less present than before, but there, nonetheless. The night after the reburial, I woke up downstairs, balancing on a chair, reaching for the matches in the top kitchen cupboard.

Every night since the matches, I stay up as late as I can, then pour this old instant coffee I found into a big mug and sip it and try to distract myself with books and TV until dawn. Once the sun rises, I figure I can sleep safely, so I get a good four hours of sleep before Traci and Jeff make enough noise downstairs that it's impossible to sleep any longer.

I watch as Aggie makes her usual non-committal descent from the ceiling. I throw one of my socks at her and it pops right through her and drops back onto the floor. She shows no signs that it bothers her.

Unlike Sabrina, who wasn't sated by the reburial like I thought she might be, and Ellis, who continues to shadow Jeff, threatening to take over his body, Aggie never takes any action. She doesn't talk at all. She doesn't seem to want anything. She lies peacefully up above while I force my eyes open.

I wish Aggie would help me decide what to do about the house. After all, she's the one who lived here longest and understood this place the best. Is she really ok with whatever will happen to her if this place burns down? If she lives in this house now, where will she go next? Or will she burn up along with the rest of it? Aggie remains absolutely neutral. As much a part of the structure of this house as the walls. She took her silence to the grave and beyond. Sabrina wants justice, but maybe Aggie already got hers and she's just waiting for the rest of this drama to play out. She's as complicit in death as she was in life.

Sabrina's words rattle around in me. *Burn it down.*

I get it and I agree; I'd want the place where I was murdered burned to the ground too. I don't feel the attachment that Traci feels to this place, either. I know that attachment is complicated— her relationship to her parents and Aggie was complicated. But if I were to burn this place down, I don't know if our relationship could take it.

How am I supposed to burn the one thing that I saw light up my mother's face this year? The project she saw as a cure-all for our issues back in the city. She thought we'd come out here and it would be easier for us to get along with a project to work on. She and Jeff wouldn't argue so much. Me and Jeff might find a way to get along. But everything's the same, if not worse, here. None of us sleep properly and this house doesn't want us to survive in its presence. It wants to collapse. It wants to break down.

There must be another way. Burning it down can't be the only way to bring peace. I've searched online "how to get rid of a ghost" but all the searches turn up scammers and conspiracy theorist sites by boring middle-aged white men. Besides, it's kind of the wrong question. I don't want to get rid of Sabrina and Ellis and Aggie. I want justice for Sabrina, for Aggie. I want to make things right again. For them, for my great grandfather, Nan, and for me. The injustice ends with me. I want a future free of hauntings, literal and metaphorical. But if that's not what Sabrina wants, who am I to deny her wishes?

As the sun rises through my window, I let myself drift off.

ঔ৯

At the doctor's office, the receptionist hands me a sheet and pen and tells me to fill it out. Pop-country plays through static in the background. My legs stick to the bright-orange plastic waiting room chairs. A girl who looks younger than me is playing with her baby in the corner. The kid keeps trying to eat the markers laid out in front of coloring pages. I look back down at my own sheet.

I don't know how to answer these questions. They're all about being on edge. Of course, I'm on edge—the dead are asking me for favors. Should I answer this questionnaire as if I'm not talking to ghosts or as if I am? And would my answers even be that different?

Traci isn't with me. The door is right there. I could walk out and say I went and that there's nothing wrong.

I almost do it.

But obviously if I walked out, the doctor would call her and say I didn't show up, which would be even more cause for concern. As much as I don't want to be here, I don't want to convince Traci that I'm any more out of control than I am.

The nurse looks up over her beige dinosaur of a computer and calls my name. I hastily circle all the zeros on the sheet. She beckons me over and I follow her through a narrow hallway.

The office is in an old factory building poorly divided into offices that make up a block of the town center. Kind of like a huge strip mall. There are posters on all the walls that say things like: "Do you have more than four drinks a day? Talk to your doctor about alcoholism" or "When was your last pap smear?" All of them feature "diverse" casts of smiling stock models engaging in everyday chores or lying in sunny milieus. If only there were one that suggested a cure for visitations from the dead.

In the office at the end of the hall, the doctor sits with her back to the door. She's gazing out the window at the enormous clouds on the horizon. The nurse knocks softly on the door. "Dr. Paul? Asha is here to see you."

Dr. Paul swivels around in her chair and reaches a hand out to shake mine. I expected my doctor to be an old bumbling white guy who'd set up his station in this town about sixty years ago. Clearly, my own assumptions got the better of me. Dr. Paul is a woman around my mother's age with soft features and light brown skin. Although her face is open and kind right now, I suspect she's just as firm when she needs to be.

"Nice to meet you, Asha! When I got the call from your mother, I couldn't believe she was back in town in that old house. How are you?" She holds out a hand for the paper as she asks this, and I hand it over. She pulls the clear-blue plastic glasses that hang around her neck up to her face and perches them at the end of her nose so she can get a good look. As I watch her squint at my messy scribbles, I almost feel bad for not taking the questionnaire more seriously.

"I'm good," I say. She raises an eyebrow at the marks on the sheet.

"Good," she replies and smiles. Then she tosses the sheet in a recycling bin.

"What—"

"I'm sorry, I think you'll have to answer the questions again." She pulls a copy of the same sheet out of her desk and hands it to me with a blue ballpoint pen. "Fill this out again. Be honest this time."

"I was honest," I mumble unconvincingly as I grip the pen and keep my eyes lowered.

"Were you?" She's somehow able to convey her disbelief without sounding rude. "Then just fill it out again. No problem."

I fill out the sheet. I answer honestly this time.

When I hand it back to her, she looks it over. "Your mother told me she found you in the woods in the middle of the night covered in dirt. Can you tell me what led up to this?"

"I went to bed."

"And then?"

"I woke up in the woods."

"Ok. And you have no memory of walking outside?"

"No."

I do. But I don't like to think about it. I don't like thinking about what might happen to me if I told the truth.

"How would you describe yourself as feeling the day leading up to this episode?"

Episode. Possession. "I felt ok." Shaky, nauseous, dizzy. Furious at Cole. Pleading with Sabrina to take control. "I guess I wasn't really feeling like myself."

"Not feeling like yourself how, exactly?"

"I don't know. Just, like, not *me*, you know?"

"Disconnected?"

I nod.

"You moved here recently. Are you making friends? People your age?"

"Not really." Cole's face surfaces, but I push the thought of her back down.

"Hard to meet people in the summer without school. I could ask my son Devon if he wants to show you around. I wouldn't mention how we met, of course, doctor-patient confidentiality. He's your age."

"We've met already."

She gives me one of those neutral doctor smiles, sets her pen down, and looks at me pointedly. "Living in this town can be difficult if you're like you or me, historically speaking. For me, that could mean being reminded how this land is stolen. For Mi'kmaw people, we never gave up this land. We're still here. For you and your people, it might mean being reminded of being stolen and brought to this land. You need to protect yourself and take care."

I've never had a doctor who's talked openly about race before. It's a relief. Usually doctors just tell me to take more vitamin D, or that I'm at more risk of certain diseases, or just straight up rush through the appointment. "I know."

"Good. I can recommend some resources to help you with that." She holds eye contact with me for a second, assessing if I'm taking her seriously, or just agreeing so I can get out of here. "And your home life. Are there any extra stressors?"

I surprise myself by laughing. "My dad's in prison."

"Yes. I heard about that. How are you coping?" Dr. Paul doesn't have the reaction I expect at all. I'm used to people doing a double take when or if I tell them at all.

"I don't know. I guess I thought I was coping ok."

"And now?"

"It's hard."

She scribbles down a note. "Anything else?"

"Me and my mum's boyfriend don't get along."

"Why not?"

"I don't know. He thinks I'm a burden on my mum."

"Are those your words or his?"

"Both? I think that's about the only thing we agree on."

"Is there any history of mental illness in your family?"

"I don't know." I think of Traci on the couch that whole week Jeff was in the hospital. And when I was so resentful of her for not paying attention to me when I was younger, but I could tell she couldn't muster the energy for me. Isn't that textbook depression? Dad couldn't be there for me these past few weeks because he couldn't bear to hear my voice on the other end of the line. Maybe he couldn't bring himself to sit in that grief. And my anger. It takes over me sometimes. I would call it possession if it wasn't so different from the disconnect from my own life that Sabrina provides. When I'm angry, I feel the surest of myself, that I'm alive, that I will keep on living. That feeling burns so bright, it holds me captive and I can't feel anything else. I want to feel other things too.

Maybe these are symptoms of mental illness. Maybe I'm just like my parents. I come from them. I thought it was just the way we all were and accepted it's the way we all would be forever. I understand Sabrina now. I understand why she would want to burn the house down. She doesn't get a future. All she gets is a past where she must live with the rage of injustice every day. That's all there is for her. But for me, for Mum, for Dad, there is a future, and there will be anger, but maybe we can change. Maybe I can experience my anger without contributing to the same conflicts. How can I forgive them? How can I forgive myself? Without forgetting and making the same mistakes we've already made. Even though I can't talk about the ghosts with Dr. Paul, acknowledging something is wrong out loud made it easier to hope that maybe there's a way out—for all of us.

"I'll ask your mother. And we'll follow up in a couple of weeks to see if these numbers have improved. I understand it's hard to live in this town. I want you to call me if there's anything. I'm here to help. In the meantime, try to stay active. Get good sleep. Eat three meals. Can you promise me you'll do that?"

"Yes," I say. And I want it to be true. But I don't know if I can do it all.

"Take care." Dr. Paul holds my gaze. She selects a few booklets from her filing drawers and hands me a stack of mental health resources. Even if I can't do it all, I know I will try my best.

*

Traci takes me for ice cream on the way home. It's this little shack on the side of the highway.

"You see that cute little farmhouse back there? Shame so much of the old architecture gets neglected." She tries to make conversation, but I can only see a corner of a decomposing fence and the hint of a roof above the dense wall of trees that border the road. She doesn't ask me about my appointment. She's waiting for me to break the ice.

I get Moon Mist on a sugar cone, just like I used to as a kid. She gets grape nut in a waffle cone. We lick our ice creams in silence on the drive home. Traci keeps glancing at me from the corner of her eye. I don't think I want to talk about it yet. I'm not sure how it went either but I'm leaning toward okay. Something in my chest loosened in Dr. Paul's office.

When we drive over the moat, my ice cream falls into my lap. I scoop it up with my hand and place it back on the cone, use some of the napkins in the glove compartment to attempt to wipe the blue-yellow-pink off my thighs.

"Oh!" Traci squeals. I look up to see if she's hit something or if we busted a tire in the moat, but she's looking at the figure that has appeared at the end of our driveway. It's Cole. She's bulked up in her orange jacket even though it's still sunny out. What the hell is she doing here? "You invited Nicole over. I'm so glad, Asha."

"Cole." I didn't invite her. My heart jumps into my throat. Something bad must have happened for her to be here.

As soon as the car is parked, I swing the door open and slam it behind me. I walk over to her swiftly, a pulse of anger throbbing behind my eyes. Something else tingles across my scalp. Relief?

"What are you doing here?" I fill my voice with as much venom as possible. But she isn't fazed.

"Can we talk in your room? It's important."

Traci waves from the door. She would never turn a guest away. "Cole, why don't you come in for a bit?"

"Fine," I say. And she follows me in.

As soon as I've cleaned up the spilled ice cream and Traci's done asking Cole what her mother's up to these days and how her father's doing and what everyone thinks of the new outlet panels in the kitchen, we go up to my room where I drop what little pretense of friendliness I was putting on.

Before I can say anything, she jumps in: "Are you ok?"

"What?" She's asking me if I'm ok after she made it clear she didn't value our friendship enough to respect my decision not to have the police involved. Didn't respect our friendship enough to apologize this whole week and now she shows up unannounced asking if *I'm ok*. I laugh.

Cole looks sorry she asked. "The bones are gone from where we found them."

"Oh." So this isn't even a little bit of an apology. Even if I did know where they were, I wouldn't tell her if it means she's going to get Joe involved again.

"Asha, I'm sorry about the other day. I was being ignorant. It's just complicated. I love my uncle but I thought a lot and read up on the law online and I think you were right?" She waits for a response. I don't volunteer one. "About not calling the cops, I mean. I thought they would fix everything for us. But it's more complicated than that for both of us. There isn't an easy answer. And when I heard that shot in the woods after your mum called my house, I thought . . ."

She takes a deep breath before continuing. She thought I was dead. I thought I might be dead too. "You have to understand what it was like to wake up in the middle of the woods holding my grandmother's bones with my bare hands. When Sabrina was in me it felt fine—that was part of me—but when it was just me, when she left me . . . I freaked out. You know it's illegal to tamper with human remains? I looked that up, too. We could be punished for moving Sabrina's bones around. But Sabrina didn't care. Or she didn't know. It felt like she used me and I was going to be the next one to go down for what Ellis did. Calling the cops seemed like the only option. Uncle Joe's always wanted to find out what happened to her. I thought I could bring him closure too. She was my grandmother and I've lived in this town longer than you. I need you to recognize that."

I'm silent and still as a tombstone. Cole rubs her hands over her eyes to wipe away the tears that are gathering there.

"And not to be a jerk, but even before we became implicated in a crime, I had my own shit going on."

Anger makes my tongue a knife. "You keep saying that, but it's no excuse—"

"No, listen. I'm not saying it as an excuse." Anger starts to creep into her voice, but she manages to temper it. I've never seen anyone do that before: communicate their anger but also their limits. "I believe you. About everything—the ghosts, not calling the cops. Just don't be an asshole, ok? I've had a lot on my mind, I'm serious. But Devon texted me and told me Meagan Hunter was at the clinic with her baby and saw you there. She's in our grade. She recognized you from the party."

Damn. News really does get around fast. How long's it been? A couple hours? And Cole and Devon are talking again? How'd that happen?

"I don't know why you were out there, but I was worried something had happened to you, and I didn't feel like I could text you to ask. That felt really bad. So, I wanted to make things right between us. I want to listen to you, but you also have to listen to me."

Stubbornness clenches my jaw even as relief pours over me in a cold rush.

"I told you. I had a lot on my mind." She's looking down at her hands. "Because even after we had that big fight, I still wanted you back. I want to support you. Up until the night with Sabrina's bones, I felt safe around you and I want you to feel that way around me too. But it's something I've been thinking about for a long time. I just kept getting caught up wondering how much easier things would be if Ben were here to talk this through . . . it's not exactly a surprise, but what I've been thinking about is important to me. Just as important as everything with this house. I wanted you to know: I'm not a girl. I'm still figuring gender stuff out, but can you use they/them pronouns for me from now on?" Their face flushes deep red. They look up to the ceiling as though they're praying. I look up too to see if Aggie's there. The ceiling is blank.

"Oh." Why hadn't I paid attention when they said they needed space? I wish I'd been more curious about what they were going through. My brain didn't have space for anything but my own mission.

If I could go back in time, I'd ask them more questions. I think of how Mum won't stop asking me about my sexuality—it's overbearing. I didn't want to be like her, but in trying so hard to counter Traci's way of being in the world, I've neglected Cole, completely ignored their needs. Maybe Traci's just been trying to figure out what I need and I haven't made it easy for her. Cole's vulnerability brings me back to myself. I should have listened when they told me they needed time and space to think. "Of course. I know I'm not Ben, and I'll never be close, but if you want to talk to me about anything, I'm here for you. Sorry I didn't pay attention. Thanks for telling me."

"I just needed time. It was never about you. So, we're good?"

"Yeah. I was a jerk, huh?"

Cole lies back on my bed, and I join them. "Yeah. And so was I, to be fair. Especially knowing what happened to your great grandfather. I should've made it clearer that it wasn't about you. But there's something else I need to tell you." They take a minute that feels like forever to continue. "That night I slept over, there was a man on my chest. I know it wasn't a dream. I just didn't want to think about it when everything else was so intense for me. He kept telling me he was going to kill me."

"Did he say anything else?"

"No. He just kept on squeezing harder. If his hands were real, I don't think—I don't think I'd still be here, honestly." I nod. "Don't worry, I'm not going to call the cops or tell my uncle anything. I know it's hard for you, and after Uncle Joe shot that deer, I don't think it's safe. He's come over every night after searching the woods, and I don't think he's doing well. He's not sleeping, won't eat Mum's food even though she cooked up the deer nice and everything. He and the other cops might just mess things up."

Cole picks at a piece of their jacket that's peeling off. Orange flakes onto my bed spread. "I'm still worried about what might happen if they find out we tampered with the site. There must be a way around getting the police involved, without the bones. And now that the bones are gone, no one would believe us unless we could find them anyway."

"Sabrina has her own plans for her bones. I don't think we should mess with them. Not that I know what she wants." She has plans for this house too. I'll have to tell Cole about that at some point.

"I just assumed Sabrina used you to—"

"She did. We reburied her somewhere else in the forest, but I don't remember where I was. It was dark, and I was . . . confused." And no matter how hard the cops look now, they still haven't tracked down the burial site where Traci found me. I think even Traci's starting to wonder if she imagined the burial mound.

Cole lets out a sigh.

"Before Sabrina dropped into me, I wanted to believe Ben would come back. But feeling Sabrina in me, and Ellis on my chest, all their unrest . . . it made me glad he didn't stick around. Even if that meant giving up on a hope I didn't know I had."

"I'm sorry you can't talk to him." It seems like a silly thing to say and not nearly enough to soothe the grief they must feel every day. "What would he think of all this?"

"I miss him, and I wish I could talk to him, but I hope he wouldn't know anything about it. He'd be far away on some university campus or in a big city playing bass in a band or unexpectedly doing the MCAT or some shit. This would be a story I'd tell him when he came home at the holidays—about the haunted house and the city kid with a garbage sense of direction who talks to ghosts. I'd tell him about how we avenged our grandmother." Cole sniffs in their tears hard.

"Do you think Ben would've liked me?"

"I think he would've thought you were annoying, just like me. But yeah. He would've liked you. You kind of remind me of him."

"The marshmallows?"

Cole laughs softly. "Not just that. You're both obsessive. Can't leave anything alone once you get started on it. You both basically drink garlic butter with your lobster too—"

"Hey!" I'm laughing now. It feels good. I thought we'd never speak again, but here we are, back to normal. Better than normal. We understand each other better now.

"I'm just saying, the rest of us need to eat too." We lean up against each other at the shoulders.

"So, you're ok?"

"I'm ok."

"Ok." I'm relieved.

"I'm so glad we're good."

"We're good?" I ask them to confirm.

"We're good."

With everything that created tension between us out in the open, sitting next to them feels so easy. They place their hand on top of mine and look intently into my eyes. "I like you," I tell them. They're nervous. Their small palms are clammy, and their fingers are gripping too tight. "When I left you in the woods, I thought I heard you say something."

Cole's face reddens again. It glows like the day they came to take me on that hike to the waterfall. My heart is racing.

"I was too angry to think about it," I continue. "I wanted to forget you ever said anything. If I could, I would've forgotten you completely. I've never had a friend like you before. Someone I want to be with all the time, someone who I want to *be* with . . ." I'm at a loss for words. I don't need them anymore, though. They nod, then they lean forward and our lips meet softly.

One time, I almost got dragged out by the undertow at the beach. When we kiss, I'm pulled under. It's like drowning, losing myself to something bigger. Saying goodbye to everything I know. And that's such a good feeling right now. To just be without consequence.

Then I pull away.

"What? Was that bad?" Cole is self-conscious, biting their lip.

"I don't know. I mean, I like you. I liked kissing you, but I don't know about . . . about *me*." Isn't this what I wanted? How could I pull back when all I want is to lean in and kiss Cole more?

"If you're queer?"

"No. I am." The confirmation slips easily from my mouth. I'm certain of my queerness. With Cole, it feels natural to acknowledge this part of myself. I'm sure of who I am with them in this moment. "But I meant more—I don't know if I'm ok."

"Ok." I thought saying it would hurt them, but they just smile. "No rush."

I'm so relieved I could cry. But I don't. We lie in silence until I start drifting off. Next to me, Cole shifts, then gets up and tiptoes to my desk. I hear the scratch of their pencil against paper as they craft the intricate details of whatever world they're imagining in their head. Sabrina is giving us privacy. I can't feel her presence at all.

Completely at peace for the first time in weeks, I drift into a dream about Nan cornrowing my hair in her backyard, her firm but gentle hands pulling me closer to her. She leans closer to me, and her breath warms my ear. "When are you coming home?"

Home. Hers? Mine? Ours . . . I've been there before. The Walker house. I shoot up, completely awake. Making up with Cole made me all soft and floppy, but my dream redirected me.

"You remember that party we went to?" I ask, startling Cole, who is deep in their drawing. "Can you show me how we got there?"

"Sure." They go back to scribbling.

"I think that house was my great grandparents' farm." I don't feel as nervous about bringing it up now that we've cleared the air. I stand up and start gathering myself, wipe the drool from the corner of my mouth.

Cole stops drawing and turns to face me. "Shit. Of course." Their face reddens with embarrassment. "The *Walker* house. You're Asha *Walker*. I never thought to make the connection. You're just Asha and the house is just the house but you're—"

"Related." I want to rush out the door and run until the house appears in front of me, but I resist. I need Cole as a guide, and I don't want to make the same mistake I did the night I dragged Cole out on the side of the road and assume they'll just come along. Besides, I don't have to wait long. They're already zipping their jacket.

"You think there's proof about your great grandfather out there?"

"I don't know. I just know I need to be there."

Cole nods. "Okay then. Let's go."

♪♪

Traci lets me go out for my walk with Cole if I promise I'll be back for dinner. The clouds that Dr. Paul watched on the horizon are getting closer, and the wind's picking up. The days are getting noticeably shorter as summer starts to slip away.

All the trees are at the peak of aliveness, and when we take a detour to walk up the mountain to the waterfall, I'm at the peak of my aliveness too. Cole's leading and telling me stories about Millie driving them crazy and their dad's return from work out west in a couple weeks. They wonder what going back to school will be like after this weird summer. We make plans to present ourselves as unabashedly queer to the rest of the school, to say fuck it to the whole town and just be ourselves. What's tying us to the past is far away.

Separate from the house, Sabrina's lurking presence leaves me. The flickering heat in my fingers dissipates. Splashing in the cool pool beneath the waterfall, I understand myself as part of this environment, as a body and as an organism in the larger body of this ecosystem.

Cole shows me the way back to the Walker house. After a summer of hanging out between trees, I'm beginning to be able to tell how to read the paths Cole follows. Last time we were here, it was so dark that I didn't see how much debris laid around its walls. Remnants of the party we attended weeks ago, and maybe a few more since, litter the ground. Beer bottles and cigarette butts and chip bags.

The ground around the house is sunken but not depressed. The house itself is unmovable, rooted, as stable as it can be, given its abandonment. If moving from the city to this town was a shock, I wonder how Nan felt moving from here to the city. Out here, secluded with her family on this hill, this town must have seemed like the whole world.

Looking back, the river valley stretches out as far as the edge of the earth, pulsating in the wind. Steeples and colorful houses are bright against the gray sky. Right below us is the ice cream stand where I got a cone with Mum. The farm she talked about behind that line of trees by the road . . . it's Nan's.

Beyond the ice cream stand, the market's a bit further off. And the river, the bridge where me and Cole jumped. When we visited, I always thought of this place as empty. Surveying the land now, I realize how deeply mistaken I was. Everything here is a participant. Even me, a small force of nature.

We try all the doors, but they won't budge. I shake the knobs in frustration. There are no working locks in sight, yet the house won't open itself to me. I just want to get inside and see where my grandmother grew up, where my great grandparents lived their lives, where I could have grown up. What could have been my home. Now it's a party house. Does it still hold any of my family's history?

"I don't think we'll get it open." Cole lays a hand gently on my shoulder. I'm breathing heavily from the effort of trying to kick in the door. "I can ask Devon if he knows anyone with the key."

They're right. I'm going to damage the place if I keep kicking. I take a deep breath into my stomach, then I decide to let it go. If this house doesn't want to open to me right now, it's not the right time. When I glance at Cole, a cool wind rustles over me, pulling up goosebumps on my arms. "Let's go back home. I'll come again later."

"You're sure?" Cole looks surprised. "We came all the way out here."

"It's fine. Maybe you can ask Devon about that key."

"Ok, I will." They take a second glance at me to make sure I'm good with leaving. I don't look back at the house. If the house doesn't want me to see inside yet, maybe it's not the only place that can prove my great grandfather's innocence, or maybe it doesn't think I'm ready to be let in on its secrets. Or maybe the house is trying to tell me proof isn't what my great grandfather needs—what I need—anymore.

We head back home. "I was gonna ask earlier: you and Devon are talking again?"

Cole nods. "Yeah, he groveled. I had to give in. We've been friends forever. Plus, Millie missed him. He's kind of like a big brother to her." It must be hard on Cole not seeing Devon because of that too.

"That's good. I talked to him, you know. At that café."

"The Riverbank? Yeah, he told me."

"He said he'd take us to the beach."

"Oh, did he?" Cole cocks an eyebrow. "Well, I guess we'll have to take him up on that."

It'll be cool to hang out with someone who Cole cares about so much. Someone who knows them better—or differently—than I do.

We head back home. I guess I'm not as alone as I thought in this town. And neither is Cole. We all have our people. Our families outside of family. Those can keep growing, shifting, morphing into what we need. Aggie and Sabrina knew that. I just wish no one had suffered for it.

CHAPTER NINETEEN

———

My phone comes alive shortly after lunch. I pick it up without looking at who it might be, assuming it's Nan finally calling back.

"Asha?" Nia's voice crashes into me like the pavement on a hard fall. My eyes sting with relief.

"Where did you go the other day?"

"Bad connection. Sorry I was so moody."

"Nothing to be sorry about. How's your mum?"

"She's good. Like I said, joyful. I think I just needed to talk about how different she is with someone, so I didn't feel like I was going crazy. How's your mum? Are you getting along with her now that you're grounded?" She laughs as though this would be impossible, but it does kind of feel like we're getting along better now.

"Actually, yeah." Even with the Sabrina incident and being grounded, it doesn't feel like a total lie.

"It's a miracle."

"How's Freetown? Like, beyond your family."

"It's perfect. It's hard." Nia often does that, puts two contradictory statements right next to each other. She's able to see the hard in the perfect, the perfect in the hard. I've always wished I could be more like that. "I miss you."

"I miss you too." I can hear the din of family in the background. "Must be busy. What are you doing?"

"We're going to market—" There's static on the line followed by Jamal and Nia's voices sharpening against each other.

"Hi Asha!" It's Jamal.

"Hey! What's up?"

"Goin' to market."

"Damn, did your voice drop?" His voice is huskier than when he left. It's only been six weeks.

"That's all people say to me! Nia—hey!" He still has that whininess though.

"Give me space! God—he's always trying to get in my business. I was trying to tell you: there's this cotton tree here. I think I sent you in a video in my email. It's huge, where our people landed when they came back to this continent. I've never seen anything like it before . . ."

"Like it how?" I glance out my window at the trees on our property. They're tall, but probably nothing compared to the cotton tree.

"It's hard to explain. There's this feeling when you're near it. Like it knows you. It knew people before me. My mum and maybe some of my ancestors on my dad's side. The roots. It's right on the Atlantic. Like the roots are reaching back."

"Whoa."

There's silence for a few long seconds. The afternoon sun beats down on the yard. It's dry yellow even though there was a brief summer rain last night. What little is left of Mum's work in the garden might be completely lost if we don't get a big rain soon. "What you texted me about ghosts? Is everything ok?"

I twiddle with a curl at the base of my neck. "Yeah. Yeah. Everything's fine."

"Do you really think the place is haunted?"

I pause, maybe too long, not sure if I should tell Nia the truth or not. It's not that I'm worried Nia won't believe me—unlike

Cole, I don't think she needs to experience the ghosts herself to be convinced of what's happening here—it's more that I don't want to worry her on the last few days of her trip. Now that I have Cole's support, I don't feel so alone. I decide to save it for a story. "No. I was just joking."

"Ok, well, send me your address. I want to put a postcard in the mail for you."

"You're going already?"

"Gotta go—everyone's ready. I'll be back soon. Love you!"

"Love you."

When she hangs up, I catch myself smiling in the mirror. Sabrina squeezes my shoulder. She's happy for me. As much as we've become close, kind of friends, even, I sense our relationship is reaching toward a natural conclusion. Her presence is a reminder of what she wants done. She wants an ending. I'm going to have to help her toward one in some way or another.

I want to continue. I'm thinking of Nia. Thinking of the beach. When we drive out with Devon and stand on the Atlantic, I'll put my feet in the water and imagine the roots of the cotton tree reaching back and connecting me to Nia even across distance and time.

*

I come into the kitchen smiling. Traci is just getting off the phone with the last mouse exterminator. Jeff is at the table scanning the business section of the newspaper. Ellis hangs over his shoulder, reading too, although I must admit, even he looks bored.

"What are you smiling about?" Traci seems happy to see me happy. The dimples we share pop out on her cheeks.

"Nothing."

"Ok." She restrains herself from asking me any further questions. There are samosas on the kitchen table. I grab one and take a big bite. It's lamb. "These are good. Where'd you get them?"

"Market."

"You went without me?" I would've gone with her. At this point, I'd do anything to get out of the house.

Jeff clears his throat and flips to the sports section. I can't believe he still buys paper copies. Probably to support the provincial overlords he works for. I'm in a good mood today, though. I try to put all the things that bother me about Jeff aside.

"Apparently there's a tornado warning," Traci tells me as she places some tamarind sauce in front of me.

The trees outside are completely still. The sky is blue. I squint into the distance. "Really?"

"You wouldn't know it." Traci sits on the side of the table between me and Jeff.

"I talked to Nia."

"How's she doing?"

"Good. She said there's this huge cotton tree in Freetown from when Black Loyalists sailed back there."

"Must be enormous."

"Mhm." I take another bite. "Can I hang out with Cole again today?"

I can see Traci weighing the risks in her mind.

"Can I at least go for a ride on my board? It's been forever."

"Skating? I thought you gave up on that."

"No, I just I gave it a rest after I got in trouble from Joe. He's not coming by today, is he?"

Jeff lifts the paper up higher so I can only see a tuft of his thinning, mousy hair. I look at Mum. "He's coming by *again*? All he does is lean against his car, smoke, and stare at the tree line. He hasn't even gone in the woods since the first few days he was here."

Mum puts her head in her hands and presses into her forehead. "Joe's been waiting his whole life for a lead like this. It's his mother. He has every right to investigate, Asha." It doesn't take much for tension to creep into her voice. Maybe she's still upset about how I reacted to Joe trying to ask me questions the other day. Isn't it my right to remain silent? Jeff's certainly exercising his rights. I haven't heard a peep out of him on the topic. Does he not want Joe around either? Maybe for once, Jeff can be my ally, although I suspect whatever his motives are, they're probably not aligned with mine.

"Jeff, don't you think Joe should give it a rest?"

He lets out an exhausted sigh and folds up his paper. "I'm not getting into this."

Of course, he decides not to pick a fight when it would benefit me. He gets up and takes my plate out from under me. There was still a corner of samosa left on there. Ellis has a snide grin plastered across his Ken-doll face.

"Ash, how's Cole? Did you two make up?" Traci is just trying to change the subject, but the way she looks at me with concerned expectation rubs me the wrong way. I know she's asking because she wants to know if we're a thing or whatever.

"Yeah."

"What happened between you?" She picks at the edge of the table where the melamine's melted. "Kelly told me you had a fight. Is that why you tried to leave that night?"

With every question, I can feel my good mood slipping away like an ice cube skidding beneath a refrigerator. "Dr. Paul said I don't have to talk about what happened if I don't want to." I know I'm twisting her words about doctor-patient confidentiality, but I want Traci off my back about Cole.

"If Joe's coming over, can I please go over to Cole's so I don't have to be here?"

Unexpectedly, Jeff turns around and says, "Traci, why don't you just call him and tell him not to come? It's not right."

"Jeff, I told you. It's his *mother*. It's just good manners."

"It's against the law. He doesn't have permission."

"He's an old friend."

The blood drains from Jeff's face. The line between him and Ellis blurs. They move into each other. It's as if the warm air is sucked out of the room. "I see the way he looks at you." It's as if Ellis and Jeff are talking as one. I haven't seen Ellis do this to Jeff before.

Where's Sabrina? Her presence was vague all morning, and now I can barely sense her drifting around. Usually, an appearance from Ellis makes her appear more solid. Without her, me and Mum might not have much protection against Ellis.

"For God's sake, that was in high school, Jeff. Do you see me looking at him like that?"

"I just want to protect you." The phrase, coming from a man sharing a mouth with a murderer, makes me shudder. This has the feel of an older argument. I hadn't realized they'd been fighting about Joe. Then again, I've been busy with other things.

"It's fine." I try to diffuse the tension. "Why don't we all go someplace?"

"Great idea, Asha. We were supposed to go to that fried chicken joint on Main Street."

"It's crap. Why don't we go for something healthier?" Jeff scoffs.

"You were all about this family being a 'united front' a few weeks back. What changed?" I can't believe Traci brought that up. I had no idea it bothered her too.

"What if Cole comes over here?"

"That whole family is bad news," Jeff says. "Asha, you should stay away from them, believe me."

"What do you mean?"

"That kid, Cole. I think she has a crush on you. Looks at you the same way her uncle looks at your mother."

"They, them—Cole's not a girl," I correct him. "And what do you mean by that?" My patience with Jeff is running out. Ellis is pulling back out of him again now. He stumbles a bit against the counter.

"She's taking advantage of you. You said it yourself. She's gay. Playing with your feelings so her family can get close to the property."

"*They.*" I glance from Jeff to Mum. "What's he talking about?"

She keeps her mouth clammed shut. Does she know about what he told me? That this land is rich in resources and he's checking it out for his own benefit?

"Soon he's going to get surveyors out here looking for the property line. Soon he's going to have his cop buddies make up reasons for you to leave. That family's always wanted this house."

"Me and Cole are just friends," I tell Jeff. "Not that it should matter to you if we were dating." So what if either of us are queer? How is he suddenly an expert on our relationship? Mum is silent. Why won't she back me up? "I just want to go out for a skate. Please." I need to get out of here before Jeff drives me up the wall.

"No." Traci's voice draws a line that I know I shouldn't cross, but I can't help it.

"Why not? I'm fine."

Traci won't look me in the eye. She tells her hands, "I told Joe you'd talk to him."

I start sweating. "You *what?*" There's heat radiating off me. How could she betray my trust like that?

"I told Joe you'd talk to him. I didn't tell you because I didn't want you to—"

"Get angry?" I stand up and my chair scrapes against the wood. Mum hates that. The anger that temporarily grew smaller, bursts back at full force. It almost knocks me off my feet.

"It's his mother, Asha, have some compassion."

"He's a cop! Plus, he believes Dad's grandfather was the murderer!"

"And he's a good man!"

"A good man? After what happened to Dad?" I realize I'm gasping for air every second word, but I can't catch up with my breath now; it's steps ahead. "You know I hate the police—"

"You can't make every cop out to be a bad guy."

I scoff. "You say that, but when did a cop ever do anything good for you? For Dad?"

"Your father was guilty."

"They *say* he was guilty."

"The court decided he was guilty."

"They jacked up his sentence because he's Black."

Jeff steps between us. "They decided on what was fair."

I wish it was Sabrina who took my arm and pushed Jeff, but it's all me. I push him as hard as I can. He stumbles into Mum. "Fuck you, Jeff, stay out of it."

Traci's jaw drops. "Whoa! Asha—"

I've already stormed out of the room and down the hall. What's wrong with me? Why would I make things worse with Jeff? This was between me and Traci. Traci is racing after me. She corners me in the living room.

"Asha, we need to set some boundaries."

"Ok, let's set a boundary. I'm not talking to Joe. Stay out of my business. Stop treating me like a little kid."

"I'm not treating you like a little kid, but you're sure as hell acting like one. How could you push Jeff like that? I taught you better. God, what is wrong with you?"

"What's wrong with me? What's wrong with *you*? Why would you bring someone like me out to a place like this and expect me to have a good time, to make friends with cops after what happened to Dad and our family?"

"What do you mean, 'a place like this?' This is our family home."

"*Your* family home. This place is—" I find my words in the hollow of Traci's dropped jaw. "Haunted with whiteness. I can't live here; it makes me crazy." We're both screaming at this point. We haven't had an argument this heated since we were back in the city. I'm tensed up again in all the places where only a day before I was relaxed and self-assured with Cole, where minutes before I was talking to Nia, happy. Is it the house or is it me that holds this anger? Or maybe we hold it together. At this point, I can barely tell the difference between what I feel and what the house does. Both of us are ready to explode. The floors groan beneath us. I need to get out of here so I can breathe again. Jeff's figure appears at the door, shadowed by Ellis.

"I know you're not doing well, Asha." Traci lowers her volume, tries to get a grip on her temper. "And I'm trying, but you make it so hard. This is hard for me too. You won't compromise, you won't spend time with me, and you're out with Cole doing who knows what? You won't talk to me about what you're feeling. Am I supposed to guess? Or what? What is it? I feel like I don't know you. I just want to help you, ok? I just want to be a good mother. I wish I had a mother when I was your age. Please, just let me take care of you."

"By keeping me locked up with no contact with the outside world and tricking me into talking to the police when you know—you *know* . . . ?"

"It's to keep you safe—after what happened—people have died out here for being . . . for being gay! What if the person who took Sabrina Levesque is still out there, and I lose you? Or Kelly and Joe lose Cole, after Ben . . ." Traci's crying too but I can't make myself care. She doesn't know the half of it, doesn't know we've been living with the murderer this whole time. She's the closest to Ellis when he attaches himself to Jeff's shadow and close enough to Joe, who put me at risk by shooting in the woods that night.

"How am I safer in this blood-soaked house than outside?" They're Sabrina's words in my mouth. I wish I was possessed but I'm not. Sabrina's presence has dissipated to nothing by the time

I lurch forward and push Traci. She pushes me back. I feel like an animal. I'm ready to really fight. But then Jeff's in between us again.

"Don't be dramatic, ladies. Let's have a rational conversation."

He couldn't have possibly said a worse thing. Both me and Traci's jaws drop at his tactlessness. "Oh. *You* think *we* should have a rational conversation? Like you with your possessiveness and jealousy over some high school fling?" I turn back to Traci. "He's keeping stuff from you."

Traci shoves him aside. She also looks annoyed that he's stepped in here. "What do you mean, Asha?"

"He's planning something. He's just using us to get to natural resources so he can become CEO of his gross energy company."

"I don't know where you got that idea—"

"He told me. Why don't you tell Traci what you told me."

Jeff is silent. Me and Traci both watch him. As the silence stretches out, I watch the tension build between them. "I never said anything about natural resources to Asha."

"Then what are those 'opportunities' you mentioned?"

"I told you—to spend more time with you and your mother." His face is so open and firm I almost believe him. I can tell Traci does. As she looks back at me, her frown deepens.

"He's lying. He's—he's planning something," I stutter. Traci will never believe me.

Traci takes a stabilizing breath. "You're always so eager to prove Jeff's a bad man. When will you finally accept him into our home?"

"*Not a bad man?* He won't even let you post what you want on social media or go out for fried chicken without his blessing. He's lying. He doesn't care about us." My voice is constricted. Anger makes me cry. I know Jeff will see this as a mark of weakness. I do everything in my power to hold my tears back.

"I have no ill will toward you or your mother, Asha. I know you're going through a hard time right now. I don't know what it's like to have a father who's absent, someone who's let you down so profoundly. I can't even imagine . . ." He shakes his head. That's my last straw. I need to be believed. I don't care if I get kicked out of this house and have to stay with Nan or Nia for the next year. Living without the truth out in the open will kill me. Not being believed will kill me. And I don't want to be another ghost in these walls.

My anger surges. I step back and grab a paperweight, then hold it up in the air as if to throw it at Jeff. He cowers, childishly, and I'm reminded of just how scared of me he is. He's scared of every part of me: of who I am, of what I can do, of what I know. I have the power. And with him gone, maybe this house will be ok. Maybe it won't need to be burned down. Ellis won't drop into me or Mum. He only uses Jeff to cause harm. *But can't he do that without Jeff too?* a small voice in my head reminds me. He strangled me and Cole without any living human's help. But he didn't leave a mark on us. Maybe it's like with Sabrina—he's stronger when he's attached to a living form. When Jeff's gone, we'll all be safe. It's either him or me that has to go.

Even in this moment, when I desperately want to throw the paperweight at Jeff—I can't justify hurting him. I turn on my heel and throw the paperweight through the windowpane instead. The glass smashes. In the silence that follows, cut by the fresh wind rushing through the window, I know I've done something I can't come back from. So, I take the next step. I turn to Traci, and I tell her: "He's cheating on you. Jeff's cheating on you. I have proof. He doesn't love you. He's just using us as a way to get a promotion or as a pity project. He doesn't care about us. He doesn't."

They both look at me with such a deep sadness that I can't even be in the same house, let alone the same room. I run to my room and grab my skateboard as Traci and Jeff's voices rise in the background. I can't be in this house with my head spinning out like this. What have I done? I can't be here. I can't be part of this household anymore.

Before I know it, I'm skating down the road to town, swerving to avoid every pothole. There's no one out. The wind pushes me further and further from the house. Faster and faster. I skate toward the edge of the world.

I fall off.

I'm gone.

CHAPTER TWENTY

I stopped skating a while ago. I was getting blown every way except forward once I hit Main Street, so I walked out here on the road's shoulder. There are no cars out, no one to see me. Everything around me becomes more transparent. I'm by the ice cream shop Traci took me after I saw Dr. Paul. The shop is shuttered up against the wind. They've rolled in the awning and the parking lot's empty. I sit down at one of the sticky picnic tables just to think about where I should go next, staring at the trees creaking and stretching almost to breaking. Then, one of them, a tall, half dead elm, does.

It makes this sound, as close to a scream as I've heard any plant make, and the part of the tree that split off razes through the other nearby trees' branches, taking some of them down with it. The wind that replaces the tree's fall fills all the land around us with a sigh.

It's a relief I don't share. My skin still prickles, electric with rage at Traci. Every time, she's chosen Jeff over me. And maybe this time she'll choose him again. Every time, she's chosen to follow her dreams without thinking about how her dreams aren't mine. Moving to this place that doesn't want me. This place I'm trapped in with no way of escape.

I stare at the shredded trunk of the elm. It's so strange that when humans die, they bleed and decompose so quickly. But that tree continued to stand in the shell of its living form until some force of nature took it down. Is that what I am to the ghosts of Sabrina, Aggie, and Ellis? Some force of nature? Some gust of wind that's supposed to return their spirits to ashes or dust or whatever immaterial substance they're composed of? Out of the house, these questions come like gusts of wind too. Not enough to bowl me over—just something I'm moved by. I'm still upset with Traci, Jeff, and myself. But I have some distance. I want to let the wind blow me off course from Aggie's house, toward Nan's old farm.

I wish I could talk to Dad about all this. We used to talk sometimes when I was on the way home from school. I'd just call him because I was bored, or he'd do the same. Walking from the bus stop to our house was only far enough to get the highlights in. It occurs to me now that these conversations were naive. I saw him as a friend, not a parent. I saw him as infallible. I trusted him. I want that innocence back. I want to go back to thinking everything's gonna be ok. I want everything to be ok. And now I don't have anyone except Cole.

That's not totally true, though, is it?

My eyes worry the gap where the elm used to be like the exposed gum after a lost tooth. I run my eyes over and over the gap until I stop seeing it and begin to concentrate on the background. A hill. An unfarmed plain of land. The little cottage with its weathered gray shingles. The roof sags into a smile. The Walker house on the abandoned farmland where Nan grew up.

I don't look both ways as I step onto the street. Luckily, there are no cars. I have tunnel vision. Any fear of ticks or poison ivy falls away as I battle through the weeds up the hill toward Nan's childhood home. Even if I can't get in again, spending time there has to be important. I'm walking where my great grandparents and Nan walked so many years ago. Even if that connection isn't justice for my great grandfather, at least I can connect to his memory. Did he imagine his great grandchild would walk the same paths as him someday?

I've found my way back to the ragged structure of Nan's childhood home all alone. This place called to me. Even when I was riding, fueled by rage and without destination, I managed to find the path back here. This time Nan's house will let me in. I can feel it.

The doorknob is bubbled with rust. It takes an extra twist to jimmy the whole thing clockwise. I don't expect it to open, so when the knob clunks and the front door opens into a dark hallway, I'm shocked. The air inside is thick with nature. It smells alive. It probably helps that people party here frequently. This space is still used, contrary to the lonely abandonment of Aggie's house.

I'm careful to avoid any spiderwebs or piles of leaves that might contain squirrels as I step through the rooms. Empty bottles of hard liquor and cans of Oland Export huddle in corners and half-formed tags are spray-painted onto walls. I hear a rustle and chatter in the walls, as if the rodents are whispering my arrival to their kin. A welcoming? A return? I hope not an invasion. My presence here is temporary.

Although the banister is rotting, the stairs look fairly stable. I imagine Nan would have slept upstairs. There likely won't be many hints about her family's life here, but I just want to have a better picture, a clearer imaginary history of this place.

There are only two rooms upstairs in this small house: my great grandparent's bedroom and Nan and her siblings' bedroom. They're on opposite sides of the hall. I imagine the patter of children's feet crossing the hall into their parents' room in the night, finding warmth in their parents' bed. I imagine what I know I would have done. What I did when I was a kid. My favorite nights were the ones where I slept between my parents. I never had any dreams.

I choose to enter the room on the right first. The window faces southwest. The glass is cloudy and melting with gravity's slow force. On sunny days, it must heat up in here, must fill with a religious glow. Was this the kids' room? I turn from the window back to the door, and that's when I notice the graffiti scrawled in blood-red against the peeling wallpaper: *murderer.*

So, this is my great grandparents' room.

I peel it all off until the wall is blank, then I visit the room across the hall.

The wallpaper in this room is softer. This is definitely where the kids slept. A pattern of lily pads and frogs repeats except where the walls are water damaged or the paper's peeled off. I imagine my Nan, tiny, with her hair coming out from its braids, playing jacks with her brothers and sister in a corner. Her laugh, which always bursts out of her chest so warm, higher-pitched and goofier. I sit down cross-legged on the floor and gaze out the window at the clouds roiling above. I watch for symbols to draw themselves with their ridges until my eyelids get heavy.

☙

My phone's buzzing wakes me. If it's Traci, I'm not answering. I don't want to think about what the fallout of my statement about Jeff will be. If she believes me, she'll be devastated. And if she doesn't believe me . . . What if I've destabilized their relationship just enough that she and Jeff live in a limbo of distrust forever? I'll have to be witness to it all, knowing that I'm right with his smug face leering at me while Traci's back is turned. Even worse, what if I've destabilized our relationship to the point that Traci can't trust *me* anymore?

I don't even want to look at my phone. But it keeps buzzing, so I pull it out of my pocket to quiet it. Then I see it's Nan on the other end of the line, as if I'd finally summoned her by connecting with her old home.

"Nan!"

"Oh, good, I got the right number. How come I haven't heard from you since you moved? You don't think of your Nan?"

"I called you, Nan. Left a message."

"Got your message. But why didn't you call again? Are you being safe? I told you don't get on any strange motorcycles."

I laugh. I know she's serious though, so I keep it quiet and say, "I won't, Nan."

"Those country boys are some else. You watch out."

"I will." What would she think of Cole? There's silence on the line. "I'm thinking of coming into the city soon. Can you do my hair like when I was a kid?"

"As long as you don't squeal like you used to. Couldn't pay you to keep still."

"I promise I won't." I hear the click of her lighter on the end of the line and a long sigh as she takes a drag of her cigarette. I used to hate getting my hair done whenever we'd go to see Nan but now the memory gives me comfort, like in the dream I had of her yesterday. The smell of cigarettes would get so deep into my hair and skin and clothes. It smelled like death to me. But now I'm nostalgic for it. I wish I could sit on one of her old pillows on the floor while she tugged at my head. "You know where I am?"

"No."

"Guess."

"I don't like guessing games." I roll my eyes.

"I'm at your old house."

"That old place! Ha!" She laughs full-bellied into the receiver and static gathers like the dimples at the corners of her mouth. "You be careful. Hope you're not going inside." Too late.

"What was it like when you moved to the city?"

"Hm. Well, at first I hated it. But then I started to like some things. Church and after school going to the corner store for penny candies. Seeing other Black folks around. Met your grandfather. Made my babies." She leaves out the hard parts. The addiction, abuse, poverty that interspersed those joys . . . all the fear . . . But I believe in the joy of the moments she does mention because I can tell she does too.

"Did you like living out here on a farm?"

"Oh yes. It was my whole world. I didn't know anything different. Go by the stream and splash around, play in the woods with my siblings. And ride the horses my dad raised out there. You know my Tamarack, the picture I have up in my living room."

"Mhm." I peek out the window at the slope, imagine Nan and Tamarack riding across the fields. "Dad told me some stuff about our family's history in this town. About how you left because of your dad getting accused of murder. Do you know what happened?" I want her side of the story. Maybe she knows something Dad didn't.

"I don't like to talk about it too much. Nothing good can come of talking about it." I hear the click of her lighter and a soft inhale as she pulls the smoke into her lungs. "But if you really want to know, they said they found a body on the property where my father worked. Took him in for questioning. Broke his leg. He didn't do it, of course. Our farm was everything for us, he'd never risk it."

"I've been looking for proof—to clear his name once and for all—"

"No point," Nan interrupts. My heart drops.

"Why not?"

"Nothing left from that time. Even then, it was his word against that Ellis Bainbridge. No one ever believed my father to be untruthful, but his word was worth a lot less. Going against Ellis might mean losing your job at the mill."

"You're sure there's nothing to prove your father was innocent?" I ask, but I know the answer before I'm even finished the question. If Aggie's whole house is like a museum, a mausoleum even, this house is barely bones left over. No one was here to preserve it.

"Why d'you need proof anyhow? Isn't knowing enough?"

"Well, how're we supposed to have justice if I can't prove it? People will still believe he did it!"

"Let me tell you something, baby—our farm fed us and half the town. But with the way people treated us after that woman was murdered, we couldn't stay. They forgot or ignored that our family built most of the houses in that town, including the one where he was a handyman. Some ancestors were enslaved, others freemen . . . and before that the land was stolen . . ."

Sabrina's words echo in my head: *Who built this house? Whose money? Whose blood?* Nan is repeating a story that's familiar to me. To hear confirmation from her, a living, breathing family member who has cared for me my whole life, makes me sure of my next steps. If I do this, I'm not doing it for Sabrina. I'm doing it for Nan. I'm doing it for me, and for Dad, and for Mum.

"My Great Aunt Aggie's house was part of that. That's where he worked."

"That's right."

"Why didn't you tell me?"

"Your father told me not to tell you all those years ago because you'd never be able to sleep in the house again. None of my business, but I thought you all shouldn't be sleeping in that place anyway. Crawling with ghosts." Has she seen them too? Doesn't matter if she believes. One day I can tell her the whole story. For now, I just need facts.

"Do you think Aggie killed her husband?"

"Oh, I know it. And good riddance. How could she live with that man after all he did? That man knew how to give people the runaround. He was scamming up and down Main from the day he was old enough to carry a wallet. And our family suffered the consequences. We were the last Black people driven out of that town by the white folks who made us build it. We made that town, and they took everything from us. You understand why I never gone back there."

"I don't want to live here."

"But you do."

"I hate Jeff."

"Don't say hate. It's not what you feel. You don't know hate. You've got to make do until the situation is over."

"I know, but I don't want to."

"You have to respect your mother's choices. There's a lot I regret as a mother, but seeing you, seeing how good you've grown up . . . Traci did a good job with you. And your father, even though he still got stuck in the trappings we tend to get stuck in . . . I'm still proud of everyone. And I know you're going to take good care of yourself and those around you because it's what I taught your father, and it's what your mother and father taught you. Look, we all get into the wrong things at different moments in our life, but it's your choice to move forward wishing others well. Justice comes fast sometimes, but most times it's slow and it's not a straight line. You're going to be just fine. You hear me?"

"I hear you. I miss you, Nan."

"I miss you too, sweetie."

There's as much silence as there could be with the wind rattling the windows of this place and the TV in the background of Nan's life feeding through. But I know this is what peace is. This moment. It's the moment before we say goodbye.

"Now, I have to go get ready for my evening. I'll hear from you soon, Asha."

"You will."

"Bye."

"Bye."

I'm left alone again. But I feel less lonely now. All this time, I've been thinking about how other people should be living their lives. Alive or dead or undead. But to move on, it's not a clear path. I've hurt myself as much as others by not understanding what I need to be able to live in this place. If I'm going to live here, no matter for how short a time, I don't want to be haunted by past violence. I don't want to forget, but I don't want to drag my feet into the future. I have to speed things up; I have to move toward the future I want running. And I have to do right by everyone I love.

CHAPTER TWENTY-ONE

I don't hit a single rock on the skate back home. The trees rush by, my leg burns. The wind's died down enough that I'm no longer blown off course. I am a ghost ship, risen from the Atlantic, captained by the dead and my force of will.

The sky is flat gray but it's as if my eyes are turning up the saturation. I see red tones brighter, with more clarity. I filter out my doubts, stand tall and strong as a mast.

I have no doubts, only propulsion. Aggie's house will not be preserved. I will not take its pain into the next generation. I will listen to Sabrina—I will burn it down. That house needs an apology that doesn't negate the truth with a fresh start. A cleansing. Ellis, Aggie, Sabrina—none of them need to reproduce their pain anymore. This house is done passing their trauma and violence on.

Before I turn onto our road, I consider for a second that I've fully lost it. But I am more solid, stable, and sure than I can remember being in this place. I am not afraid. Continuing to live in that house has far worse, inevitable consequences of harm than what I'm about to do. The only choice is to act.

Me and Sabrina will end this together. I know this is her right. A right she wasn't allowed by Ellis who murdered her in a violent rage, or by Aggie who must have wanted her around as company in that house all those long years alone. She preserved those old columns and antique furniture as decoys. Their extravagant presence consumed any hints at a life that wasn't proper, any hint of what shouldn't have been love but was. Each curtain was pulled closed. All that was good in her life was left for the mice and insects to nibble through for decades, until only a photograph remained, slotted into a crack in her bedroom wall. To live without moving on from this history of concealment is to betray myself. I cannot let myself be consumed by this place. All I want is to move past this time into another. All I want is for everyone I love to be free of what holds them captive in the past. I want that to be possible for all of us: a new foundation of care.

♫

As I approach the house, I'm ready to step up on a kitchen chair and grab the matches, ready to set everything aflame as soon as I can get Traci and Jeff out. I'm ready to walk in and burn it all down, with Sabrina by my side.

Except Cole is sitting on the front steps. "What are you doing here?" I ask them and they raise their head from where it's hanging between their knees. They're the picture of Sabrina. The picture I couldn't stop staring at, that I found a friend in. When we make eye contact, I know it's not Cole blocking my entrance to the house, but Sabrina.

I repeat myself, shorten my earlier question to: "What are you doing?" I thought Sabrina would leave Cole out of this. But again, she's gotten to Cole before me.

Sabrina speaks through Cole's mouth. "You're making the right decision."

If she thinks I'm making the right decision, then why is she blocking the entrance? Only a few weeks earlier I wouldn't have been able to tell the difference between Cole and

Sabrina-dropped-into-Cole. But now I can. I know the way Cole holds their face tough when they're scared and how they hold themself a little less confidently than Sabrina does. Sabrina is older, saw more shit in her lifetime. Watching her move in Cole's body fills me with a deep sadness. Sabrina embodies and guards in her body a collection of traumas I hope Cole never has to house.

"I want to end this house but not only because of you. And not if you're going to use Cole to do it."

Sabrina nods. "You have your own reasons. I have mine. Our common goal is freedom."

"What does that look like for you?"

"True rest."

"The reburial wasn't enough?" I know it wasn't enough. She's been trying to tell me so through reaching for fire. I just hoped we might find a different solution.

"I want real death. And all the birth that comes with it."

"We have to make sure everyone's safe first."

Sabrina nods slowly. "I will set the fire if you help my grandchild provide a distraction."

"Did you even ask them if it was ok to use their body?"

"Of course." She looks almost offended.

"I don't want Cole to get hurt. Take me instead if you have to." I don't trust Sabrina the same way I used to after I woke up in the woods. What if Cole doesn't remember agreeing?

Sabrina purses her lips. "That's not your decision. Cole has already agreed to draw Ellis out."

"How?" My heart leaps. "Why would Cole agree to put themself in danger?" They've already drawn his wrath once, in peaceful sleep. If they're going to do it fully conscious and ready to fight back, things could get out of hand.

"If I can't convince you they agreed, then they can tell you." Sabrina's voice drops off, and Cole's body sways. In the moment they drop back into themself, they blink slowly, acclimatizing to being back in their form, and then they see me, and smile their bucktoothed grin. I can't help but smile back. Knowing they're in this with me makes me feel safer.

I'm also worried. "You ok?"

"Not bad."

"You let Sabrina drop into you? She didn't force you to do it?"

Cole shakes their head. "No. I want to be a part of this."

"You could get hurt."

"*You* could get hurt."

"Me and Sabrina can do this alone. You don't have to let her use you as bait."

Cole has a stubborn look on their face. "If I can't have a relationship with my grandmother, I can at least bring her justice. You taught me that. Both our families need this. I can't control what the ghosts decide to do in the end, but if there's any way I can help stop all this violence so we can heal, I'm in."

I rush forward and squeeze them. "Thank you."

"No problem," they say, but I see how hard they worked to get here, how difficult it was to come to this conclusion. After tonight, if we climb up the mountain again, we won't see this house's miniature on the toy landscape below.

"So," I say, grabbing their hand to pull them over the rotten step. "How're we going to do this?"

∂ρ

The plan is simple: we recreate the night Cole slept over.

Because Cole comes back inside with me, I'm spared a lecture from Traci and Jeff. Besides, I can tell some sort of eruption took place after I left. The curtains are ripped off the rod and one of the blue velvet antique chairs has two splintered legs. Traci is in the den, scrolling through her phone. She doesn't look up as Cole and I pass. I wouldn't have known Jeff was here except for his slate Tesla still in the driveway and the way

264 • A HOUSE UNSETTLED

the door to Traci's room is shut tight in its frame. His shadow moves back and forth against the floor as he paces.

"It's cold in here," Cole notes, sliding their clammy hand into mine.

I sniff the air. "Do you smell that?"

Cole turns their head up to the air and takes a long whiff. They crinkle their nose. "Smells like mildew or something. I thought the mold guys finished up weeks ago?"

It's as if the walls themselves are decaying. As we get further from Traci and Jeff's room, the smell abates. My room is torn apart completely. Every drawer, every corner is covered in my belongings.

"Whoa, messy room."

"This wasn't me." Who did this? I grab clothes at random and attempt to stuff them back in my drawers. Not that it matters. Everything I own is going to go up in smoke soon. Putting it all away is a force of habit. I try not to miss anything. When I see Dad's basketball jersey, I pull it on over my t-shirt, like armor. I'm able to keep my fury under control with Cole here and with the knowledge that the violence brewing in this house will end tonight.

"Ellis?"

"I don't know."

"What happened? Where were you? I came by and Sabrina told me you were gone."

"Had a fight with Traci and Jeff."

Cole looks around the room again, then scans me up and down. "Are you ok?"

"I'm fine." We've made our decision. "All of this ends tonight. Are you ready?"

"I'm ready." Our eyes meet and any last uneasiness I have dissipates. We'll all get out of this place. We're finally letting go of it. Soon, we'll all have rest.

We wait out the night watching cartoons from our childhood. It's all flat. None of the jokes land and neither of us is really paying attention. It's a miracle we even fall asleep. Even in the face of danger, lying next to Cole, it's easier than I expect to fall away from consciousness. Next to each other, we're able to create a little warmth.

♪

This time, Cole doesn't scream. Ellis's hands aren't the only ones around their neck. Jeff's hands are squeezing the life from them too. At first, I wonder if I've woken too late, only because one of Cole's flailing arms smashed into my nose. It's streaming blood, coppery, into my mouth. Cole gurgles and attempts to gasp in air with no luck. The life's squeezing out of them with every passing second.

No time to waste. This time my silence breaks, and I am wrestling with Jeff as Cole struggles beneath him. I realize I'm screaming, "Mum! Mum!" but she doesn't come running. She can't be sleeping through this. I manage to break Jeff's grip and push him onto the floor. Cole gasps for breath, pale at the edge of passing out.

"You want to destroy my home," Ellis growls through Jeff's teeth. I grab Cole. We stumble past Traci's empty room and down the stairs, a mess of knees and ankles.

"Where's Sabrina?" I ask, half to Cole, half to myself. I thought this was Sabrina's plan all along. Did Cole know Sabrina using them as bait also meant they'd have the exact same marks around their neck that Sabrina did when she was buried?

Ellis uses Jeff to barrel down the stairs behind us, yelling incomprehensibly. I remember how Jeff's body reacted in proximity to ghosts last time and I wonder if he'll be able to withstand Ellis dropping into him.

Cole continues toward the door, with Ellis close behind, and I split off toward the kitchen. As confident as I was earlier that we could do this, now my hands are shaking.

"Mum?" I call out again, into the dark of the house. "Mum, get out of the house!" Where is she?

I climb up onto the counter, and like I've done in my dreams before, I reach for the box of matches on the top shelf and fumble them with my numb fingers. The box falls and the matches scatter on the kitchen floor.

A crash comes from the front of the house. "Asha, hurry!" Cole's strained yell reaches me as I gather up as many matches in my fist as I can and grab the box. Where's Sabrina?

I dash back to the front of the house. Ellis has Cole cornered in the den, somehow bulking up Jeff's small frame to seem as broad as he was. Cole is holding a fire poker between them. I can see the vintage Tiffany lamp they smashed on the floor, shards of its jeweled carapace glittering like freshly exposed organs. Ellis is reaching for a knifelike shard of glass, slowly, daring Cole to do harm to Jeff's body. I'm paralyzed. I need to make sure neither of them gets hurt. I need to burn the house down.

Come—Sabrina's earthy presence settles behind me. She grabs my hand and pulls me into the living room. *May I?* I nod, and she drops into me one last time.

She steadies my hand and moves it with the grace of her own toward those ugly, dusty curtains me and Traci just couldn't seem to get rid of. With my fist of matches, she strikes against the matchbox and a fire lights between our hands. Gently, she places it onto the fabric. It begins its ascent.

"Stay away from me!" Cole's voice comes to me from a distance.

Sabrina leaves me. *I'll tend to the flames. Keep my grandchild safe.* I don't have time to wait for my body to settle back into itself. Heat and smoke are collecting in this room. I stumble toward the front door, where Cole is turning the doorknob frantically, trying to get out, as Ellis limps toward them as fast as he can, a wide gash in the thigh of his pants. It's my emergence from the den that draws his eye. Just as he's about to reach Cole, Ellis notices the fire spreading behind me. Ellis's connection to Jeff wavers for a moment, before he tightens his attachment to Jeff's body, and they lurch toward the living room.

"No!" I rush after Jeff as the fire spreads from the curtains to the walls. I try to pull him back by the shoulder, but Ellis snarls and rips Jeff's body away from my grasp. Smoke is billowing out of the room. The fire's spreading faster than natural, popping up in places where it shouldn't be, as if Sabrina is throwing it across the room.

"Asha, come on, you're going to get hurt!" Cole yells from the doorway.

"Help me," I shout back, choking on the thickening smoke. "We need to get Jeff out of here!" Sweat evaporates off my face as fast as I can produce it.

Cole hesitates for a moment and then is by my side too. With both of us holding onto Jeff, we're able to pull his body out of the house. Ellis protests the whole way, thrashing and cursing until the threshold, where he becomes weaker. He gives out one last snarl before Jeff's body goes limp and Ellis's ghost pulls away with a pained wail, and races into the flames to fight Sabrina.

It's too late for him to stop it. The fire's spread far enough that not even a supernatural force could stop it. Cole and I turn away. The rest is up to Sabrina. We focus on dragging Jeff to the edge of the moat where we drop him. He regains consciousness and scrambles to his feet in the muck.

"I'm sorry." He's looking at Cole. Tears are streaking through the ash and dirt on his face. He keeps repeating it.

"It's okay. It wasn't you." Cole tells him, but they keep their distance.

I turn away from them both and begin to run back toward the house, but Cole stops me. "What are you doing?" they ask.

"My mum—"

Cole's face falls. They let my arm go. I race back toward the house, ready to run into the flames. Why didn't Mum come when I called earlier? Was she sleeping that deep? I need to get her out. I need her. I need to save her. How could I let this happen? How could Sabrina let this happen? How could Aggie let this happen? I need her.

I call for her through the flames. They've engulfed the door now. I fall to my knees.

Then Jeff's behind me, lifting me up and shouting Traci's name. "You take the right side of the house, I'll take the left." He pushes me gently to the right side of the house and we both walk frantically through the thickening smoke, yelling Traci's name between coughs.

And then I hear her calling me. I turn, and she's running up over the hill by the garden, through the patch of poison ivy. And I run to her in the heat of the flames. Jeff joins us as he comes around the other side of the house. We pull each other to safety. Glad to have each other's lives. It almost escapes my notice that a second, glowing shadow peels off Mum's as we approach Cole, and floats its way back to the house.

Mum pulls me into a hug as soon as we're out of danger, on the edge of the moat. "I thought I lost you." She rocks me. I thought I lost her. "I don't know how I got outside. I just woke up on the other side of the garden." I watch the glowing shadow join with the smoke, then evaporate into nothing. *Aggie.*

As the fire department arrives, the house sighs and collapses in on itself.

CHAPTER TWENTY-TWO

*A*fter the fire, we stayed with the Levesque-Gergeses. Until it felt too much like imposing, we were comfortable there. Cole had to wear turtlenecks for a while to mask the bruises that bloomed on their neck following Ellis's attack. Since it's getting cooler, no one asked questions.

I slept on Cole's floor, sometimes in their bed, and things were good. Quiet. We found an easy understanding of each other's presences in the small space, Cole's drawings multiplying and improving while my piles of books grew. We became used to each other's sleeping patterns—Cole an early riser, me *definitely not*—and grew closer. Without Aggie's house to drive a wedge between us and raise my temper, we've found ways to talk about hard things without hurting each other. Even better, we have more time to joke around and just be teens. It's our last chance. Next year, we'll both be eighteen. Where life will take us after high school is anyone's guess.

Mum and Kelly grew closer too; they talked deep into the night about all their years apart. Mum and Jeff still see each other occasionally, but less and less frequently. He had a brief hospital stay after Ellis possessed him the night of the fire, but he's recovered since and moved back to the city, closer to his work. Their entire relationship, I thought the end would be a bang, but here we are, at the end, and it's more of a fizzle. Even me and Jeff reached a sort of peace. I didn't feel so threatened by him after seeing him taken over by Ellis. I realized that even though he's older than me, he still has a lot to learn. It's up to him to decide if he wants to. He got his promotion. I don't think he'll ever change much, but I can leave him in the past knowing I made my peace with his flaws. If I see him in the future, the ball's in his court.

Mum is planning on breaking things off for good next week. Finally, it did come out that he was planning on getting surveyors out on the land to see if there were resources that could be extracted from Aggie's property, expansive as it was. Even with the house gone, Mum couldn't bear to let him take advantage of the forest that way. Maybe on some level, she could understand that he was taking advantage of us too, to try and soothe his insecurities. We haven't really talked about him cheating on her since I blurted it out in anger. Maybe we never will.

The Saturday before school starts, we go back to the market for blueberry pancakes and head down to the dock. We stick our feet in the water, like the first time we came here. It's colder. After a few minutes, I can feel my blood starting to chill and rush up my legs. I pull my them out. Mum reveals a folded wad of paper from her pocket.

"What's that?" I ask.

"Open it up."

It's a land deed, I can see that from the first page, but I don't recognize the address. "Where is this?"

"The insurance money for Aggie's came in. I bought the farm back. For you. Well, for you when you come of age. For now, if your Nan and father want to live there, or spend their summers there, that's up to them. Your father will need a place to go when he's released."

It's instinct; I pull Mum into a tight hug. She wraps her arms around me tight too, and rocks me a bit, just like when I was a little kid. "We can fix it up. The structure's not in bad shape. Aggie's was grand, but your Nan's old house is solid. It's filthy inside from those parties kids have, but that's easy enough to clean."

"I can't wait to tell Nan about this!" I splash my feet around in the water again. "How'd you find the house?" I hadn't shown her or even mentioned where I went when I left her and Jeff after our blowout.

"Cole helped me." Mum smiles mischievously. The two of them kept a secret from me—a beautiful secret I'm happy to receive. "They're a good friend to you, Asha. They brought it up to me, actually. Then they showed me where the property was. Hidden in plain sight. I did the rest."

Mum protects the papers by stuffing them back in her jacket. I never expected her generosity to extend to Dad and Nan. I never expected her to understand what I wanted or needed. But here we are.

"Asha," she takes a steadying breath, "I know it's hard for you to talk about, and you don't have to say anything. I just need you to know that after everything, I'll always be here for you, ok?"

I nod. I know she believes this. My throat tightens as I think about all the ways she hasn't been here for me in recent years, because of her own baggage, because of circumstances beyond our control, because she doesn't understand some things that I do, and one day, I won't be able to talk to her anymore, even if I want to. Where I used to feel resentment is a big pool of grief.

"I think, sometimes, maybe you can't be there for me." Tears start dripping from my eyes. I don't try to hold them in.

I expect Mum to disagree with me, to tell me she *does* understand, that everything's going to be ok, because she'll be there for me one hundred percent from now on. Instead, she pulls me close and lets me lay my head on her shoulder. She sniffs my scalp.

"I know I don't always understand what you're going through—I never will, probably, because we're different." Mum's voice is tight too. "You know so much more about what you need than I did at your age. You don't let people cross your boundaries. I wish I knew I had boundaries when I was your age.

"I try to help you. I try to know what you need. It was easier when you were a little kid—you'd just cry if something felt bad, smile if something felt good . . . Now it's so hard when you won't tell me what's wrong." She stops to wipe her eyes and nose. It's my turn to pull her close in a hug. She feels small in my arms. I guess having a kid who's almost grown is a kind of grief too.

"Sometimes I don't know how to tell you. I'm scared of what you'll say." It's honest and I can see it stings for her to hear. "I know you love me now, but what if one day you don't because of something I do or say?"

She pulls away from me and makes me look her in the eye. "Asha, I promise I'll always love you and I'll always believe you when you say you're hurting. That will never change, even if I get hurt sometimes too."

It's time for me to ask the question I've been holding back since our early days here. "Why couldn't you see how much it was hurting me to be in that house?"

"I could see something was hurting you." She admits. "But I thought I knew what you were feeling. When I moved in with Aggie, I hurt all the time. I was on edge, cranky, angry—like you. You know, I thought I used to see ghosts—" My heart jolts as Mum chuckles to herself. "—but it was just growing pains. I didn't think I'd ever be able to go out in public again after my mum died. I thought people would be able to see how broken I was inside just by looking at me. But Aggie gave me time, and I got better. I made friends, I started going out too much, even.

That grief never went away but there was space for it to reside in the house, space for it to reside in me, if that makes sense?"

I nod. "There was no space for me at Aggie's."

Mum takes a deep breath. "I know. I know that now. I hurt you, and Jeff hurt you and living in that house with its history hurt you, and I wasn't listening. I'm sorry." She places a hand over mine. "There were things I knew I should have shared with you. I just thought you'd never come with me if I told you. I thought I'd lose you if I told you your great grandfather worked at the house and was accused of Sabrina's murder or told you the rumor about Aggie murdering Ellis . . . I was worried that if you knew how complicated our family's history is in this town, how much of it is contrary to your identity and values, that you wouldn't even want to stay with me for a short time. I convinced myself life would be easier the less I told you. We'd be able to start fresh. Now I know the only person I was protecting was myself."

I let her words sink into me. Neither of us was able to start fresh. Even though that's what we both wanted, I don't think that's what either of us needed. Now, sitting here, I feel like I'm finally getting to understand where Mum is coming from and she's actually listening to me.

"I'm sorry too," I tell her. "I'm sorry I made this move hard and living with Jeff hard. I was scared of losing you too."

"You don't have to be sorry. I'm just grateful I still have you." Mum holds me for a while. I breathe in her apple cider breath, the bacon smoke wafting down the path.

I'm still not ready to tell her the full story. I might never be. There are parts of it I told her, the photo I found of Sabrina in the wall, her and Aggie's relationship. Other things, I kept to myself, like the possessions and the intentional fire. How me and Cole's relationship has shifted to something more than friends, something less than together. For now. I honestly think Mum knows, but it feels good to have a part of my life that's separate from her. And a few things remain a mystery to me. I never did learn if Aggie murdered Ellis.

Whatever happened, it's over now and I'm ok with not knowing. I've let go of trying to understand everything. Like Nan said about her father, sometimes justice is fast, but most times it's a slow and winding path.

When we're ready, we head home. We're staying in town now. Mum signed a lease for an apartment on Main Street. When she asked me if I wanted to move back to the city, I said no. I still want to give this new life with her a chance. I could tell she was happy to stay in this place too. She's starting to make new friends in town, and she got a job organizing events for the county.

The place we moved into last week is much smaller, on the top floor of a pink Victorian house. I haven't seen any ghosts yet, but maybe it's just because I'm too zonked after school to wake up during the night. Sometimes I fall asleep in Mum's bed next to her, just like when I was a kid. It feels good to fall asleep and wake up next to her.

The breakup was hard on her, but not as hard as the relationship was. We still fight sometimes, and this is by no means the fresh start Mum or I envisioned, but it is the continuation of the best parts of us into a new phase of life.

Nia's back and planning on driving up to visit me in a couple weekends. It'll be her first road trip alone. I'm excited for her and Cole to meet. She's bringing pictures from her trip and sketches. Even better, stories. We're going to spend all night talking, the same way we used to before this long, exhausting summer.

Mum took me to visit Dad. It was good to see him in person. I realized as soon as I saw him that even though he's locked up, he still loves me just as much as he did when he was outside. I was able to stop worrying about whether he did the crime or not. It doesn't matter. He's still my dad and if he could, he'd show up for me when I needed him. If he did do it, he will have to repair the relationships with the people he hurt, and if he didn't, those relationships will repair in time. The system is unjust. But the entire carceral state is harder to burn down than a single house . . . maybe my life's work is haunting oppressive systems until they turn to ash for some better future to rise out of.

School here isn't so different from the city. Same dramas, same conflicts, different cast. Cole and I share a few classes. Sometimes we jig and drive out to the ocean, walk along the red rocks and try to discern the Bay of Fundy's horizon from the fog. Every so often, Devon will join us. We're becoming a little friend group, opening to more people in the community, more sure of ourselves, and where our lives are headed.

After school, I get off the bus with Cole, and we walk in the woods. Sometimes our hands or lips reach for each other, other times we talk, or walk in silence. We've been making new paths and letting the old ones grow over.

It's by accident today that we take one of our old paths. We end up at Sabrina's grave. Neither of us knew how to get there. She chose a well-hidden spot to rest, and I don't remember much from the darkness of the night I buried her. We don't notice right away. We almost step over it before we feel our bodies jerk back and a familiar dizziness washes over us. I don't know if it's really *her* or a different kind of ghost, something closer to memory that affects us. It doesn't matter. We stop and look down in silence at the red and gold leaves decorating the surface of the earth that contains her bones.

And then there's a rustling. A rabbit emerges from the dead matter, soft, tiny, frightened. Both Cole and I kneel to watch it without threat until it calms, acclimates to our presence. We stay even after it calms. Its breathing slows, and it hops away. So, then, as is our new habit, we part ways at sunset, knowing we will see each other tomorrow and the day after that.

ACKNOWLEDGMENTS

Writing is a kind of possession. It's taken over my life the past two years and lived in my body. Now in physical form it's been exorcised—it belongs to you now, if you want it. Thank you for reading. I'm so lucky to have had the space to collaborate and wrestle with the questions about legacies of violence and paths to justice in this book.

Thank you to my editors, Claire and Khary, and to Genevieve, Kaela, and Mercedes. Thank you to everyone who worked on this book in small or large part at Annick for helping me bring my vision of this haunting to life and for questioning the elements that needed work. The care and mentorship you've provided me has changed me and helped me grow as a writer.

To my parents and all intergenerational supports in my life, thank you for trusting me and nurturing my love for writing.

Simone, you have revolutionized my world since 1998. My imagination lives half in your head. All of my work exists because you are my sibling.

Vi-An, thank you for teaching me love and softness and for supporting me through this process.

To my friends: our bonds have sustained me and allowed me to understand love as a current that brings us back to each other when we need it. To MG, PD, TB, LS, JM, laughing through high school with you saved me.

To rural New Brunswick: your beauty is home and hell.

A House Unsettled is set on unceded land of the Mi'kmaq, Wolastoqiyik, and Peskotomuhkati nations covered by the Peace and Friendship treaties. Black Loyalists landed in 1783 in the lands of Peace and Friendship and our continued survival is intertwined with the decolonial politics of those lands. This book was written in Tiohtià:ke. Here, the Kanien'kehá:ka Nation is recognized as the custodians of the lands which have long served as a gathering place for many First Nations peoples, including the Kanien'kehá:ka of the Haudenosaunee Confederacy, the Huron/Wendat, the Abenaki, and the Anishinaabeg. Thank you to these lands for caring for me.